Daring Rogues

Reformed rakes find romance!

Carrick Eisley and Logan Maddox may have once put their lives on the line with their wild, daring exploits, but when it comes to putting their hearts on the line, that's one risk these former rakes aren't willing to take. Until they are confronted with the women who will change their view on love, and their lives, forever!

Read Carrick and India's story in:
Miss Claiborne's Illicit Attraction
Available now!

And look out for Logan and Olivia's story:
His Inherited Duchess
Coming soon!

Author Note

Carrick and India's story is about second chances and starting fresh even though that does not mean being able to erase the slate. The past is always with us and it shapes our present just as it shapes Carrick and India's present. It's set against the early days of the decline of the coaching industry as trains became a more accessible means of transportation, which I think is a suitable backdrop especially for Carrick. He's a man who has retired from racing but still finds ways to stay active in the racing circle through his carriage designs.

Like so many folks these days, Carrick is starting a second career and it's a bit scary—carriages are slowly becoming a hobby for drivers instead of a primary means of transportation. Like many of us over the past few years, India has had a new "job" thrust upon her when her prior life is ripped away from her through tragedy. Now, she's parenting her younger brother and trying to preserve an estate she was not raised to manage. She's had quite the learning curve and it's changed her. She and Carrick are not the people they used to be and they have to get to know each other all over again, blending the old with the new in order to forge a lasting connection.

A fun note about Benson: this was the home of the Benson Driving Club and it was indeed housed at the White Hart Inn in Benson. The scene between India and the inn's proprietress features the actual proprietress, Mrs. Shrubb, who ran the inn until 1852.

BRONWYN SCOTT

Miss Claiborne's Illicit Attraction

ISBN-13: 978-1-335-72354-3

Miss Claiborne's Illicit Attraction

For questions and comments about the quality of this book, please contact us at CustomerService@Harlequin.com.

Harlequin Enterprises ULC
22 Adelaide St. West, 41st Floor
Toronto, Ontario M5H 4E3, Canada
www.Harlequin.com

Printed in U.S.A.

Bronwyn Scott is a communications instructor at Pierce College and the proud mother of three wonderful children—one boy and two girls. When she's not teaching or writing, she enjoys playing the piano, traveling—especially to Florence, Italy—and studying history and foreign languages. Readers can stay in touch via Facebook at Facebook.com/bronwynwrites, or on her blog, bronwynswriting.blogspot.com. She loves to hear from readers.

Books by Bronwyn Scott

Harlequin Historical

Daring Rogues

Miss Claiborne's Illicit Attraction

The Peveretts of Haberstock Hall

Lord Tresham's Tempting Rival
Saving Her Mysterious Soldier
Miss Peverett's Secret Scandal
The Bluestocking's Whirlwind Liaison
Under the Mistletoe
"Dr Peverett's Christmas Miracle"

The Rebellious Sisterhood

Portrait of a Forbidden Love
Revealing the True Miss Stansfield
A Wager to Tempt the Runaway

The Cornish Dukes

The Secrets of Lord Lynford
The Passions of Lord Trevethow
The Temptations of Lord Tintagel
The Confessions of the Duke of Newlyn

Visit the Author Profile page at Harlequin.com for more titles.

For Rowan—
always choose your passion.

Chapter One

London—spring 1839

Some men were born wild. Some had wildness thrust upon them. Of the two men standing amid the dust of humanity and horses at the improvised starting line along the Richmond Road, Logan Maddox was of the latter persuasion, while Carrick Eisley, born as wild as an autumn tempest, with his auburn hair and storm-grey eyes, was quite obviously the former.

'By the saints, I swear the competition gets younger every year,' Logan muttered, stepping out of the way to avoid being run over by a careless driver who pulled his curricle into place alongside Carrick's with barely any acknowledgment for the man on the ground.

Carrick flashed his friend a cocky grin from his curricle seat. 'Younger and easier to beat.' He surveyed the forming line of vehicles. Twelve in all. Only half were familiar to him. The other half were all new bucks come to try their luck at illicit racing—*not* illegal racing, mind you. There *was* a difference. No one said you *couldn't* race to Richmond in the broad light of day, it just wasn't recommended. But what could the authorities do? It was a little bit like duelling—which was indeed illegal, Carrick liked to note. Neither was supposed to happen, but everyone knew both did and there was nothing anyone could truly do about it.

Unsanctioned road racing had become a rite of passage of sorts for the young bloods of London. Such racing wasn't overtly advised, of course, because of the danger associated with it. Daily traffic had a habit of getting in the way. In that regard, the daytime version of the midnight race to Richmond was more challenging. At midnight, a driver contended with the darkness, but had an empty road in exchange. At the height of the day, though, the driver could see, but faced an enormous amount of slow traffic. Such traffic made the race difficult and dangerous in daylight.

Carrick stretched his arms over his head in an exercise intended to loosen his back. With a groan, he finished the stretch and extended his leg out in front of him, resting it on the dashboard.

'How *is* your knee?' Logan nodded towards the outstretched limb.

Carrick shrugged, dismissing Logan's concern. 'Fine, a little stiff this morning, but it will shake out. It always does once I get warmed up.' A driver down the line caught Carrick's eye and tipped his hat in acknowledgement before turning to say something to the driver next to him.

'An admiring fan?' Logan was all wry humour.

'Maybe.' Possibly. Hard to say. Carrick didn't know him, but the man had apparently recognised him. He'd been racing carriages so long and *winning* those races for so long he'd become something of a living legend. His body had paid for that legend. Along with the victories, there'd been accidents, too, like the time he'd been thrown out of a carriage when he'd taken a turn too fast and broken his arm. A normal man would have ended his racing season right then, maybe even his 'career' in racing notoriety. Not Carrick. He'd finished the dubious season driving one-handed to victory a week later. He'd been twenty-three though, a mere stripling on the town, ten years younger than he was now.

'That knee's going to go one of these days,' Logan cautioned with a frown.

'But not today.' Carrick laughed. He tried not to think about his knee or any of the other aches he had. Thinking about them meant admitting to them *and* admitting to all they represented: he was getting too old for this.

'You *hope* it doesn't go today.' That was Logan, the practical cynic. One of them had to be and it certainly wasn't him. He was an optimist by necessity, otherwise he would have stopped racing years ago. It was optimism that fuelled him now. Optimism that he would win today, that his knee would hold a while longer. Racing, horses and carriages were all he knew.

'Ho! Carrick, is that you?' a man called out, pulling a bright yellow phaeton around to Carrick's far side. 'I thought I might see you here today.'

'Landon Fellowes, by Jove!' Carrick reached over to take the other man's hand, his spirits buoying at the sight of his friend. 'Look who it is, Logan, it's our soon-to-be newlywed.' Carrick winked at Landon. 'I'm surprised the lovely Miss Claiborne has let you out of her sights with the wedding looming.' Whatever doubts the day might have held were banished now. The sun was out, the sky was blue, there was racing to be had, a purse to be won and Landon, one of his best friends outside of Logan, was here beside him to share in the thrills.

'Wedding's on Friday.' Landon grinned, emanating a ridiculous amount of happiness. 'She's getting a final fitting today for the gown. I just dropped her off, in fact. It's hard to believe I'll be an old hen-pecked husband this time next week.' But it didn't look to Carrick that Landon would mind it much. His friend bore all the signs of a man in love. The Fellowes–Claiborne wedding was the talk of the Season thus far, a grand romance as much as it was an alliance of two wealthy families with two handsome children to wed. Fairy tales didn't get much better. 'You'll be there, for the wedding? Yes?' Landon asked.

'Wouldn't miss it.' Carrick grinned back at his friend. 'You're a lucky man. Miss Claiborne is a lovely woman.' She was also popular, well connected and rich, too, by all reports. Her parents were sparing no expense for the wedding and had even bought the couple a home in London in exchange for their daughter marrying an heir to an earldom. Landon Fellowes had somehow managed to have it all: good looks, a beautiful bride he was madly in love with and the finances he needed to live his dreams without worry. And in time, he'd have a title, too. Until then, he was a hell of a racer, the perfect Englishman, living the perfect life.

Carrick liked racing Landon. Landon was a good

driver who knew how to push him. By the look of it, Landon would be doing that very thing today. Carrick studied Landon's team, two well-muscled Cleveland Bays. 'New horses?' Carrick enquired appreciatively. They looked good, up to any pace set by his own team.

'New team, new carriage. All of it a wedding gift from my father.' Landon beamed proudly. 'This one on the right with the tiny star is King and the other is Sabre. These boys are fast and this carriage is the latest, a new French design. I might just take you today.' he chuckled good naturedly.

'You might,' Carrick joked in return. But he thought his chances were still good. He was partial to his team. He'd bet on them any day. He'd raised them from colts, he knew every inch of them, what they could and could not do. 'Loser buys the first round in Richmond?'

'You're on.' Landon flashed a wide smile, the sun glinting off his blond hair, his laughter full of life. He nodded at Carrick's team. 'Still driving the Holsteins? How old are they now? They're probably thinking of retiring.'

'Still, always. They're ten. They haven't failed me yet.' Carrick chose to ignore the comment about retirement. They were no closer to quitting than he was. Bronte and Sterope, named for the immortal horses that pulled the sun god's chariot across the sky, were closer to him than some people. There was no pair like them. He'd cross bred their Holstein dams with a thoroughbred sire of great speed. The colts had been born two weeks apart.

The starter gave the final call for racers. Logan stepped back from the line of curricles, shaking his hand and then Logan's. 'Drive safe, you two. I'll see you at the finish line.'

Carrick flexed his knee, forcing himself to ignore the mounting evidence. Time *was* running out. He'd been glib with Logan this morning, but his knee hurt more often than it used to. He'd turn thirty-four in a few…*in a short while*. He pushed the thought away. He couldn't afford such thoughts today. He needed to think about winning. Winning was financially and socially lucrative. Winning kept his other dreams alive, kept them hovering on the periphery, waiting for the time when they could be claimed: the farm, the horses, a decent life building carriages. An admittedly quieter life. Perhaps that's why he resisted. He was not the quiet type. Deep down, he knew he craved the reputation he'd built. He wasn't ready to disappear into the country. Not yet. But some day…some day he'd succumb to its appeal.

Carrick gathered the reins, steadying his horses for the start. It was important to go out fast and not get trapped behind the other racers. He knew from experience how that could change a race. Too much experience. In his saner moments he *did* think about retiring from this dangerous gentlemen's game. But when the wind was in his hair, the road speeding by and he the master of it all—of horse and carriage, the angles of the road—the conclusion was always the same: *Not yet.* One more season; one more season as London's fastest driver, London's riskiest driver, most daring driver, the one the men cheered for and the one the ladies swooned for; one more season as London's biggest winner. He'd made sure he lost at nothing, that he didn't know how to lose.

The starter raised a white handkerchief. 'Gentlemen, take your marks!' Harnesses jingled. Carrick steadied himself. 'Go!' He was off, surging to the fore for all he was worth. He had a legend to perpetuate and a reputation to protect. After all, if he wasn't London's most reckless rake, who was he?

Bronte and Sterope thundered to the front, taking advantage of the early start straight away. They would fly now while the road was empty and straight. They'd have to slow around the curves. One never knew what was coming on the other side of the bend. He passed a farmer with a heavy cart who swore as he sped by. He slowed his team to a trot for the first curve, the other drivers already dropping into a pack behind him with a handful of drivers still on his wheels, Landon among them. He took the curve on the inside, the team turning well, the carriage smooth on its axels.

Carrick's joy soared. This was everything! The feel of a team, a driver, a carriage all in beautiful synchronicity with each other. The wind pushed his hair back from his face and he felt the sun on his skin. The curve behind him, a stretch of empty, visible road ahead of him, he gave the horses their head. They were ready for it, had been begging for it. They loved to run.

Two-thirds of the way to Richmond, only Landon with his light phaeton was left to challenge him. They were both forced to slow as a group of market wagons took up the road. He could hear Landon cursing behind him over the traffic. Carrick laughed. He eyed the road, finding a narrow strip on the shoulder wide enough for a curricle to pass between the outer wagon and the verge. It would be tight, no margin for error. The verge was uneven ground. If he went too far to the right, the curricle could tip over. Too far to the left and he'd be on top of the dray.

Carrick would chance it. He swerved to the right, knowing Landon would follow him, taking advantage of the work he'd done forging a path, but so be it. The wagons would block the other racers behind them, ensuring it would be a two-carriage race now, just him and Landon the rest of the way to Richmond. Sterope and Bronte were steady as he manoeuvred through the narrow lane, unfazed by the other horses and the general busyness of the road. He squeezed past and then he was free!

Carrick flicked his reins and was off, finding more speed. The last curve to Richmond loomed, Landon thundering behind him, pushing him to increase his speed and the risk. He'd been lucky so far. The curves hadn't presented any oncoming traffic as yet. How fast to take this one? It was nearly noon. The recent traffic had cost him. He had no significant lead on Landon now. Landon would pass him if he slowed too much for the corner, then it would be a mad, reckless dash. Carrick kept his speed and moved to the centre of road. It was an old, familiar tactic. At least he could block Landon out and dominate the road. By driving in the middle, he prevented Landon from going around him wide or inside and it gave him better visibility if indeed anything was oncoming.

Feeling confident, Carrick let the horses run. Faster times called for faster measures, after all, and Landon was indeed pushing him today. Out of the corner of his eye, he saw Landon pull even and make his move.

Good lord! The man was crazy! He was going to pass on the inside and use the tighter turn to edge out a lead. It was sane in theory, insane in practice. Theory didn't account for the risk. If there *was* someone coming, Carrick would be able to swing left, but Landon would be pushed into the ditch along the verge. Unless…unless Carrick gave way, dropped back and ceded the road. Hell, no! He was not giving way. This was a race, Logan had managed wagers on his behalf. He needed the win, the money. This was his career. He wasn't going to give way because Landon Fellowes was driving with the devil beside him.

Chapter Two

Carrick laughed and whipped up his team. Let Landon try, just let him try! Landon threw him an exultant look as he raced between Carrick and the ditch, pushing his new Cleveland Bays. He called out, 'What's good for the goose, is good for…'

On the outside, with better visibility, Carrick saw the oncoming vehicle first. 'Landon!' Carrick called the warning, sawing hard on the reins to make a wide left, avoiding the vehicle. Recognition flashed: Noon! The Richmond coach! The world narrowed to a series of images that came too fast. He could do nothing to stop the disaster in motion: Landon's speeding phaeton overbalancing and tipping into the ditch, the horses going down with it, Landon thrown violently from the vehicle. There were sounds, too: the scream of frightened horses, the crunch and crack of the phaeton coming apart as wheels spun out into the road, the dashboard separating from the main body.

Carrick pulled his team to a halt in the safety of the left-hand verge and raced across the road, shouting orders to the driver of the coach. 'Send someone back for help! Get Logan Maddox.' Then, he was calling for his friend, hoping against impossible hope that Landon would rise from the wreckage. He scrambled into the ditch. The horses tried to rise in their panic, but were unable to move because of the unwieldy angle of the carriage. What to do first? He couldn't see Landon and the horses needed help. He clambered awkwardly to their heads, hands fumbling with the harnesses. Someone was with him in the ditch, perhaps a passenger from the coach. They had one horse free, the one with the blaze. King. The bay lurched forward, limping. The other one neighed, hurting and frustrated. This one had taken the brunt of the flip. Between them, he and the stranger got the carriage bar off the animal's back, got the harness off. The horse tried to rise, fell back, tried again.

'Leg's broken.' Carrick assessed grimly. This beautiful horse would never leave the ditch. But first, he had to find Landon.

'I've got a pistol,' the stranger said numbly.

'Wait, we've got to find the driver.' Carrick put a hand on the man's arm. Carrick stumbled over the rough weeds of the ditch, half crawling, half staggering towards what remained of the carriage body. 'Landon!' he called hoarsely. By now, the rest of the coach passengers had disembarked and joined in the search, but it was Carrick who found him, fifty feet from the carriage at the bottom of a sloping embankment, an impossible distance to imagine, and impossible to imagine anyone would survive it.

Carrick slid down the embankment, incoherent sounds

coming from his throat. He couldn't make any words. There was no impossible hope. He could see that even at a distance. The unnatural angle of the body, the awkward curve of his leg. But that didn't stop him from hoping anyway. 'Landon, I'm here. Landon…' He gathered his friend in his arms and almost dropped him, horrified. Landon was gone already. His neck had snapped on impact. All that remained was a limp bag of bones.

That was when he began to cry—huge, uncontrollable, racking sobs that rocked his entire body as the enormity of what had occurred swept him. How had this happened? They'd been laughing together, riding the wind together and then…the last vision of Landon torn from the carriage seat made it hard to breathe. He raked his hands through his hair as if gripping his head would stabilise him. But nothing would stop the wild howls that ripped from his throat.

He was still howling, hands locked in his hair, when Logan found him, when they—strangers he didn't know, would never know—took the body from him. He might have howled all day, all night, if Logan hadn't forcibly dragged him back to the road, to the wreck. There was quite a crowd. The other racers had stopped and were milling about. A few came forward to talk to him.

'Good God, man, can't you see he is in no shape for a conversation.' Logan growled on his behalf, pushing him up into the curricle, away from the crowd. 'I'm getting you to the inn.' Logan took up the reins, calling out to Sterope and Bronte with brisk efficiency.

Carrick didn't know how he would have managed the first horrible hours after the accident if it hadn't been for

Logan. Logan had a room arranged, a hot bath, a stiff drink, a warm meal and patience unending while the shock settled, while his mind grappled with the scenes it couldn't erase, couldn't put away.

Carrick stared at the amber liquid in his glass, vaguely aware that evening had come along with the return of reality, lurking like shadows on the periphery of his grief. 'He was supposed to get married this week.' Carrick muttered the words, numb, but not nearly numb enough as other implications rolled over him. *India. Dear God, India.* 'I'll have to tell her.' But how? The dazzling India Claiborne, whose smile lit up ballrooms across Mayfair, who had spent the morning at a final fitting for her wedding gown, would be devastated. Her world had been all light and perfection when she'd awakened and now that perfection had been shattered, suddenly, irrevocably, without warning. She'd had no chance to brace herself. He knew too well what that shock felt like and how helpless one felt.

Something painful surfaced from deep within him, memory twisting and turning in his gut along with the brandy—the memory of losing the most important person in the world to him, the memory of a fifteen-year-old boy losing his beloved father, a man who'd been vibrantly alive one moment and dead the next and he unable to stop it just as he'd been unable to stop Landon's death today.

'Devastating' was unequal to the description of grief that followed the realisation of what dead meant: gone for ever. No chance to say goodbye, to say all the things that should have been said long ago. India would be feeling all that and more. He would not wish it on anyone, especially not on her, a girl who'd had everything to live for, to look forward to, a girl who was the epitome of what it meant to be alive. When one was with India Claiborne, one could not help but feel alive, too. In that, they were alike. They shared a passion for living.

It had never been a chore to have her tag along on Landon's adventures once they'd become engaged. Carrick enjoyed her company. They were friends, thanks to their mutual acquaintance with Landon. But now Landon was gone. He should be there with her, to comfort her, to tell her. She should learn of it from him.

'I have already sent word to the appropriate parties.' Logan put a hand on his in comfort. 'You needn't worry.'

Carrick jerked his hand away, his temper blazing, his body feeling the first painful returns of emotion as he stared at Logan. 'No, don't you understand? *I* have to tell her. It was my fault. I should have ceded the road.' Would she ever forgive him for it? She would certainly blame him for it, how could she not?

Logan fixed him with a stern stare. 'I heard the story from the coachman. That's not the tale he tells. Landon took the risk, Carrick. *He* could have ceded to *you*, but he chose to pass on the right. He was an experienced driver and he knew the danger of such a move.'

'I forced him to consider it,' Carrick challenged, not swayed by Logan's argument. Landon Fellowes was dead, the man with the perfect life was dead before he could live it. 'One moment, he was flying past me, yelling some nonsense about what was good for the goose, and the next…' Carrick choked on his brandy '…he was flying through the air and he was gone.' Flying was too tame of word for what had happened.

'The doctor said his neck snapped,' Logan said quietly, matter of factly. 'He…'

'I *know.*' Carrick pushed his chair back, sudden and rough. He sent his tumbler, full of brandy, hurtling into the wall, shattering in a violent cascade of glass and amber. He pointed his finger at Logan, his body shaking with rage. 'Don't! Don't you dare say he didn't feel a thing as if not *feeling* the last moment of his life slip away is a consolation that's supposed to make *me* feel better.'

Logan held up his hands in retreat. 'All right. I won't say it.' He reached calmly for the decanter and a fresh glass, pushing it towards Carrick.

'The horse?' Carrick took a healthy swallow of the new drink. Surely numbness would come and oblivion would follow. If only he could drink faster, it would come sooner.

'I put him down myself. The other one is in the stable here at the inn.'

Carrick nodded, his throat thick. 'Thank you.' He wondered if there was enough brandy in the innkeeper's cellar to help him find peace. Probably not. The best he could hope for was temporary escape. Those moments would be with him for ever. Nothing would be the same. 'Tomorrow, I'll go to Miss Claiborne.'

'If you feel you must, although I should warn you, she may not receive you,' Logan cautioned sternly and they sat in silence for a long while.

'How much money do I have in the bank?' Carrick

asked at last. He never handled his winnings, never knew exactly how much he had. That was Logan's job. But surely he had enough by now.

'Depends,' Logan replied, wary. 'What do you want it for? You can't be thinking of giving it to Miss Claiborne. She has plenty of her own.'

Carrick drew a deep shuddering breath and finished another glass of brandy, his fifth? Maybe sixth? Did it matter? 'Can you arrange the deal? I want the carriage works in Benson.' He wanted to be away from here, from this world suddenly full of tragedy, one of the two things he'd sworn to avoid when his father died. The second was that he'd promised himself he'd not allow for the creation of such ties that permitted such extreme loss again. To love was to lose and losing was the one thing Carrick did not tolerate. And yet, today's events had caused those very things to rear their ugly heads.

'Are you sure? Would you like to think it over?' Logan counselled. 'Perhaps this is not the best time—'

'No,' he cut Logan off decisively. He didn't want to think. Carrick reached for the decanter, his hand unsteady, his stomach starting to lurch. He couldn't quite manage to pour a glass. Brandy sloshed on the table. He'd missed the tumbler completely. Carrick swayed on his feet. 'Logan, I think I'm going to be…' He didn't get the word out before the contents of his stomach came up all over Logan's polished boots: every brandy, every bite of food, every ounce of remorse, none of which he could take back. The enormity of the day, of what he'd done, swept over him yet again and now he knew the answer to his question. If he wasn't the reckless rake of London, what was he? He was a murderer. He'd killed his friend, stolen the bright future of a young woman and rattled the cages of his own demons. Never mind no one else seemed to see it that way. He would for the rest of his life.

Chapter Three

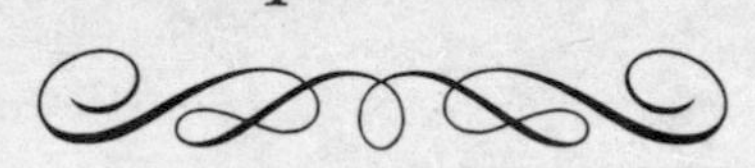

Benson, Oxfordshire—autumn 1842

She could do this. She could go downstairs and attend her first official afternoon tea in three years. India Claiborne halted on the stairs, listening to the hum of voices from the drawing room below. Once, the prospect of an afternoon tea spent exchanging news with a group of ladies would have filled her with anticipation. She would have agonised over which gown to wear, how to do her hair, how to sit to show herself to best advantage. Today's tea, though, brought out none of those anticipatory feelings. This was merely an event to be endured.

When Elizabeth had invited her to the autumn hunt party at Foxfields, attending had seemed like a good idea. She hadn't had a holiday since her parents had died. Where better to go than to her friend's home? Elizabeth had promised the house party would be small, the pressure to socialise minimal and, best of all, no one there would know her or the tragedies that surrounded her: the public tragedy of Landon's death followed less than half a year later by the boating accident off the Isle of Wight that had killed her parents.

Quite understandably after that double blow, she, who had once craved society, had withdrawn from that society out of a preference to avoid pitying stares and the repetitive barrage of questions. She'd also withdrawn out of necessity. There'd been no time for a hectic social schedule. Someone had to untangle her father's financial affairs, which had been more disorderly than one might have expected of a beloved knight of the realm. Someone had to keep an eye on her younger brother, Hal. Someone had to ensure there was an estate left for him to inherit when he achieved his majority. That someone *had* to be her. There was no one else, no one she could entrust with the task, at least.

There was Cousin Victor, but his offer of help came with a price she was unwilling to pay and with motivations he'd not taken enough care to disguise. No, she did not trust him with her home or her brother's inheritance. In fact, it was quite the opposite. She feared him and probably would until Hal was twenty-five and firmly in possession of Belle Weather. *Seven more years*. Until then, she had to stand in the breach.

'There you are, my dear!' Elizabeth gave a wave as she emerged from the drawing room, spying her on the stairs. Elizabeth swept up the steps and looped her arm through India's. There'd be no escaping now that Elizabeth had her in her gentle bonds. 'You look lovely, India. Pink has always been your signature colour.'

India looked down at her dress. To her mind it was more of a dark rose than a pink. She'd chosen it for its subdued sophistication as opposed to its colour. She'd not thought of it being pink when she'd put the gown on. She'd not thought of anything except getting through the afternoon. She could have done without the comment or the reminder of a past when she'd been the belle of every ball. Those were days gone by. She was not looking to reclaim them.

'I'm sorry, I didn't mean to remind you of anything... unpleasant,' Elizabeth offered apologetically, realising her mistake too late. 'I just meant that you looked lovely.'

India squeezed Elizabeth's hand. 'I know.' She was being touchy. Her friend had intended the remark only as encouragement, perhaps out of a misunderstanding for her reticence to join the party. India knew unequivocally Elizabeth wanted only the best for her. Elizabeth was as loyal a friend as there'd ever been all through childhood and even when their paths had diverged. At eighteen, India had gone to London for two high-flying Seasons while Elizabeth had stayed home. When Elizabeth had married, India had been her maid of honour at a quiet country wedding to Godric Blackmon. Elizabeth was supposed to reciprocate the role soon after. The two of them had never dreamed it would not come to pass.

Even amid tragedy, Elizabeth had been a constant source of support over the last three years, one of the few friends who'd remained true. Elizabeth had never forgotten her, never pried into the accident that had claimed Landon's life and India's own happy ending when she had been close-mouthed about the details. Elizabeth had simply been there, offering comfort and support, as had Elizabeth's brother, Laurie. Between them, they'd seen her through. India would be grateful for ever.

'I have good news for you,' Elizabeth whispered as they moved down the stairs. 'Laurie's arrived. He'll be a friendly face among strangers.'

Tall and trim with steady brown eyes, Laurie—Lawrence Benefield—was a welcome sight to India as they entered the drawing room. He stood by the fireplace, talking with the other men, his friendly gaze finding hers almost immediately. He offered her a smile and a nod. She smiled back and felt herself relax.

It wasn't that she was anxious about meeting people. India had no pretensions towards shyness. She'd dealt with plenty of people in the past three years who would agree; relatives who'd hid their greed behind a gossamer veil of good intentions, to solicitors who felt it beneath themselves to discuss business with a woman. It was more that she no longer had the patience for small talk anymore. Even as Elizabeth introduced her around to the guests, the empty conversations grated on her. But something else grated on her as well, especially as the circuit of introductions came to a close. Her brother was not present.

'Has Hal not come down yet?' India asked Elizabeth quietly as they moved to the last group of guests. It was after four, Hal should have made an appearance by now. At this point, he was well past being fashionably late.

Elizabeth furrowed her brow and scanned the room. 'I admit I don't know. I'm sorry, I wasn't keeping track.' Of course not. She was the hostess; she had a thousand details to see to. She didn't have time to keep an eye on a wild eighteen-year-old. That was *her* job, India scolded herself, and she'd been lax in it today, allowing herself to indulge in her own worries. She'd dawdled upstairs, reluctant to come down. Apparently, Hal had taken advantage and slipped away.

Elizabeth completed the introductions, ending their circuit at the fireplace where Laurie stood with Godric. 'Have either of you seen Hal? India is worried about him,' Elizabeth enquired on her behalf. A look passed between Godric and Laurie, so swift one might have imagined it.

'No, but I wouldn't worry, Miss Claiborne,' Godric assured her with a placating smile that bordered on fatherly before his kind, dark eyes turned towards his wife. 'Afternoon teas aren't exactly events of interest for young men his age. In fact, I know several grown men who feel the same way.' That was what worried India: the events that did hold Hal's interest. 'Of course, a tea doesn't hold the same appeal for them as it does for me.' Godric chuckled, taking his wife's hand and raising it to his lips for a kiss, the affection passing between them unmistakable after four years of marriage.

Laurie laughed and cleared his throat. 'Perhaps Miss Claiborne and I should take a turn outdoors. Shall we? We can look for your brother while the weather favours us.' He offered her his arm and India took it, grateful for a chance to step out for a moment, away from the party as well as a chance to search for Hal. As usual, Laurie had read her thoughts and answered her need without being asked.

'Godric's right, you know,' Laurie said as he manoeuvred them out to the garden. 'A tea isn't likely to hold Hal's interest. He's probably holed up somewhere, perhaps in the hayloft, waiting for the afternoon to blow over.'

India slanted Laurie a look of dubious disagreement. She wished it were that simple. But Hal and trouble had a way of finding one another. It was a longstanding relationship that had become more pronounced since their parents' deaths. Despite the five-year difference in their ages, she and Hal were usually quite alike in temperament, both of them outgoing, social creatures, and once upon a time, both of them thrill seekers after their own fashion.

But they were not alike in this—the 'afterlife' as she referred to the years since Landon and their parents' deaths. In that, they'd become polar opposites in how they had dealt with the loss of those closest to them. Where she'd withdrawn from thrill seeking, Hal had engaged it, seeking trial after trial against which to test himself.

Laurie guided them down a gravel path that boasted flowers in the summer, but was quite stark now in the grips of autumn. 'In regard to Hal, I am surprised he's here at all. I thought he was supposed to be at Oxford this term.'

That was a touchy subject with India these days and she felt herself prickling even at Laurie's polite enquiry. By rights, Hal should have gone, it had all been arranged, but he had been fiercely resistant to the point of threatening to run away if she sent him until it hardly seemed worth the effort to pack him off.

'We compromised,' India offered firmly. 'He'll start in the winter after Christmas.' Even with Laurie, a friend, she was conscious of appearing weak, vulnerable, as if she wasn't capable of managing her own brother.

'And in the meanwhile?' Laurie prompted. 'A compromise consists of *both* parties getting at least part of what they want.' She could tell he was disappointed in the decision, perhaps even disappointed in her.

She raised her chin in a defiant tilt. 'He's learning the estate books at Belle Weather.' It was hard to tell how much was sticking with him. She'd been unable to get him to sit down with the steward as regularly as she preferred, but it was a start.

Laurie studied her, perhaps guessing what she'd omitted. 'He's at a crucial age, India. He needs structure,' Laurie offered kindly. He would never presume to lecture her, but he would advise if he felt strongly about a subject. She appreciated that about him. Laurie understood she needed her autonomy if she was to hold on to any authority as a woman alone in a man's world. But today, she heard the concern and the scold in his words. She also heard what went unsaid, the message between the lines.

'You mean he needs a man in his life who will take him in hand,' India surmised bluntly, her gaze challenging.

Laurie met her eyes evenly, unfazed by her directness. 'Well, yes, India, not to put too fine a point on it.'

She bristled at that. 'I am doing the best I can.'

'You are,' Laurie was quick to assure her, 'but there are limits to what you can give him and you are fast reaching them, despite your best efforts. It brings me no joy to tell you these things, but as your friend, I think it's my responsibility to help you see the reality.' He paused, a grimace passing over his fine features. 'Forgive me, India, if I've overstepped my place. It was not my intention to come out here and quarrel with you.'

Her irritation subsided as quickly as it had sprung up. She was prickly today on several accounts and definitely not at her best. She flashed him an apologetic smile. 'Of course, Laurie. There's nothing to forgive. I cannot cut up at you simply because you tell me the truth.' It was an unpleasant realization, but one she'd known for quite some time. She'd been Hal's sister long before she'd had to become his parent, a role she was admittedly not ready for.

How did a twenty-year-old girl become both a father and mother to a fifteen-year-old? Even now, she often wondered how a twenty-three-year-old maintained that role as that one-time adolescent now edged towards adulthood? She found herself in the dubious position of needing to condemn behaviours she'd once championed and antics she'd once laughed at. Hal thought her quite the hypocrite.

They reached the end of the gravel path and stopped beside a rose trellis, the wooden shape of it fully exposed, the framework devoid of its covering of waxy leaves and profusion of blooms. India ran her hand over the wood, its nakedness too obvious a parallel to her own. Landon's death had exposed her heart, but her parents' death and the aftermath had stripped away all the trappings that had kept her cosseted, secure.

She'd been naked for so long now, she barely recalled what it felt like to be any other way, to be like those people inside the house who dressed themselves in manners and politeness, who thought that somehow they were better protected against the world than their lesser counterparts, that they couldn't be touched. It was hard to believe she'd once been like them. What a lie they told themselves! Everyone could be touched. The past three years had taught her that. No one was safe from grief, from the revelation of secrets, from the hurt of loss.

'You needn't bear the burdens alone,' Laurie said quietly from the stone bench where he'd taken up residence.

She turned and smiled at him. 'I don't. I have you and Elizabeth.'

He shook his head. 'That's not what I mean. Have you given any thought to re-entering society?'

She stiffened. 'Why would I do that? I haven't time for parties and balls, for being away from the estate for months on end all for the sake of pleasure-seeking.' Although, once she had. The Season had been the centre of her universe, something her life had depended on.

Laurie crossed his booted legs at the ankles, gazing at her thoughtfully in a manner that put her on alert. His words came slow and filled with intent. 'For the same reasons other young women enter society. Marriage.' India made a stern face at the mention of the taboo topic. Usually a grimace was enough to warn Laurie off the subject, but not today. Today, he pressed on with unusual persistence.

'It's been three years, India. Surely you've thought of it? You can't remain alone. You needn't make a grand return and go to London. There are quieter places that would suit just as well. Bath, perhaps?' His gaze lingered, refusing to break from hers. 'I had hopes that your presence here at Foxfields might signal such a return. Am I mistaken?'

'I have no intentions of marrying, you know that.' She was disappointing him. Again. For the second time that day.

'Perhaps you should revisit the merit of that decision.' Laurie's brown eyes, usually a soft shade of chocolate, were now reminiscent of the hard agates that lay in the stream bed at Belle Weather. 'There is no arguing the benefits of a husband if only from a practical standpoint. He would lift the burden of Belle Weather from your shoulders, he would keep it safe for Hal.'

His voice dropped low and private as he softened. 'A husband would keep you safe, too. He would stand between you and Victor. Your cousin frightens you more than you admit, I think.' Laurie rose from the bench and came to stand beside her, his tone sincere. 'There would be other benefits, too. You deserve a life of your own, India. The right husband could give you that—a home, a family.' Laurie had never spoken on the subject so passionately before.

The quiet intensity of his words caused her to look at him anew, the fine Benefield features, the brown eyes that reflected care and intelligence along with sternness when warranted. There was strength in Lawrence Benefield along with compassion. But for the sake of their friendship she did not dare lay claim to it if indeed her instincts were right and he was testing the waters before openly putting himself forward as such a candidate.

'It wouldn't be fair to such a man, if such a man existed,' she warned, her gaze never faltering. 'I could not give my heart.' Her heart had died with Landon and Laurie deserved so much more than she could offer.

Laurie seemed to consider the importance of that for a moment. 'Perhaps the right man could do without your heart. Perhaps he'd understand and be happy with whatever you *could* offer.'

She shook her head. 'A smart man would realise it is a poor trade for him. I've made my decision. I will never marry,' she said firmly.

Laurie slanted her a look, temporarily resigned. 'Never is a long time, India.' It was. She knew. She'd lived it in perpetuity since Landon had died. She had not been Landon's wife, but she felt very much that she was Landon's widow. She felt the loss of him and her parents every day. They'd been her bulwarks and they were gone now, for ever. That was another very large amount of time. For ever and never. Always and nothing. Two sides of the same eternal coin.

'Speaking of a long time, we've been out here quite a while. Perhaps Hal will be back by now from wherever he's been hiding,' India suggested, desiring to move the conversation away from the difficult space it had wandered into.

'Yes, perhaps he is.' Laurie turned to head back inside, but she did not miss the hesitation before he'd answered. His eyes gave him away and she froze on the path.

'What is it, Laurie? What are you not telling me?' A knot of worry formed in her stomach. 'You know where he's at.' Her temper flared. 'All this time, you knew and didn't tell me.'

'I don't know that he's there for sure. I didn't want to tell you, India. I wanted to protect you.'

'By protecting Hal?' India railed. 'Where is he?'

Laurie seemed to debate with himself and then relented. 'You won't like it. Several driving clubs are in the village for a series of carriage races and Hal fancies himself quite the whip.' Even with the confession, he didn't say it outright. He was letting her put the pieces together to a horrifying conclusion. *Carriage racing.*

The knot in her stomach tightened to Gordian proportions. No wonder she hadn't been told. She understood better Godric's almost patronising look this afternoon. 'Does Elizabeth know?' She swallowed hard, feeling betrayed on all sides. These people were supposed to be her friends. They were supposed to be on her side. Laurie shook his head. Well, that was something at least.

'You men decided to keep it to yourselves,' she scolded. 'How dare you decide that on my behalf? I thought better of you, Laurie.' She surged ahead of him on the gravel path, only to feel his grip close about her arm, forcibly halting her.

'Wait, India, what you going to do?'

'I'm going down to the village and bringing him home, assuming he's not been hurt or trampled.' Dear lord, anything could have happened to him. He could be dead, even now. How dare Hal do this to her? He knew what carriage racing meant to her, the awful nightmares, the memories she had of that day, of standing in her wedding gown on the modiste's fitting block when the news had come. *There's been an accident on the Richmond Road...* Even now tears stung in her eyes at the memory, at the thought of having to live through such a thing again. If anything happened to Hal, she wasn't sure she would survive it.

'What do you think that will accomplish?' Laurie said sharply. 'If you go down there and drag him home by the ear, embarrassing him in front of those men, he will not forgive you for it. A young man's pride is often all he has at that age.' It was yet another reminder that she was not cut out for the task of taking her brother in hand.

'He'll be alive,' she retorted, but she saw the wisdom in his counsel. Her relationship with Hal was already stretched. Stretched too far and it would break. Besides, it was likely too late to extricate him from the race without him losing face.

'Hal's a good driver. He'll be fine. Let him be, India. If you must question him on it, do so in private.'

She nodded and let Laurie walk her back inside. There was nothing more to be done until Hal returned. All she could do in the interim was hope her brother didn't do anything stupid or drive too fast.

Chapter Four

The village of Benson, England

'Damn. The kid's fast.' Carrick lowered his binoculars and whistled in appreciation as the carriages neared the finish line in a cloud of dust at the second annual Oxfordshire Regional driving championships. Beside him, Logan, acting as the event's official organiser, tossed him a smug *I-told-you-so* grin.

'Fast and stupid,' Carrick qualified his appreciation as the crowd screamed wildly for the champion, a fair-haired young man who was perhaps twenty years old only under the most generous of terms despite his claims to the contrary on the entrance form. If the boy had lied about his age, what else might he have misrepresented? It made Carrick wonder if the boy's name—Hal Whiteacre—was false as well. Not that it mattered overmuch to Carrick. He had no connection to the boy.

Whoever he was, he gave the concept of driving with 'reckless abandon' new meaning. He'd cut off three racers in a dangerous swerve that took him across the wide expanse of road in the home stretch to secure his victory, a move worthy of Carrick in his younger days.

Logan shrugged off the remark, letting the crowd and the racer have their moment of celebrating before the official victory ceremony. 'It's not his fault he's reckless. He doesn't have any mentoring. Think what he could do if he had a master to teach him?' He gave Carrick an arched glance full of implication and challenge. 'Now, if you'll excuse me? I have a cup to present.'

It was a hell of a remark to drop and then leave. Logan knew very well Carrick was done with it all. A man had died on his watch. Carrick let himself drift to the back of the crush, watching the victory scene with detachment. Well, almost. Three years on, and the thrill of victory, even vicarious victory, had never quite left him even though he'd left racing. Days like today were complicated for him, as he suspected Logan well knew.

Logan had believed from the start that he'd left racing too precipitously, a knee-jerk response to tragedy instead of a well-reasoned one. It was ironic considering back then Logan had been the one who'd nagged him about his knee while he'd been the one reluctant to acknowledge the encroaching finality of his racing career.

Carrick almost believed Logan had organised this annual event just to remind him of how much he loved the sport and how he'd left too soon. Of course, Logan might also have organised the event because it gave him an excuse to see his friend a few times a year, or because it gave that friend some popular exposure for his carriage works, or because it was good money for Logan.

Not that Logan needed the money. Logan had wealth aplenty as Viscount Hailsham. But wealth alone was not enough. Logan also needed the thrill of the challenge. Just like he did. It was one of the things they'd bonded over as boys at school together. Neither of them had outgrown that or the loss of their fathers—the other thing they'd shared.

Carrick watched the crowd hoist the tow-headed champion up on their shoulders, bearing him with raucous cheers towards the platform where Logan waited with the cup, a great shining silver behemoth with careful, elegant engraving commemorating the occasion. Carrick had a case full of cups just like it, displayed in the privacy of his rooms above his carriage shop—a reminder of pleasure and pain, the thrill of racing and all it had cost him. The case was a private penance.

He slipped into the side streets away from the crowd, making his way to his shop where it would be quiet, where he could be away from it all. There would be drinking and celebrating at the inn, but the shop would be empty tonight. He'd given his workers the day off to enjoy the racing and to study the carriages—what technologies had performed well? What could be improved upon?

Maybe he would work, though. He'd have the workshop to himself and he had several orders to complete by the end of the month. He prided himself on never missing a deadline. Or maybe he'd indulge in the luxury of working on improving his phaeton design, a phaeton with a release lever that could be used to separate the horses from the carriage in an emergency. Just the thought of it brought a smile to his face. He should enjoy the peace while it lasted. If he knew Logan, Logan would find him eventually. They had a conversation to finish.

* * *

True to form, Logan found him a few hours later, fitting a wheel on to an axle. 'You should be at the White Hart, drinking with the victors.' Logan strolled into the workshop with feigned idleness, stopping to study a wheel here, a crane-necked tongue there. Only a novice conversationalist would think Logan didn't have something on his mind. 'You have as much right to celebrate as anyone. Your carriages showed well today in all the divisions. You should be pleased.'

Carrick nodded and stepped back from the wheel, wiping his hands on his leather work apron. 'No lost wheels, no broken axles, no overturned carriages, no injured horses. A good day indeed.' Safety first. That was how he defined good racing these days. He followed Logan about the shop with his eyes.

'So, why aren't you celebrating then?' Logan turned from his scrutiny of a harness to fix him with a stare.

'I am not one of them. Not any more.' Carrick began picking up his tools. He wouldn't get any more work done tonight, not with Logan on the prowl. His friend wanted something. As for what *he* wanted, it wasn't that Carrick didn't want to go to the White Hart and drink with the victors. It was that he couldn't. He feared what it would do to him, how it would stoke the hunger to an unmanageable level. It was like asking a man who suffered from too much drink to go to the tavern and watch other men indulge while he languished from a thirst he couldn't quench.

'Celebrating is good for business, especially with the memory of your carriages fresh in the minds of excited men whose pockets are full and whose hearts are already thinking about next year. You could sell some carriages tonight, make some new contracts.' Logan put down the harness and began to stroll again. Carrick was not fooled by his friend's nonchalance.

'I've already got enough orders to keep me busy for the next two years and more coming in every day,' Carrick argued. He knew what Logan was driving at and he wouldn't make it easy for his friend. He couldn't. The temptation loomed too great, too powerful.

'Then hire a few more apprentices.' Logan chose to ignore his rebuttal. He reached into an inside breast pocket of his coat. 'I have your share of the profits.' He pulled out a wallet, thick with bills. 'The event is catching is on. I'm thinking of expanding it to three days next year, maybe adding a horse-racing component. There's interest in some other counties, too. They want their own regional championship. There's a chance you could expand the carriage works, maybe open a second shop in one of those counties.'

Carrick did not miss the slanted look Logan gave him as he laid the wallet on the table. 'We're at a point where it makes sense to form a syndicate and a travelling team. People will turn out to see racers and local whips will pay big money to prove themselves against professional drivers with publicised reputations.'

Carrick chuckled, non-committal, trying to hide how tempting it was. Regardless, he couldn't give in. 'You always were the one with the ideas, Logan.'

Logan slapped the table with his gloves, irritation evident. 'Don't play coy with me, Carrick. Look me in the eye and tell me you don't miss it. The women, the excitement, the thrill of victory, the wind in your hair.'

Carrick stopped his puttering and faced his friend. 'Whether or not I miss it is irrelevant. A man died trying to pass me.'

'Oh, sweet Lucifer's balls, Carrick, are you *still* carrying that around with you? It's been three bleeding years.' Logan was genuinely exasperated. 'You didn't *make* him pass you. He took that chance all on his own.'

Carrick shook his head. 'Why do you care so much if I race or not, Logan? Weren't you the one who wanted me to retire? You were always mothering me about my knee.'

'Retiring and quitting aren't the same thing. *You* quit.' Logan didn't back down. 'I am worried about you. You didn't just quit racing, you quit living. You didn't come north with me last Christmas to see friends. We all missed you.'

He'd missed them, too. But Carrick hadn't been sure he was up to all the festive cheer of Christmas and it was easy to use the excuse of work to avoid the trip. He'd let the season pass quietly with a pork chop and a few tankards of Christmas porter at the White Hart. Carrick sighed. 'I'm not joining the racing team, if that's what you're angling for.' This was an old conversation and it wasn't the first time Logan had asked.

Logan nodded, seeming to consider this yet again. 'All right. I won't ask you to join, but there's a place for you, of course, should you change your mind. There are also other ways you might consider being involved, for now. There's the syndicate. I'd like you on the board. We could use your expertise. You'd get a percentage of the profits. Regardless, you'll be the carriage sponsor for our racers. They will all drive your creations. It will be fabulous advertising. You'll have more orders than you can manage. You can expand at a time when other carriage-makers are struggling for business.'

It was a generous caveat. But it wasn't done solely out of friendship and Carrick knew it. Logan was using it as a breadcrumb, to lead him slowly back to the racing world, to move him off that world's periphery and back to its centre. Carrick blew out a breath. Even outright rejection didn't stop Logan when there was something that man wanted.

Carrick raised his head to refuse once more when he caught sounds in the outer yard. A white-haired blond head poked into the workshop, eyes landing on him, and then searching until the intruder found Logan. 'Mr Maddox, is this a good time?'

Mr Maddox? The address had Carrick on full alert. He watched Logan straighten up, his demeanour changing immediately, a wide smile on his face, all consternation over the polite feud with him fading. Logan's hand was outstretched as he strode towards the newcomer. 'Hal, of course! You found us all right? It's so good of you to take time out of your celebrations.'

The young man stepped into the workshop, shaking Logan's hand. In the light, Carrick recognised him as the winner of the carriage race. He held back, letting Logan make the introductions. 'Hal, this is Carrick Eisley, the man who made many of the top finishing carriages. Carrick, this is Hal Whiteacre, our curricle division winner.' Up close, twenty was generous indeed. Did the lad even shave? Carrick was quite sure he'd faked his age and his name now on the race entry. Which meant two things: the boy had likely sneaked away from somewhere to race and he was trouble. Boys that sneaked away from home were usually followed by angry guardians.

He was going to shoot Logan. Never mind that Logan was a pistols expert. How dare his friend invite the enemy into his camp? But Logan merely grinned, quite pleased with himself. 'Mr Eisley saw your race, Hal.'

'Did you?' Hal reached over and offered his hand to Carrick, forcing Carrick to extend his own with less enthusiasm. 'What did you think, Mr Eisley? I would like your opinion.' Carrick saw through that little overture immediately. The boy was cocky. Adulation was more likely what the boy was looking for. This boy wasn't interested in an opinion as much as he was interested in winning some praise. Well, he might be in for a surprise. Carrick decided not to hold back.

'I think you were reckless. What you did endangered three other drivers and your own team.' There. Now he'd see if Hal wanted his opinion after that.

Logan shot him a scathing look, 'Certainly Hal is untutored, Carrick.' Logan opted for the high ground, giving the boy an apologetic look in the case the remark hurt the boy's well-armoured ego.

Carrick narrowed his gaze and crossed his arms over his chest, his tone stern. 'How old are you, Hal? And don't tell me you're twenty because you're not. I want the truth.'

His tone must have worked. Hal shifted on his feet, his gaze darting between him and Logan. Logan gave a short nod and Hal cleared his throat. 'Eighteen,' the words came out in an adolescent croak. 'As of last month.'

'Eighteen?' And barely. It was even worse than he

thought. Sweet mercy, Hal Whiteacre was a *boy*, hardly even a young man. What was Logan thinking to let him race? To let him lie about his age? To bring him here to the carriage works? Carrick fixed both of them with hard stares of censure. Age did not excuse recklessness.

The *boy* didn't like that. He set his hands on hips, his jaw set hard. 'I haven't wrecked anything yet, sir.'

Carrick raised an eyebrow. '*Yet* would be the key word in that sentence. You keep racing like you did today and you will.' He did not have time for a cocky boy who wasn't even old enough to shave more than once a week, *if* he was lucky.

'You have something against my racing?' The boy gave him a sharp up-and-down appraisal full of disrespect. 'I'd like to see you behind the ribbons, old man. You pull off what I did today and then we'll see who can criticise whom.' Hal spat on the floor in a show of imagined male bravado. 'Besides, most people who have a problem with my driving are just jealous.' He gave a mean grin. 'You jealous, sir?' Then he tried out his arrogance on Logan, 'I thought you said this man would want to train me, that he was any good.'

'Train *you*?' Carrick didn't wait for Logan's response. He exploded, splitting his disdain between the two of them. Logan must be out of his mind. 'You told him I wanted to train him?'

'He does want to train you, Hal,' Logan asserted, meeting Carrick's gaze firmly as if he could forestall another argument. 'Mr Eisley just doesn't know it yet.' Logan's eyes glimmered with mischief as they challenged Carrick to deny him. '"Yet" is the key word in *that* sentence,' he parroted, tossing Carrick's words back at him.

Carrick answered with a false smile, his own gaze steely. 'Perhaps Mr Maddox is forgetting that I am not in the business of training boys.' Or anyone.

'Come on, Carrick. He's got good instincts. If you don't want him to wreck anything, you should train him,' Logan said. 'How is he supposed to get any better? Any safer?' Ouch. Logan was stabbing hard now if he was willing to invoke the safety argument.

'For starters, he's too young.' Carrick ignored the appeal to safety. Hal Claiborne was too young and too arrogant. Those sorts never took instruction well. In short, he was far too much like Carrick was at that age.

'Too young?' Logan scoffed with mild good humour edged with sharpness. 'Since when have *you* become the arbiter of what is too young? Was sixteen too young for losing your virginity in a whorehouse? Was seventeen too young for racing your first horse? Was eighteen too young for—?'

Carrick cut him off with a scold. 'Apparently, thirty-six isn't *old* enough for having one's secrets aired in public. Good lord, Logan, show some discretion.' But the point was taken. Who was he to say what was too young? At eighteen, he'd resented any limitation put on him.

Carrick looked at the cocky youth before him, the gangly arms, the long coltish legs. He was slender still, not yet full come into his size. Not that the boy realised it. Carrick knew too well a boy his age already believed he was a man. Hal would be a tall, well-built man in a few years. He'd have trouble keeping the girls away then. Probably already did. Probably didn't mind it too much. Goodness knew *he* hadn't minded it at that age, or any age really.

Carrick could feel himself start to relent. What could it hurt to help him out a little, especially if it got Logan off his back. If it helped keep young Hal Whiteacre safe, so be it. Perhaps the boy's safety, and those he raced with, would be a worthy trade off.

And maybe you should be careful, the voice of caution whispered in his mind. *Maybe it's just another justification to take one step closer to returning, the beginning of a slippery slope.*

Carrick sighed. 'Maybe I could give him a couple of tips.' To the boy he said, 'Come back around noon tomorrow, as long as your parents agree to it.'

'My parents? Oh, they'll be fine with it,' Hal assured him. Good. Angry papas and worried mamas were bad for business, especially if they were of substance. Carrick had not missed the boy's polished grammar: *then we'll see who can criticise whom.* Hal Whiteacre was educated. Carrick shot a hard look at Logan, drawing his line. 'I'll offer a couple of tips, *but* this in no way constitutes formal training.'

Logan grinned, clapping a hand on his shoulder. 'Of course not. I wouldn't think of forcing you into anything.' Carrick raised a disbelieving eyebrow. The hell he wouldn't. A man had to watch himself around Logan or he'd end up doing all sorts of things he'd promised himself he wouldn't do.

'I think a drink is in order.' Carrick moved to a cupboard and took out three glasses and a bottle of the good stuff. Usually, he saved it to toast important sales. His buyers liked the idea of having a drink to seal the deal. He thought he might need more than a drink after tonight, but it was a good place to start.

Carrick raised his glass, feeling obliged to offer a toast. 'To your victory today.' That seemed appropriate, safe and non-committal.

Then Logan had to go and ruin it. 'Here's to new beginnings.' Giving a boy a few pointers didn't constitute new beginnings. Carrick would make sure of it. His racing days were long behind him and he was not looking back, no matter how thirsty he was.

Chapter Five

She'd looked everywhere for Hal. India was beginning to think she'd never find her errant brother. He hadn't been in the Foxfield stables, or in one of the many inns Benson boasted. It was a rather large village, to her mind, and to her feet now that she'd walked most of it from the High Street to Littleworth Road. It boasted a tidy selection of shops selling dry goods, foodstuffs and clothing.

Most of all, it boasted inns: the Crown with its wheelwrights and blacksmith's forges; the Red Lion at the corner of the High Street and Mill Lane; the Castle, appropriately named for its location in Castle Square at the centre of the village; the Sun Inn on Chapel and Watlington which had been her first stop on the edge of town. All with no luck. No one had seen Hal or anyone like him meeting that description.

Now, she was down to the last two inns: the small Three Horseshoes, next door to the rather large edifice of the White Hart, an inn she'd saved for last on purpose, although she probably ought to have started there given that the White Hart was the home of the Bensington Driving Club which had been a sponsor of last weekend's race.

She stepped out of the autumn sunlight into the dim interior of the White Hart Inn. She gave her eyes a moment to adjust. She'd spent most of her afternoon trying to track him down and the tracking had taken her to unencouraging places, places she'd rather not find Hal. Perhaps if she was in a less pessimistic mood, she'd be buoyed by the fact that Hal *wasn't* in those places. But she was quite cynical these days when it came to Hal. She wasn't at all confident she'd like what she found when she found him.

She surveyed the sparsely populated inn, taking in the billiards table at the back where two men played, the empty mid-afternoon tables in the taproom. He wasn't here. No one was here. That meant he wasn't shooting billiards or drunk. That was the good news. The last thing she needed was for Hal to be keeping company with the driving club. It would only add fuel to his fire to race.

'Can I help you, miss?' a friendly female voice called out from the bar, which both startled and surprised India. Usually, people—men—found her presence in public houses unwelcome.

She approached the long, polished bar. 'I was just looking for someone, Hal Claiborne? I'm India Claiborne, his sister.' She offered a brief description. No one who'd ever met her brother would forget his wild, white-blond hair, the sharp blue eyes, or his easy laughter.

The woman's smile broadened. 'Ah yes, the tow-headed lad who raced last weekend. He's quite the whip, put on a good show.' She wiped her hands on her apron. 'I'm Sarah Shrubb, proprietress of this establishment. I know all the club drivers. Your brother was here with the carriage-maker for lunch. They left a while ago to go driving on the Oxford route. They should be back soon.'

Sarah Shrubb's openness and kindness were a relief even if the news about Hal was not. 'Thank you. Is the carriage works near here?' At least now she had a destination.

'It's just a street away. The carriage-maker takes all his meals here. The man used to be a racer himself. Your brother's in good hands.'

India thought that was debatable. Clearly, Mrs Shrubb had a different opinion of carriage racing than she did, but the woman had been kind to her. She thanked her and made her way down the street with a brisk step as if by hurrying she could put a stop to something that was already in action. In reality, she could undo nothing. The verdict was already certain.

Her brother was up to no good if he was out practice racing a stranger behind her back. And it was definitely behind her back—he'd told her he was out riding when in truth he was out *racing*. As if entering that competition this past weekend hadn't been bad enough, as if he hadn't sheepishly promised her that he'd be more careful when he'd flung open his bedroom door to find her waiting for him when he'd returned, trophy in hand.

Not even four days later after a dressing down that had taken the better part of an hour, he was at it again and likely had been all week under the cover of going out riding. Instead, he was risking his damn fool neck. Just like Landon had, like her father had. Such risk taking had killed them both *and* her mother. She didn't want her brother dead, too.

She'd lost everyone, she wasn't going to lose Hal. What would the past three years have been about if she lost Hal? If all of her protection came to naught? The thought propelled her down the street.

India reached the shop, its shingle painted with a black carriage silhouette and elegant spidery tracings announcing: *Benson Carriage Works, established 1809.* The shop front was neat red brick with two white-paned windows on either side of a clean white door, a pediment overhead; it was eminently respectable in appearance. She supposed carriage-making itself was indeed a respectable occupation. It was what gentlemen *did* with those carriages she took issue with.

She took a moment to gather herself and draw a calming breath. She needed to appear firm and commanding, not hysterical. If the past three years had taught her anything, it was that one must deal with men firmly from a position of overtly demonstrated strength. There was no room for weakness. If she'd shown any sign of vulnerability, she and Hal would have lost Belle Weather and been bundled off to distant relatives.

The bell tinkled as she stepped inside, announcing her to no one. So much for appearing firm. There was no one to appreciate the effort. The small front office was empty, but she followed her nose and her ears, tracking the scents and sounds of lumber and the forge to the back where the shop opened out into a large work yard filled with carriages in various states of production.

She found Hal immediately, the sound of his laugh leading her eyes to where he stood. His back was to her as he talked excitedly with the man beside him. Seeing Hal so happy poked a bit at her anger, threatening its sustainability, and India tightened her grip on her resolve. Happy or not, Hal had lied to her *after* he'd given his word and he'd jeopardised his own safety.

The man beside Hal shook a dark auburn head and made a motion using his hands to explain something, broad shoulders lifting beneath a cotton work shirt. The gesture, the hair—an auburn so rich it looked like an autumn forest on fire—awakened a sense of familiarity that suggested quite improbably she knew this man. But how could that be when she'd never been to Benson and when her association with men over the past three years had been limited to the family solicitor, the land steward and various relatives, Cousin Victor among them? All of them over forty and many of them living embodiments of dry sticks.

This man was none of those things; neither over forty, nor a dry stick. He gave the appearance of being very much...*alive*. Vibrantly so. She would leave it at that. The billowing folds of his shirt were tucked into the narrow waist of dusty breeches that hugged well-muscled thighs and long legs that tapered into equally dusty boots, the dust further proof, if she had needed any, that Hal and this man had been out driving. It was a further reminder, too, that her sense of reproach was not unwarranted.

India cleared her throat and raised her voice to be heard over the general din of the workspace. 'Hal Claiborne, what do you think you are doing here?'

At the sound of a feminine voice in a decidedly masculine setting, the yard went silent. Workers stared. Hal and the man turned, Hal looking surprised and abashed at having been caught out. The man beside him fixed her with an intense grey stare, the kind of stare that could leave a certain kind of woman breathless. She *knew* those eyes, that hair, that easy, vibrant grace. Her intuition had not been wrong. A leaden ball of betrayal settled in her stomach as disbelief swamped her, flooding her with fury and unlocking memories in its wake.

Carrick Eisley. London's most reckless racer, rake extraordinaire whether it was behind the ribbons of a fast team or tempting debutantes with his flirtatious charms. Landon's close friend and the man who had been the last person to see Landon alive. The man who had literally driven Landon to his death.

A thousand emotions rocketed through her: bone-deep sorrow, abiding grief, hurt, dismay, a fury born of fear that fate had come again to play a cruel trick on her, perpetrated by perhaps the same man who'd stolen not just Landon's life from her, but had stolen her own life from her as well. Nothing had been the same. She would never forget how it had felt, how it still felt every day since. It was the fury that she latched on to, the fury that kept her upright. India mounted her attack with a single word. *'You.'* She met his storm-grey gaze with the ferocity of her own. 'How dare *you* come near *my* brother?'

'India?' The word slipped out before he could think better of it or think at all, so great was his surprise. It wasn't the shock of seeing her that undid him—he'd recognise those blue eyes and that defiant tilt of a head anywhere—it was the shock of seeing her here of all places, in his carriage yard, the very last place he'd ever expected to see her. How had she found him? Why had she found him? What was she doing here? His brain started functioning again. He knew the answer to those questions. She'd not been looking for him. She'd been looking for Hal Whiteacre, only Hal wasn't who'd he'd claimed to be. Hal Whiteacre was actually Hal Claiborne. 'Your brother?' His gaze slid a scolding glance in Hal's direction, 'You lied about your name, Hal?' And more. Likely, he'd lied about his parents' approval, too.

Another layer of shock settled on Carrick at realising what he'd done: he'd agreed, albeit unwittingly, to take on *India*'s brother as a protégé. If he'd known who Hal really was, he might have resisted Logan more firmly. *No, you wouldn't have*, his conscience whispered. *You'd take any excuse to race again.* Would he? Was that what lay behind taking on a protégé or was there something more? Or perhaps it was a little of both.

There was a lot to sort through. It was hard to focus on Hal's deceit and his own motivations when India Claiborne stood before him, the past rushing up to meet him in living colour. Here stood the woman Landon had loved, the woman he had taken it all from with a single decision made in the heat of a reckless moment; the woman who'd refused to receive him when he'd called after the accident to make amends, a woman who'd not forgotten him and clearly had not forgiven him. A fate that put India Claiborne in a carriage yard in the middle of Benson, Oxfordshire, was a cruel fate indeed. Of all the small villages in England, she'd found her way into his, or rather her brother had. What could he possibly say to her?

'Hal, step outside. I will speak to Mr Eisley alone.' Her china-blue eyes, once sparkling with laughter, were hard and unyielding, never leaving his as she gave her order.

Hal looked about to protest. Carrick was swift to intervene. 'Hal, go.' He waited until Hal had huffed out of the office, slamming the door behind him before he spoke again. 'India, I had no idea.' She must be reeling although she gave no sign of it. 'I know how this must look to you,' Did he? How did this look to her? His words seemed empty.

This was not how he'd ever imagined their first conversation since the accident. He'd certainly not imagined having it in the middle of his shop. What must she be feeling to discover her brother in his company? Did she know Hal had been racing? That would not sit well with her. He didn't need to be a genius to know she'd lay the blame for that at his doorstep, too, as soon as she made the connection.

She crossed her arms, eyes flashing. 'You know absolutely nothing, Carrick Eisley.'

'He said he had your parents' permission.' He tried to placate her and defend himself all at once to no avail.

She gave a little snort. 'Did he? Then that's two lies he's told you. Our parents are dead. I'm Hal's guardian now.'

The words stunned him. Implication after implication rolled over him. She'd lost everyone. 'I didn't know.' He automatically stepped towards her, wanting to comfort her out of instinct. She stepped back out of reach, her gaze steely. 'I'm sorry.' Were there any two less effective phrases in the English language than 'I didn't know' and 'I'm sorry'? Yet he was relying on them to convey layers of meaning.

He *was* sorry he'd taken on the boy under false pretences of approval, sorry that her parents were dead. His brain did a quick calculation. Losing her parents would have been quite a blow, coming in such close proximity to Landon's death. Even not knowing the dates, there could not have been much time between the tragedies. She was not dressed in mourning today and it had only been three years.

He was sorry, too, that at such a young age she was now responsible for raising a brother who might have been just fifteen when his parents had died. It was a critical age to lose one's father at, as he knew too well from the loss of his own. It made a boy desperate for manhood, desperate to prove himself, desperate to fill that void.

Most of all, Carrick was sorry for her. The India Claiborne he'd known was not this woman with hard eyes who stood before him. At some point, she'd lost herself, too, and that was probably his fault as well.

'I didn't come for your pity,' she snapped. 'I came for Hal. Now that I have him, we'll be leaving.' Leaving? Just like that? With no consideration for the past?

Remember, she wants nothing to do with you, the voice in his head railed at his finer sentiments. *Let her go. Let the boy go. You don't want this. You don't need it. You promised yourself no more attachments and that's what you're inviting here.*

The words were easier said than done. Despite the defiant tilt of her chin, India Claiborne was in need of help and he owed her…owed her so much.

He could never completely atone for what he'd done, for what he'd cost her. One didn't have to be a parent to see the problem with her approach. No eighteen-year-old boy wanted to be commanded by his sister in front of men he'd spent nearly a week with, men who'd treated him like an equal.

Carrick shrugged as if he didn't care if she walked out the door. 'Hal will be back. He raced last weekend.'

'Do you think I don't know he raced?' She bristled.

'You didn't know he was here for four days,' Carrick replied drily. There were few people he tolerated such an attitude from. 'Your brother is a touch arrogant. I can see where he gets it.' Carrick reached for a towel and wiped his hands. 'He's a good driver, India. He won't settle for being dragged away by his sister. He's already lied to us and to you in order to race. He'll keep at it until he gets what he wants.'

'To us?' She arched a blonde brow. 'Who is "us"?'

'Myself and Logan Maddox. He's the race sponsor.' Carrick could see she didn't like that. No doubt she was remembering the trouble the two of them and Landon had once managed to get into.

'You and Logan are in it together? I should not be surprised. The two of you were always neck deep into some scheme.'

'Schemes you participated in on more than one occasion,' he reminded her. 'Your brother has talent. Logan introduced us after your brother won. I've taken him out a few times this week.' Hal had been instinctively good with the ribbons, surprising Carrick with his level of intuition when it came to the horses. He'd hate to see Hal go, although it surprised him to admit it.

'Don't do it again.' India was white with indignation. In other circumstances, Carrick would have taken offence at anyone walking into his establishment and telling him what to do and who he could do it with. But this was not arrogance. This was fear masquerading as conceit. Her eyes gave her away. Her fear was understandable and obvious, at least to him. Carrick wondered if she saw it as clearly. She was afraid of losing Hal. Did she see how ill-suited her solution for that was, though? The more she sought to shelter him, the more her brother would rebel.

It was what he himself had done in the wake of his own father's death. Hal was already lying to her, already sneaking around, using false names. Did she think the deception would end? If she pushed her protective agenda, Hal wouldn't stop there in his bid for freedom and independence.

'Hal has talent,' Carrick said again carefully, exceedingly aware of his position and his lack of credibility. She did not want to hear anything he had to say and yet he was exactly the person who should be saying it—a man who'd also lost a father, a man who had been addicted to risk and the adulation of the crowd that came with it.

'A talent for what? For dying young?' India was fierce, her gaze unwavering. She gave him a cold half-smile.

'Not if done right,' Carrick argued, an idea coming to him, his motivations becoming clear to himself. He could not give her back Landon, but perhaps he could help her brother, show him how to race effectively and safely. Perhaps this could be his private penance, a meagre attempt at atonement.

'I suppose *you* know how to do it right?' India snapped. 'Why should I believe that based on your record? Why should I *allow* that?' She'd begun to pace in her agitation, some of her coolness slipping. She'd been lovely in a classic sense when he'd known her in London: pale skinned, blue eyed, flawless manner, dashing wit and all that spun white-gold hair. The past three years had taken all that beauty and transformed it, chiselled away its soft edges. Where she'd once been a Muse, she was now a Fury. Beautiful and terrible to behold in the protection of her brother.

'Do you think I am so naive as to think you want to teach him to drive out some sense of altruism? That you saw his talent last weekend and thought, "I'll take him under my wing"?' She gave a toss of her head. 'I am sure Logan, and perhaps yourself, made plenty of money on my brother. I know how this works. I know men like you and Maddox. You see a boy with talent and you don't stop to ask what's best for the boy.'

Carrick glared, his own anger rising at her accusations. There were many things she might accuse him of that he would endure because they were true. But using a boy for money? To feign friendship for personal gain? Never. The insult was not to be borne. 'Men like me? Do you know me so well that you can draw such conclusions? It must be nice to read minds, Miss Claiborne, to be so sure of oneself that one never makes a mistake when judging people.'

He advanced on her then, gratified when she took a step back, some of the fierceness in her eyes replaced with wariness. 'You have no idea what these last three years have been like for me.' Did she think there'd been no pain for him? No day that didn't pass with regret? He wanted to yell that he'd dedicated his carriage works to designing the safest conveyances possible so that accidents like Landon's didn't claim lives.

'Very well. We agree. We know nothing about each other. I'd just as soon leave it that way.' She turned, finished with the conversation. Carrick let her go, but not without a few parting words.

'You do know you can't stop him. Your brother will make his own decisions,' he called after her.

She turned and faced him, gaze burning. 'And when Hal does, you can make yours.' A gauntlet thrown if ever there'd been one. Now that he knew of her displeasure, he could not take refuge in ignorance a second time if Hal came to him. To take Hal out driving again would be to deliberately court her wrath. But to not do it, would do her a greater disservice even if she didn't realise it. Hal was brilliant, but dangerous.

'Hal will race with or without your approval, with or without decent instruction, and that would be a recipe for disaster.' He'd not meant to take on a protégé, but that was before he'd known who Hal was. That changed everything. He owed India Claiborne. He'd cost her Landon and the life she'd imagined. He would not be responsible for her losing her brother, too. Perhaps giving her a well-trained brother was the very least he could do and he *would* do it, preferably with her approval, for all their sakes.

Chapter Six

'You disobeyed. You broke your promise. How could you? You gave me your *word*, Hal!' India only waited long enough for the village to fall behind them on the ride back to Foxfields before she gave vent to her scold, the anger she'd turned on Carrick now effectively channelled towards Hal. Anger was a conveniently sustaining emotion, she'd give it that. Without it, she might have gone to pieces in the carriage yard. Anger would get her back to Foxfields and up the stairs to her room. Then she could give in to the other emotions—shock, fear, dread—but only when she was alone. That was her rule. No one was allowed to see her vulnerable.

'I promised you I wouldn't *race*.' Hal drew his horse alongside hers with a long-suffering sigh as if she was the one in the wrong, as if she was the one causing trouble. 'For the record, I *was* out riding.' Riding to the village, riding to meet a man who had a reputation for trouble.

'That's just semantics. Don't insult my intelligence, Hal. You knew very well what I'd think and it was not that you'd be riding into the village to meet with a racing sponsor,' she snapped. 'You were out practicing racing techniques. Worse, you were doing it behind my back, not just once but all week.'

All week. A new wave of fear swept through the armour of her anger. Hal had been with the man who'd caused the accident that had killed Landon. *But not the last part on purpose*, her conscience nudged. Scolding him for disobedience was one thing—scolding him for being with Carrick was another. Hal couldn't have known who he was.

Hal was quiet, stoically enduring her scold, or ignoring it altogether. Sometimes it was hard to tell. She was braced for Hal's response, expecting a tirade about his desire to be independent. She was not prepared for what came instead. 'India, who is he? You knew him. He upset you, perhaps more even than finding me there.'

Dear lord, what to say? And yet, telling Hal might be the deterrent he needed to stay away. 'Carrick Eisley used to race with Landon. That should be reason enough to discourage your association.' Or perhaps knowing Carrick's *ton*nishly fabled past as a risk-taker extraordinaire would just push Hal towards him more firmly, forbidden fruit being what it was.

When Laurie had spoken of Hal needing a male mentor in his life, neither of them had been imagining a man like Carrick Eisley in the role. 'Promise me you won't see him again.' She was already considering how fast she could pack and leave, taking Hal with her back to the safety of Belle Weather.

Hal shook his head, displaying a rare seriousness. 'I can't promise that, India. It was wrong of me to have promised as much as I did the first time.' He glanced her way, looking far older than eighteen. In that glance, she had a glimpse of the man he might be in a few years, a man of determination and integrity if she could keep him on the right path.

'Perhaps you need to trust that I know my own mind and I'll make the right decisions for myself. I am a racer, India, although I know it's not what you want to hear. It's in my blood and I'm good at it,' he argued in earnest, showing a strength and a maturity she'd not seen along with the stubbornness that, lord help her, she had seen displayed rather often. That frightened her. Her brother was growing up. *He will make his own decisions.* Carrick's warning echoed in her mind. *You cannot stop him.*

'Good? At racing? Like Landon? He ended up dead.' She might as well be blunt about it if the gloves were off.

'Better than Landon,' Hal corrected quietly. 'I won money, India. Money we could use for Belle Weather.' He gave her a sly look, a little grin quirking his mouth to lighten the tension that had risen between them. 'Remember, I've seen the ledgers. I know how close it is. We *need* an influx of income for the roof, for the repairs on the tenant cottages, and we need to be thinking about investing in some of the new farming implements if we want to maximise the crop yields, especially with more tenants moving off the land.'

That was a rather impressive summation of the situation at home and surprising too. She favoured Hal with a wry smile, torn between pride in her brother's thorough grasp of the estate's economics and the inconvenient timing of him displaying his knowledge. 'So you *did* learn something this autumn.' She allowed herself a little teasing. Perhaps her compromise with Hal had not been in vain after all. She'd have to tell Laurie.

Hal did not tease back as she thought he might. His grin vanished. 'I learned enough to know how difficult it's been for you to keep things going and how hard you've worked. You've done incredibly well to turn things around. I never guessed how dire the financial straits were, how close to the edge Father had been economically.' India heard the censure in Hal's tone for himself, as if a boy off to school most of the year should somehow have known.

She was aware of Hal's gaze on her, studying her perhaps for a response? Worrying over what that response might be? Perhaps he, like herself, was aware that this was the first time the two of them had openly addressed the situation Father had left them in. She offered what absolution she could. 'He hid it too well from all of us.' Each of them had been guilty of ignorance when it came to the family finances.

'I don't think even Mother knew. I didn't.' She shook her head, still unable after all this time to give herself the absolution she offered so freely to Hal. 'I was caught up in my two Seasons in London. When I think of all the money spent on dresses I wore once or twice, on matching shoes and fans, and silly fripperies simply so I could be the belle of an evening, it almost makes me ill. It was money spent on foolish things when there were such greater needs.' She'd been self-focused and unaware in those days of what it took to power the life she recklessly led in London.

'You're too hard on yourself. How could *you* have known?' It was apparently Hal's turn to offer absolution. She smiled softly at her brother's intuition, another sign he was growing up. 'But once you knew, once you understood the predicament, you've done well for us—not just for me, but for our tenants. I think you've made up for whatever girlish frivolity you accuse yourself of.' Hal fixed her with a solemn blue stare. 'Now that *I* understand, it's my turn to help as well. I am old enough. I *can* contribute. There's money to be made in carriage racing.'

It was an elegantly constructed argument, India gave him credit for that. He'd skilfully taken their mutual concern over Belle Weather's finances and combined it with a desire to come alongside her as a partner, something she'd been emphasising all autumn with wanting him to learn the ledgers. Only, he'd come to a far different conclusion than she about how best to achieve that. She drew a steadying breath. Anger wouldn't help her here. She needed to reason with Hal. 'It was only one race. One win does not a rich man make.'

Foxfields came into view with its white fences marking the pastures and the long stable block that housed Godric Blackmon's well-curated string. Hal shrugged unconcernedly and India had a sinking feeling her brother had an easy answer for her. 'There can be other races, other wins, more money. *Regular* money. Logan Maddox is forming a racing team. I've been invited to travel with him. I can send money back to you.'

India's hands curled tightly about the reins. The ghosts were crowding thick today. Logan, quieter than Carrick, more circumspect in his behaviours, was no less dangerous. That was only the first thing wrong with Hal's announcement. The second was that Hal was going to leave her and it *wouldn't* be for university as they'd agreed upon. He would have to eschew his schooling in order to travel with Maddox's syndicate.

Then there was the principle of the matter. She could not accept racing money with a clear conscience. It would validate Hal's choice and his disobedience. She returned her brother's stare, determined to make him feel guilty enough to comply if need be. 'If you want to help, then do it at the estate. I need you there. Belle Weather will be yours. A gentleman needs an education, not a racing career.'

'A gentleman needs funds. A gentleman doesn't sit back and sponge off his sister. I can contribute, India, and I can do it with carriage racing.' There was a bit of heat and bite to his words now as they neared their destination. He was not backing down and neither was she. 'I am not Landon, India.'

'No, you're not. You're my brother. My last living family.' She ground the words out as a headache took up residence behind her eyes. 'Everything I've done has been for you and all you give me is disobedience.'

'Disobedience? You think I was betraying you, but I wasn't trying to hurt you. I was trying to protect *you*.' Hal raised his voice, matching her chagrin.

'I do not need protecting.' She was tired of men protecting her. Her father had tried to protect her. It had left her ignorant and nearly bankrupt. She'd almost lost her home. Cousin Victor wanted to protect her in exchange for her subjugation. Laurie thought she should marry again, primarily for protection and ease. She'd rather fight her own battles even if it meant being alone. It was the only way to keep her and Hal safe.

She kicked her horse into a rapid little trot, relieved that Hal had enough sense to let her go. He couldn't possibly guess everything the afternoon had meant to her. She'd come face to face with her past, with a man who'd changed the trajectory of her life and now threatened to change it again. She wanted to run as far from him and the unresolved emotions attached to that time as she could. India rode the rest of the way in silence, marshalling the remainder of her mental reserves. She could only fight so many battles in a day and there was still another one waiting for her at Foxfields. This one with Elizabeth.

'I swear I didn't know who he was. I barely knew Benson had a carriage works.' Elizabeth sat on the edge of the bed in India's room, aghast over India's revelation. Her face was pale with dismay. 'You don't think I'd deliberately invite you here knowing that such a spectre of your past was nearby?'

India reached for her friend's hand, regretting that she'd given voice to the thought. 'No, of course not. How could you when I never shared any names, any details?' This was her fault. When her friends had gathered around her after the accident, she'd withdrawn in all ways, not just retreating physically from London, but retreating mentally, closing off the horror by not talking about it.

Elizabeth had never pressed for those details. Now, that decision was coming home to haunt her. For all of her efforts to protect Hal, he'd ridden into the lion's den quite literally. She could have prevented at least part of it if she'd told him more about the accident.

That Elizabeth would marry a man who'd acquired an estate a few miles from the small village where Carrick Eisley had purchased a carriage works after he'd disappeared from London was a random coincidence, proof only that Fate had a cruel sense of humour. That India herself would visit that estate, her first trip anywhere in three years, only added to that irony. The latter piece might have been prevented. If Elizabeth had known, India might never have been invited to Foxfields, might never have gone into the village and encountered him. But today, she'd tripped all those wires.

'Seeing him has unnerved me, I must admit.' India drew a deep breath. She was still unsettled from the encounter a few hours later. 'It was like coming face to face with the living embodiment of the worst part of my past.' She shuddered. 'There he was, so vibrant, and seeing him made the past leap to life.' Carrick had been Landon's close friend, always at the centre of everything they did. In those days, a room came alive simply because Carrick entered it.

Against her will, memories rose of the last time they were all together. They'd stolen away, a group of eight of them, to a deserted parlour at the Durhams' ball for a wild game of truth or dare just two weeks before the accident. The game had been Carrick's idea and it had been wickedly good fun.

Today, he'd been more sombre than she remembered him, but no less magnetic. He still exuded an eye-drawing, breath-catching brand of masculinity standing in the work yard, even dressed simply in a shirt and breeches—tight breeches that showed every muscle and sinew of those hard legs. His was not Landon's sleek, elegant, blond, ballroom male beauty, but there was no denying he had a rugged appeal of his own. In London, women had lined up to dance with him, to feel that grey gaze on them, those hands on them, as he guided them about the ballrooms, shoulders straining through the confines of his tailored evening jackets.

Mamas warned their daughters about him for good reason. India could testify first-hand he waltzed divinely despite his rugged build and size, seduction in every movement. Not that she'd been affected or that he'd ever exercised that potential on her as his friend's intended, but it had been there all the same, always simmering below the surface as if it couldn't be entirely contained.

'Was it the past that unsettled you or the man?' Elizabeth asked, carefully pleating the blanket's folds with her fingers. The question was bold for Elizabeth, who made it a practice to never pry. *The man?* India paused before answering, wondering at the implications beneath the question.

'Both, perhaps. I'm not sure I can separate the two. Carrick *is* part of the past, part of its pain and its pleasures.' He was embedded in both the good and the bad. Her response to him today had been based on that, but there was no denying he was an attractive male. Was that what Elizabeth meant? She'd never thought of Carrick that way before. She'd never needed to, there'd always been Landon, and now there was the accident between them, creating a gulf of its own, a gulf that had only widened with time.

India was quick to disabuse her friend. It seemed both Elizabeth and Laurie had the same idea for her, that she ought to marry *someone*, ought to seek out a man to stand between her and an uncertain future. 'He might appeal to a certain type of woman, but not me. He's a reckless rogue and I'm done with such behaviour, such men.' She was done with men in general. Those closest to her had failed her, Landon in dying and her father in providing for her.

Even if she were interested in finding a man, Carrick would not be a suitable candidate. Life required stability and financial security and it was up to her to provide those things for herself and her brother. She didn't need to make another mistake by putting her trust directly or indirectly in another man just because he had storm-grey eyes and shoulders broad enough to carry the world. She was a woman of that world now, not a dewy-eyed girl who believed in fairy tales.

Chapter Seven

'I swear I didn't know. How could I? Hal didn't even use his real name. Had I known…' Logan shook his head, shooting Carrick a look of disbelief over ale at the White Hart, his words trailing off as he returned once more to the other realisation that had floored them both. 'India Claiborne is *here*? In Benson? After all this time?'

His words mirrored the train of thought that had run through Carrick's mind since the moment she'd stalked into his shop, angry, defiant, as stunning as ever. Perhaps even more stunning. Now, there were sharp edges to go with the sharp tongue that had once entertained him.

She'd been a saucy but naive debutante when she'd taken London ballrooms by storm. Her cheek had made him laugh back then, even as he'd understood there was a certain naivety behind her repartee. She did not understand half of what she nuanced. She was not so innocent now. Where once she'd looked upon him as an interesting friend of her fiancé's, today she'd looked at him as if he'd been the very devil. She was not wrong there.

Logan took a long swallow of his ale. 'Dare I ask—how was she?' Neither of them had seen India Claiborne in three years. She'd disappeared from the social scene two days after Landon's accident and had not resurfaced. Then again, neither had he. Carrick understood that need to vanish. His carriages made more social appearances than he did and he was fine with that. Tragedy had a way of reshaping a man and perhaps a woman, too.

'Prickly. Furious. She doesn't like us, as you might imagine.' Carrick leaned back, allowing the barmaid to serve his pork chop and potatoes while she flirted with him. 'She doesn't hold with racing, but she holds me responsible for Landon's death.'

'Did she actually say that?' Logan picked up his fork and knife and cut into his meat.

'Not in so many words, but she was not thrilled to see me and she was eager to protect her brother. That protection said it all.' She'd been like a fierce mother bear. It was well meant, but she needed to be careful. Her brother wouldn't thank her for it. 'Don't worry, she doesn't like you either. You are responsible for taking advantage of her brother.'

Logan looked up from his meal. 'Exactly how am I doing that? The boy pestered *me* to enter the race. I hope you pointed that out to her?'

Carrick chewed his pork chop and pointed his fork at Logan. 'You are making money off him, exploiting his talent and tempting him away from whatever she's got planned for him.'

Logan grimaced. 'I'm starting to rue the day I let him talk me into allowing him to enter the race. Hal Whiteacre wasn't nearly as troublesome as Hal Claiborne is turning out to be. Perhaps it's for the best that he'll be moving on. Once the visit to Foxfields concludes, they'll go home.' Logan waved his tankard for refill. 'It's too bad, though. I could have used the boy for the syndicate and I think he could have used the syndicate, too, if you know what I mean.'

Carrick did know. The syndicate would help Hal grow up, find an outlet for his cockiness, experience the world of men where an eye could be kept on him. Despite India's worries, Logan ran a tight ship. His racers behaved. The syndicate would give Hal a chance to gently untie the apron strings India had him tethered with. That decided it. Between Hal's talent and need and his own debt of guilt to India, the decision was clear. He met Logan's gaze. 'I want to train him.'

'Train him? Four days ago you didn't even want to give him tips on driving and now you want to make him your protégé? Don't tease me like that, you know that's what I've been hoping for.'

Carrick leaned across the table in earnest. The more he'd thought about it this afternoon, the more he wanted to do it. 'It makes perfect sense. You said yourself that he'll race any way. He might as well do it right. I want him to do it right. I owe India that much. I can't bring Landon back for her, but I can help her protect her brother from a careless disaster.' He lowered his voice. 'Logan, I *need* to do this.' He couldn't decide if the need stemmed from penance or absolution. Perhaps it didn't matter.

'It will mean stepping back into racing,' Logan warned.

'Maybe. For a short time. Just long enough to see him

taken care of.' Carrick needed to be careful with himself here so that he wasn't doing this for his own gain, that this offer didn't come from some convoluted desire to justify what his heart had never stopped hungering for. He'd settled with himself on the craving for adulation, the addiction to victory and popularity. But deep down, the real hunger, the hunger for the wind in his hair, the thrill of the flight, had never left him. Teaching Hal was *not* to be an excuse to re-engage that part of him. It would, however, be a test of his fortitude to resist that lingering temptation.

'India won't like it.' Logan thrived on playing devil's advocate even when he was being offered something he wanted.

Carrick gave an irritated grin. 'Whose side are you on? I thought you wanted Hal for your syndicate? This way everyone gets what they want. Hal gets to race, you have your driving prodigy and India gets to keep him safe.' And he got to do his penance. All around, a good deal.

'You'll have to convince her.' Logan polished off his pork chop. 'I'd like to be a fly on the wall when you try to persuade her the two of you are on the same side.'

Logan was right. He needed India's compliance. Now that he knew Hal had gone behind his sister's back, he could not in good conscience continue to train him as if he had permission to. While it would be true for anyone he offered his services to, it was doubly true given these unique circumstances. He'd unwittingly hurt India once already. He'd not consciously repeat that. It was part of what he owed her.

'You think I can't do it.' Carrick felt the old hum

of competition start to thrum through his veins. He grinned shamelessly. 'Is that a wager, old man? A quid says I'll have her agreement. Come along tomorrow, if you like, and watch the master at work.' Even as he joked with Logan, it wasn't all humour and competition. There was a seriousness, an urgency beneath it all. He *needed* to do this. Tomorrow, he would call at Foxfields and somehow persuade India he could help her by helping Hal. Tomorrow he would have a chance to put something, no matter how small, into the balance against his guilt. He would not allow her to turn him away this time. The remorse of a survivor outweighed the fear of potential attachment. The latter he could guard against. He could do his penance without being drawn into the emotion.

A man's long-nursed guilt was a powerful tool, conjuring images that haunted him long into the evening and made for restless sleep. That night, Carrick dreamed of her, of that horrible day following the accident in brilliant, detailed colour…

Carrick glanced up at the four soaring storeys of the Claiborne town house already featuring a black mourning wreath. Did he look presentable? He gave his cuffs a final tug and straightened his dark jacket before mounting the steps at a funereal pace. This was not a call he wanted to make. But it must be done. He must see her, must try to explain.

Carrick straightened his shoulders, gathered his courage and lifted the heavy bronze leonine knocker. Perhaps he should have brought flowers? He was regretting that he hadn't. His hands suddenly felt empty, or perhaps that was just a physical reaction to the desperate urge to give her something. It was too late to do anything about it now. The door opened, a stern-faced butler stared at him, daring him to speak.

Carrick cleared his throat. 'Mr Eisley to see Miss Claiborne.' The butler shut the door. Carrick waited. The wait seemed interminable. When the door reopened, the butler looked even sterner.

'She is not receiving.' The butler gave him a curt nod and made to close the door.

Carrick stuck his foot out, jamming the action. 'Her father, then. May I see Sir Randolph?' He craned his neck in an attempt to see around the butler, searching for any sign of movement. Perhaps India had come downstairs at the sound of his voice? Perhaps if he called out to her and she was nearby, she might intervene and allow him admission, assuming these orders were from her parents and not her.

The butler looked affronted and shifted his stance to deliberately block Carrick's gaze, but not before he'd caught sight of copious arrangements of flowers in the hall. 'We are a house in mourning, Mr Eisley. I've been instructed to ask you to leave.' But others hadn't been turned away, it appeared. From the looks of things, the family had indeed been receiving condolence visits. Sympathy was welcome, just, apparently, not from him.

'Just tell me, then, how is Miss Claiborne holding up?' He was desperate enough to beg news secondhand if he must. He could not leave without knowing that at least.

The butler's eyes widened as if he'd committed an

egregious atrocity. 'I would not presume to say, Mr Eisley. Good day.' There was an emphasis of finality to those last words that warned he was on the edge of being removed forcibly from the premises if he persisted in this most ungentlemanly conduct.

Carrick handed the butler his card with whatever elan he had left under the mounting insults. 'Please tell the family I've called.'

Carrick turned from the door before the butler could shut it in his face and trudged down the steps, the message clear. After a year of being welcomed into this home as a dear guest, he was suddenly persona non grata. The Claibornes hadn't even bothered to dismiss him to his face but had sent a servant to do it for them. He was officially beneath them.

At the foot of the steps he looked back up at the house one last time. He scanned the windows, looking for a face, hoping that he might catch a glimpse of India, but there was none, not the slightest twitch of a curtain to indicate anyone had even been there. He could not restore Landon to her or turn back the clock. But he could give her what she'd asked for today—his absence from her life. He would not seek her out again, in person or by letter. Perhaps this abrupt severing was for the best. Pressing their association would only cause her grief and his to linger, each other a constant reminder of what had occurred.

Carrick woke in a sweat, his breathing laboured as his mind sought to separate reality from the dream. She had come to him at long last and by extraordinary circumstance. He had a chance to make amends and he would not fail her again.

* * *

'There's a gentleman to see you, Miss.' One of the Blackmon maids announced, slightly breathless, her colour high. India set her pen down and sighed, taking in the excited sight of the maid—Dolly, she thought the girl's name was. India had seen that reaction in enough women to know what it meant: Carrick Eisley was here. It was the one thing she'd hoped wouldn't happen but had fully expected anyway.

Carrick was tenacious and determined when there was something he wanted and she'd seen yesterday from the set of his jaw and the stubborn folding of his arms over that broad chest of his that he wanted Hal. Add to that his naturally competitive nature and it hadn't taken her long to conclude that Carrick wouldn't be satisfied with how they'd left things at the carriage yard. Carrick didn't like to lose. The question was just how would he go about winning? Would he go around her back and tempt Hal to further defiance covertly or would he approach her directly? Apparently, he'd opted for the latter.

'Put Mr Eisley in the blue salon.' India reached for the pounce pot and sprinkled the letter containing instructions for her land steward with sand. 'I'll be there momentarily, as soon as I finish with this note.'

Dolly's eyes went round. 'How did you know it was a Mr Eisley? I never told you his name.'

India gave her a rueful smile. 'You didn't have to. Now, let's not keep our guest waiting.' She shooed the girl away and took a moment to gather herself. She smoothed down her skirts and mentally ran through the agenda that had no doubt prompted this meeting as she made the journey to the blue salon. She knew what he wanted and she knew she could not allow him to have it. She would not give Hal to him. She would stand her ground and dismiss him as quickly as possible before anyone came home.

Elizabeth and Laurie had taken Hal out riding to a folly at the far end of Godric's property and several neighbours had joined in, making the most of the good weather. She'd been invited, too, but she'd refused on the grounds she wanted some time alone. It wasn't a lie. She had correspondence to take care of regarding Belle Weather, that much was true.

But also, she'd not wanted Carrick to hunt her down in a group. If she had to face him, she wanted to face him alone, although there was a bit of risk in that as well if she were caught. The last thing she needed was word getting back to Cousin Victor that she'd been entertaining a man alone. Although, the chances of that happening were slim if she dispatched Carrick with haste. Twenty minutes of politeness ought to do it.

Dolly was still in the blue salon, chatting amiably with Carrick as if such behaviour between a maid and a guest was standard protocol, when India entered the room. India supposed she couldn't blame Dolly entirely. Carrick did have that effect on people. He could put the shyest wallflower at ease and coax even the most strait-laced bluestocking out of her corset. It was a good reminder to self, especially when faced with Carrick Eisley polished and dressed for an afternoon call in clean, tight-fitting buckskin breeches and a double-breasted green wool coat cut for riding, a dark blue waistcoat and pristine white linen making up the layers beneath.

His stock was tied neatly but simply, his russet waves were tousled, proof that he'd ridden over hatless. He'd never liked hats. She'd always privately agreed. Who would choose to wear a hat when one had such glorious hair to show off?

'Tea, Dolly, please.' India gave the girl a verbal nudge as Carrick's attentions swung in her direction.

'India, thank you for seeing me.'

'Miss Claiborne,' India corrected him as Dolly left the room. She settled on the blue damask sofa near the fire. 'Be careful with such familiarity, Mr Eisley. You'll set Dolly's tongue to wagging below-stairs. That's how rumours start and that can hardly be what you wish.' It was certainly not what she wished. Cousin Victor watched her every move, just waiting for her to fail, and there were so many ways for a woman alone *to* fail. Not just economically with Belle Weather, but in how she protected her reputation. So far, she'd given Victor no room for complaint on either front.

Carrick took the tall, wing-backed chair across from her, his grey-eyed gaze assessing, perhaps registering the change in her. Once, she would not have cared if he'd indulged in such familiarity. She would have laughed at any concern such an action prompted for her reputation. She was no longer that reckless girl, she no longer had Landon's name, Landon's honour to protect her. She had only her own. She had to tread more carefully now. There was too much at stake.

He gave her a short nod, crossing one long booted

leg over his knee. 'Forgive me... My manners are rusty. I am not out much in society these days'

'As am I.' She offered a polite smile that didn't quite reach her eyes.

His russet brows arched. 'You seem quite sharp to me, Miss Claiborne. Yesterday *and* today, I might add.'

'I meant I am also not out in society,' India clarified. 'There is much to do with the estate. My brother and I are only here at Foxfields for a short visit. Hal will start university in the new term.' She held his gaze steadily, willing him to take in all the information she'd imparted in those three short sentences.

I am not the girl I used to be. I am running an estate and it is my life now. Soon, Hal will be beyond your reach, don't waste your time. She'd packed a veritable biography of her past three years into those words.

Carrick sat back in his chair, looking thoroughly relaxed, a smile playing easily on his lips. 'You always were direct. That hasn't changed. I understand you well...very well.' Humour flirted in his eyes and stirred her temper. He was laughing at her when she wanted to be taken seriously. 'You're warning me off.'

Dolly returned, bearing the tea tray, and set it between them on the low table. India gestured that Dolly should stay. No one could say she'd been unchaperoned if the maid was present. 'I'm not warning you off, Mr Eisley,' India corrected. 'I'm trying to save you time. Hal is too busy for Mr Maddox's racing syndicate and whatever else the two of you have cooked up together.' She poured tea as she spoke, automatically adding a healthy amount of milk and sugar to the cup before handing it to him.

'Thank you. You've an excellent memory. You remembered I take my tea white when forced to imbibe.'

She managed a wry smile, 'It's hard to forget. Your tea hardly looks like tea when you get done with it.' The delicate pink teacup looked ridiculous and fragile in his hands, a reminder that she did not entertain a citified dandy, but a *man*.

'You seem quite sure it's Hal I've come to discuss.' His smile broadened and yet managed to become more private despite its openness as if he smiled just for her.

India's own hands stilled on the second cup at the implication that perhaps he'd come instead to discuss *her*. Did he think she was shallow enough to fall for such an appeal to her vanity? 'We both know it's Hal you've come for, just as we both know that I've asked you to stay away from my brother, so your visit is moot. Do not think you can outflank me with a little flirtation.' In the past his flirtation had been a game only, something they'd done to pass the time and to sharpen their wits on one another. But this was different. Today it was no game.

She met his eyes over the rim of her teacup. *Remember, if you know me, I know you. I watched you work your tricks often enough in the old days.*

He gave an easy chuckle, clearly more at ease with the conversation than she was. That worried her. Was he at ease because he felt *he* was in control? 'I am not seeking to outflank you. I have come out of respect for the fact that you are Hal's guardian, something I was not aware of until yesterday. Now that I am aware, I have no desire to act against your wishes.'

'No, your desire now is to *change* my wishes,' she

parried with a touch of steel in her tone, but he did not retreat.

'Exactly so. Yesterday, you were shocked and I was surprised. We got off to a poor start. We couldn't see that we were really on the same side.'

She'd not expected that. It was hard to debate with someone who agreed with her, but that couldn't be. It made no sense. 'You think we are friends?' She managed the words with a cool neutrality that disguised her disbelief over his audacity.

'We were. Once. Why should we not be again?'

That was too bold. He'd gone too far, now. Her cool neutrality slipped. 'That is insolent, even for you. How dare you come here after what happened with Landon and think you can move on to an untried boy like my brother who has no notion—'

He did not let her finish, cutting in swiftly. 'It is *because* of Landon that I am here. Your brother is a good racer, but he's reckless and that's a danger to himself and to those who race with him. I don't want to see him in an accident, too.' He paused and leaned forward. 'Let me help you by helping him.' His grey eyes were in earnest, his words tugging at her. In all the time she'd known him, Carrick had been wild, but he'd never been mean or dishonest. How she wanted to believe him! How easy it would be to lay down this one burden for a short time, to let someone else take Hal in hand.

But to what end? And should the man to do so be the man who'd been on the road with Landon the day Landon died?

The questions whispered in her mind, followed by the one question she always asked herself these days—

what will it cost? What did Carrick want? No one did anything without reason.

'What exactly are you proposing?' India asked carefully.

'I propose that Hal works with me at the carriage yard. It would be beneficial for him to learn how vehicles are made. The more he understands weight distribution and balance, the better he'll understand a vehicle's limitations. I have a place out in the countryside where he can practice with me and be well supervised on the weekends.'

Weekdays at the carriage yard. Week*ends* with Carrick in the country, racing. Did he think she didn't see how that would go? 'University would lose its appeal.'

'You don't know that,' Carrick replied. 'I'll be honest with him about the risks, I'll show him the dangers. Eighteen-year-old boys think they're invincible. I'll show him he's not before he learns it the hard way. He may change his mind about carriage racing.' Carrick paused, his voice softening. 'Either way, it's *his* mind to make up.'

'He's a gentleman's son, Mr Eisley.' What would her father think of Hal working at a carriage yard? Working, having a trade, was not what her father had planned for Hal and it would come to nothing. One day he would have an estate to run.

'So am I. I am not above doing work that I enjoy.'

India shook her head, his words a reminder that he'd been born a gentleman, but he was like no gentleman she'd ever met. 'Your offer is expansive, but I am wary of such generosity. Why would you do such a favour?'

His grey eyes stilled on her, their usually restless

depths quieting. 'It's not a favour. It's penance. I owe Landon this and I owe this to you as well. I cannot bring him back for you, but I can make sure it doesn't happen to anyone else you love.' He was as solemn as she'd ever seen him. She had underestimated him. These three years had changed him, too, in ways she was only beginning to discover. Perhaps neither of them was who they used to be.

'I've waited a long time to pay my debt, India.' Her name was a soft caress on his lips and this time she did not correct him. They'd managed to talk around Landon and what had happened, but now Carrick's words brought him to life here in the room with them as surely as if he'd sauntered in, fresh from a ride.

More than that, his words brought to life other things that had lain dormant—uncomfortable things such as the knowledge that Carrick had been there when Landon died, that he'd been the last person to see him alive, to hear his last words. What had those words been? What had Landon said? Had he cried out for her? Perhaps she was craven to want to know, or worse, perhaps she was morbidly demented? Those unknown moments haunted her. What had those last moments been like?

Even now at times his death seemed surreal. How was it possible he'd been with her, laughed with her as he'd dropped her off at the modiste's and then less than two hours later he was gone? Vanished from her life in a most permanent way. How was such a thing possible? They'd had their whole lives ahead of them and it was as if he'd disappeared into thin air.

India rose and strode to the window that overlooked the garden, taking the opportunity to compose herself.

She did not want Carrick to see the chasms his words had pried open in her. She could not go through such loss again should something happen to Hal. She was barely surviving this. And, she suspected, Carrick was right. Hal would race with or without her approval. 'You'd best put your offer to Hal, then. As you said, it's his decision to make.'

She heard the sounds of Carrick rising and taking his leave. 'Thank you, Miss Claiborne. Have your brother report to me tomorrow.'

She managed a nod of her head and did not turn until she was sure Carrick was gone. She'd promised herself she'd keep Hal safe. Perhaps this was the best way to do it. But she was also keenly aware that Carrick had got his way. She'd need to tread carefully to ensure she didn't give up further ground. Hal *would* go to university come winter term. She'd need to write another letter to her land steward, informing him that her stay at Foxfields would be prolonged. She would not leave Hal alone here even if it meant facing the ghosts of the past.

Chapter Eight

'I'm glad you decided to stay. You would have missed all this.' Laurie made an expansive gesture with his arm as they strolled up the drive of Foxfields, the brilliant autumn leaves overhead filtering soft sunlight in a bright blue sky. It was the sort of day made for long walks and time outdoors. Autumn had indeed been blessed with splendid weather this year and there was no arguing it was the best season in which to enjoy Foxfields, vibrant colours outside, warm fires inside, good meals and even better company. Under other circumstances, her enjoyment would have been complete.

'I hope your sister is glad.' India laughed. 'I don't want to become the guest who stayed too long.' It had been two weeks since Carrick's proposal regarding Hal. The other guests had gone home, the small hunt party officially concluded.

'No, hardly. A friend can never overstay their welcome, you know that, India. Lizzie has been wanting to have you here for ages. She'll be loath to let you go.' Laurie patted her arm where it slipped through his as they walked. 'I will be, too.' When she'd announced her intentions to stay, Laurie had quickly amended his own return, saying his own estate and business ventures could easily be managed from Foxfields a while longer.

It had made for amiable mornings. She and Laurie took breakfast together, before adjourning to a sitting room Elizabeth had generously turned over for them to use as an office, where she and Laurie took care of their individual estate business.

'It has been good to be among people,' India admitted. 'I don't mean socialising. I don't need teas and parties. But there is something comforting about having people about who aren't servants or land stewards or solicitors. One lot is looking to you for direction and the other lot is waiting to critique you, waiting for you to make a mistake.' At home, every day was like walking a tightrope. Despite her worries about being gone from Belle Weather, it had been undeniably pleasant to be away.

Laurie slid her a soft smile. 'You are alone out there, too much. I worry for you. I want to help.'

'You *do* help, you *have* helped, you and Elizabeth both,' she assured him. 'I appreciate your letters and your advice.' Mostly because Laurie had mastered the art of waiting to be asked for advice before offering it and was never offended if she opted to go a different direction. Advising was a conversation with him where there was room for her ideas, as opposed to one-sided lecture. Unlike Cousin Victor, whose letters and advice were unsolicited and who was upset when that unsolicited advice went, in his words, 'unheeded'.

'I would like to help more.' They stopped beneath

the flame-red canopy of a spreading oak, rays of sunlight turning Laurie's brown hair to a polished walnut sheen. 'We have been friends for a long time, have we not? And now I find that I have something on my mind. Actually, it's been on my mind for quite a while and I feel I need to talk about it.'

'This sounds serious.' India was all immediate concern. Laurie asked so little of her in return for his friendship and constant, quiet companionship.

'It could be.' He gave a short laugh and took her other hand, a new, almost nervous look shadowing his gaze. He began to speak, but the rumble of carriage wheels and the jingle of harness overrode his words as a phaeton came into sight, turning on to the drive. Two figures were on the bench, one tow-headed, the other red.

'It's Hal!' India exclaimed, a burst of excitement filling her at the sight of her brother. He'd not only gone to work for Carrick, he'd gone to live over the carriage works as well and she missed him. It was practice, she told herself, for when he left for university. But still, the chance to see him was a wondrous surprise.

'And Mr Eisley,' Laurie put in, dropping her hand and stepping away, but not before she caught Laurie's disappointment over the interruption. But he was all smiles as the team came to a halt.

'We've come to take you on a picnic, India,' Hal called down from the high seat, all smiles himself. Working in town clearly agreed with him. India could immediately see the changes in him. He was happy. Gone was the surliness that had been too often about his mouth and in his posture. He climbed down. 'I'll ride on the back, India. Take my spot. Mr Benefield, would you care to join us? You and I can both squeeze on the back.'

'No, thank you, Hal. It's good to see you looking well.' Laurie smiled at her brother and turned a softer version of that smile on her.

For a moment, she was torn. Laurie had wanted to talk. It seemed bad form to desert him on the road and yet she wanted to see Hal, to hear what he'd been doing. It had been hard to give him his freedom, to not find a reason to go down to the village and check on him.

'Go on, India. I can find my way back to the house by myself.' He laughed as if it was of no matter, but the disappointment lingered in his gaze.

'We'll continue this tonight, Laurie,' India promised, reaching out to spontaneously take his hand in an offer of reassurance. Then she had a foot on the wheel rim, Carrick reaching out to help her the rest of the way. Carrick skilfully turned the phaeton and they were off, back down the drive beneath blue autumn skies. For a short while, the girl she'd once been began to stir, brought to life by the crisp air, the bright perfection of the day and the breeze in her face. It lasted only until they rounded a turn that had her gripping the low seat rail and remembering.

'You're going quite fast.' She had not been up on a phaeton for ages, not since Landon had taken her out. It was an old joy from an old life. She'd forgotten how it felt to be so high above the ground, how one could see so far down the road, the world unfolding towards an endless horizon.

Without comment, Carrick slowed the horses, but she felt his gaze on her for a fleeting second before it returned straight ahead. 'We're nearly there,' was all he said. He turned off the road, the ruins of an old castle coming into view along a sparkling ribbon of river. He parked the carriage and set the brake before coming around to help her, his big hands at her waist, strong and competent as he set her down.

Hal joined them, carrying a wicker picnic basket. 'This is a great spot, Carrick. Is that the Thames?' The two of them were easy together, she could see that as immediately as she'd seen the change in Hal. Hal called him Carrick, not Mr Eisley, proof of the quickly established familiarity between them. India wasn't sure how she felt about that. Had Carrick told Hal about Landon? If not, that might be quite a blow to their new friendship.

Don't borrow trouble, a little voice in her head whispered. *Can't you just have a good day? Can't you just enjoy your brother's happiness? Can't you just enjoy the moment? You used to be able to. Does everything have to be doom and gloom?*

Surely that wasn't true? Surely she'd not become *that* person. Certainly, she was practical. She had to be. It wasn't the same thing. She had no choice.

'How about here?' Hal surveyed a space between the river and the castle where they might set down a picnic blanket. Carrick and Hal spread an old quilt on the ground and she busied herself with the basket, setting out cold slices of ham that could be piled on thick slices of bread, a jug of cider *with* mugs, she noted, somewhat surprised they'd remembered the mugs. She reached in one last time and pulled out an apple pie, holding it aloft. 'I'm impressed.'

'Thank the White Hart.' Carrick stretched out along

the blanket's edge, his length on display. Hal settled near her and wasted no time making a ham sandwich. His appetite was still insatiable, that hadn't changed.

'Well?' India asked once food had been assembled and silence had fallen over their picnic. 'How is it going, Hal?' It was awkward to ask such a thing with Carrick sitting right there, just as it was odd to think of Carrick being back in her life, if only for a short time while Hal got his on track. It was odd, too, to think of Carrick back in the centre of that life, which he most assuredly was if he was involved with Hal.

The past three years had been about Hal and Belle Weather. Anything and anyone who was involved with either was at the centre of her attentions. Carrick had been there before, with Landon, because of Landon. She'd exiled him from that centre for the same reason. She'd not thought he'd be back, that she would ever invite him back to the centre of her world again. He'd destroyed that world once. Was she a complete fool to give him the chance to do it a second time? Hence the awkwardness.

If anyone else felt the awkwardness, they didn't show it. At her question, Hal held forth in an unstoppable stream of words about all he'd learned, talking over her head about the structure of a carriage, the import of balance, the curse of light construction, which allowed Phaetons to be fast and at the same time contributed to the danger of overturning, and why elliptical springs were better, although so hard to come by since they had to be individually fashioned.

'Fortunately, Carrick has his own forge and can make them at will. But it's still not standardised production,'

Hal concluded, finishing off his third ham sandwich with the conversation.

'He's a quick study.' Carrick flashed Hal a smile, entering the conversation for the first time, and she watched her brother straighten his shoulders a little at the praise. A look of admiration and comradery passed between them and with it an unspoken understanding of something she didn't quite comprehend, that she might never grasp. She had the suspicion they were keeping something from her and India felt distinctly *de trop*.

A little stab of jealousy poked at her as the realisation came: Hal was in the club now—the universal brotherhood of men, no women allowed. It was going to happen eventually, she told herself. It would have happened at university. She'd just not thought she'd be on hand to see it happen so directly. Perhaps if Landon had lived, he might have been the one to offer that first important, male mentorship-cum-friendship to Hal. Instead, through a quirk of fate, it was reckless, wild Carrick, even though there were other men on hand, Laurie for one.

She reached for the apple pie and cut generous slices for Carrick and Hal and a smaller one for herself. 'And the racing? How is that going?' She intercepted another look between them. So, she had been right. They were keeping something from her, something they'd meant to not discuss with her, at least not yet.

Carrick cleared his throat. 'It's going well. He's got good instincts, but there's a lot to learn. We've only been out to the track at the farm a couple times.' He polished off his pie and gave Hal a meaningful look. 'There are some good views along the river, even a bit of fishing if you want to give it a try. Your pole's on the back of the phaeton.' Hal leapt up and set off.

'That was not subtle at all.' India gave Carrick a sharp look.

'Subtlety has never been my strong suit.' Carrick gave an easy shrug and helped himself to another slice of pie. It begged the question of where did he put it all? He was a big man, but his stomach was flat. Three years had done nothing to change that. Cousin Victor was forty-two and the years were starting to show. But Cousin Victor didn't work in a carriage yard, smithing elliptical springs and hauling carriage wheels. 'I wanted some time with you. Just you.'

Chapter Nine

His words caught her off guard, or maybe it was the smile that he'd flashed with them. In another time, with another woman, those words would have been an overture to flirtation, to seduction even. But with her, she sensed they were simply honest. Perhaps she saw them that way because they could be nothing more. If he intended them otherwise, he would be disappointed. 'I thought it might be better to talk if it were just the two of us,' he explained.

'About Hal?' Her brow creased with instant worry. 'Is something wrong?' She suddenly feared Carrick was regretting his offer. It would break Hal's heart.

'Not at all. Hal is wonderful.' He smiled to ease her worry. 'That's what I wanted to tell you. I felt it was something not to say in front of him. I didn't want Hal to think the compliment was condescending, or that I see him only as a child.'

She nodded her understanding. 'That's very insightful of you. Thank you.' Who would have guessed the flirtatious, fun-loving Carrick Eisley had such intuition when it came to a young man's pride?

He gave a shrug, a gesture she'd seen him make countless times as if to say something was not worth mentioning. It was a reminder that she knew him and knew him not, this man who had been her fiancé's close friend and who had spent so many fashionable evenings in her company.

'I remember being eighteen. It's an awkward age. I felt I was a grown man, but I was not a grown man in the eyes of my family—my mother and my older siblings. My father had passed at that point and my brother was the baron by then, the head of the house.' He said it casually, too casually to let it pass. She knew so little about him beyond his rakish reputation and his ballroom skills. She knew nothing of his family, or his background.

'Your father died young then?' Perhaps that explained his penchant for helping Hal. It moved her to think that his offer was motivated by a genuine affinity towards her brother, even as such a motivation revealed a surprising depth of character she'd not expected.

'When I was fifteen, like Hal.' He gave another shrug, but she was not fooled with his nonchalance. These comments should not be easily dismissed.

'How did he die?' she asked quietly, sensing Carrick might talk, *really talk*, if she probed gently. Of course, they'd talked on the dance floor every night during the Season, but not like this, not about something that mattered, that actually revealed the truth of a person. Ballroom conversation was designed to cultivate an outer image, not to reveal one's inner soul.

Carrick shook his head and for a moment she thought he might not answer. 'A chicken bone,' he said at last.

'He choked on a chicken bone at supper and no one could do anything about it. We just watched him die. Technically, he suffocated. It was a senseless, stupid death, entirely unworthy of a good man.' Surreptitiously, India watched his fist curl in the folds of the picnic blanket. He'd loved his father.

She reached a hand out and placed it on his knee in a gesture of support. 'You miss him. A good father is not easily replaced.'

The tension on Carrick's face eased. 'He was a good man, the only one in the family who had time for me. I am the youngest of five, three boys and two girls. My two brothers are fifteen years older than me and I was born five years after my youngest sister. Everyone was busy with their lives when I came along; my brothers were off to school. But my father always made sure I was not forgotten. He took me shooting, he oversaw my riding lessons personally. He was the one who taught me to drive and cultivated my interest in carriages.' Carrick was smiling now and she smiled back, encouraging him to talk. For him, because he needed to, she told herself, but in actuality, it was as much for her. She was aware her posture had her leaning forward and she was intent on every word.

His smile dimmed. 'By the time I was fifteen, my sisters had both married as had my brothers, the first grandchildren were born. My mother flitted from house to house, helping my sisters with the new babies. I didn't see her for months on end. I didn't mind, I had my father all to myself when I was home from school. Then, he died when I was home during one of the holidays, a rare occasion when all of us were together. And I was rather quickly reminded of my position in the family. To everyone else, I was still just Carrick, the baby, especially to my mother.' He paused and changed the direction of the conversation. 'I can see you're having difficulty picturing that. I had the same difficulty at the time.'

She gave a soft laugh and let him get away with his redirection, sensing the topic of his family and his father was closed. 'I do admit I imagine you like Athena, born fully formed, springing from Zeus's head instead of having parents like the rest of us.'

'Do you miss your parents, India?' He'd captured her hand where she'd left it on his knee. He lifted her hand now and threaded his fingers through hers, an intimate, casual gesture. She wasn't sure what undid her the most, his touch or his question.

'Of course. They were lively, fun and, whatever their flaws, they loved us. There was no doubt of that.' She gave a small smile. 'It is no small thing to be raised in love, to know what it is to be loved. That's the one thing I hope to pass on to Hal. I hope he feels raised in love—even if I am bound to make mistakes, the love will be there.' Just as it had been with her parents. Despite their mistakes, there had been love, always love. 'I miss that most of all. Love makes one feel…safe… that all is right with the world.'

A strange look passed across Carrick's face. 'It could not have been easy for you to step into the role of parent. You were only twenty yourself.' His gaze dropped to study the pattern of the quilt, as if his words were too bold. 'It occurred to me, rather belatedly when I considered Hal's situation, that if Hal was alone, you were, too.' His grey gaze suddenly looked up, holding hers in soft invitation. 'Would you tell me about it? What you and Hal have been doing for the past three years?'

For a moment he thought she was going to refuse him, scold him for such boldness, even though she'd been bold with her own questions earlier and that boldness had prompted perhaps the most intimate discussion he'd had with another in years. But he'd misread the shock in her eyes at his enquiry. It was not because he'd overstepped his boundaries, but because he had *asked.* His heart lurched against his will. Exactly how lonely was she? Was there no one? The India Claiborne he'd known was not made for isolation.

'Why do you want to know?' She was wary of the invitation and her wariness moved him at the evidence of her need to respond defensively. What the hell had happened to turn the carefree girl he'd known into this woman who was shrewd to a fault, always questioning motives? She'd questioned him in the blue salon, too, the day he'd offered to take Hal on.

Only the truth would do if he meant to win her trust. He met her gaze. 'Because I care what happens to you and I care about what *has* happened to you.' That was a dangerous truth to admit to himself. Caring led to attachments and attachments flirted with loss.

He was skating dangerously close to the edge there, an edge he'd promised himself he'd guard against when he'd taken on the task of mentoring Hal. He was to train Hal to drive safely, nothing more. But this was fast becoming 'something more'. Firstly with Hal, a young man who'd also lost his father and loved to drive carriages, and India, a woman whom he…admired. Admiration he could admit to. It was allowed. He'd admired women before.

'I wish I'd known about your parents, India.' He fumbled for words. He *did* wish he'd known, but what would he have done about it? What would she have permitted him to do about it at the time?

She gave her head a little shake of absolution. 'We kept it as private as possible. It was so soon after Landon's accident. They'd gone out to the Isle of Wight in the late autumn with some yachting friends to try out a new boat. Hal was at school. I was at Belle Weather. Anything we know of the accident was told to us second hand. Apparently, a squall came up and my father put too much strain on the boat engine trying to outrun it. The engine exploded. There were other boats nearby, but by the time they reached the wreckage there were only bodies to save: my mother, my father and the crew. I got word the next day.'

It was a concise telling, the kind of compact story one trotted out to appease the curious with the horror carefully sifted out of it to make the tragedy palatable. It wasn't really what Carrick wanted to know. Dead parents meant orphans. It was the 'after' he was concerned with.

'And now? You haven't answered the question, India. I asked about you and Hal. What have the two of you been doing these past three years?' There was so much *to* ask. Were they still at Belle Weather? Had they'd been able to keep the estate? Sir Randolph Claiborne did not have a hereditary title, but his estate was entailed. What did that mean when his only male child had been barely fifteen? A minor, hardly of age. Had there been anyone to help them?

She gave him a cool smile. 'We've managed.'

No, that was not good enough. He did not want to settle for the answer she likely gave to anyone who enquired.

'India, please. You can tell me. You can trust me.' He dropped his voice conspiratorially. 'You once trusted me to see you safe in London's ballrooms.' He sobered, setting all teasing aside. 'Truly, India, who do you confide in these days? Mr Benefield, perhaps?' A little twinge of envy poked at him. He told himself it was only the naturally competitive twinge of having been supplanted, nothing more. He gave her a sly look, trying to tease a confession out of her. He rather thought he'd arrived right on time today. The tasteful Mr Benefield had appeared to be on the brink of a serious conversation. For reasons he couldn't pinpoint, he was glad he'd interrupted it. Was she or would India rather have heard what Mr Benefield had to say?

'Laurie?' She laughed and then cocked her head, thinking. 'I suppose so. He's been there to guide me with the estate management, especially in the beginning when I had so much to learn.' What was Laurie Benefield to her? A friend? A suitor? Did she have a suitor? If not Mr Benefield, perhaps someone else? That idea sat poorly with Carrick. 'He and I are friends, as Lizzie and I are friends. My mother and her mother grew up together, they wanted their daughters to know one another. Our families have always been close because of that,' she explained.

'Fair enough,' Carrick acceded, but he was aware that

he wanted such privileges, too, just as he understood such privileges would not be easily given. He'd have to earn them. This afternoon had shown him just how big of a step it had been for her in letting Hal come to train. It had also shown him how deeply the changes in India Claiborne ran.

For a person raised in the safety of a love-filled home, she was far too used to being on the defensive. She'd become a woman who didn't trust, a woman who'd been betrayed, a woman who felt she was better off alone, a woman whom men had failed. Even more devastating was knowing that he currently numbered among those whom she perceived had failed her, while the elegant Laurie Benefield did not.

He would right that perception of himself if he could, prove to her that she could trust him. The reasons for it worried him. He wanted it not just to assuage his own guilt, but because she intrigued him, because there was something he might do for her, personally. She was indeed much changed and yet, beneath those changes, the girl he'd once known still existed and was begging to be freed.

He'd seen the glow in her eyes for a short while in the phaeton this afternoon. Those blue eyes deserved to glow again. He wanted to be the one to make them spark with life once more. 'Will you come driving with me some time?' he asked.

'We'll see,' India offered non-committally. 'Things are different now.' Things were different? Or *she* was different? 'I have Hal to think about in ways I didn't before.'

'It's just a drive, India. A chance for us to talk.' Her

answer confused him. He had the distinct impression that behind her words there were things she wasn't telling him.

Hal came up from the river, pole in one hand, a small string of fish in the other. 'We can fry them up for dinner, Carrick,' he announced, a reminder that afternoons were shorter in the autumn and this one had fled. It was time to return India to Foxfields where Laurie Benefield waited with his unfinished conversation and his friendship privileges.

Chapter Ten

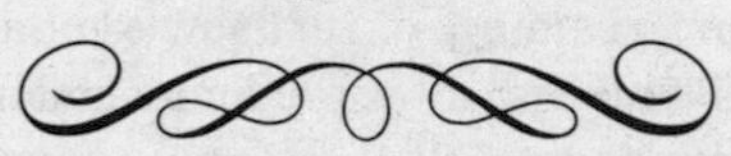

As it turned out, Benefield's conversation and the fish fry would both have to wait a bit longer. Thrilled to see Hal, Elizabeth Blackmon invited them both to stay for dinner, an invitation Carrick was quick to accept simply because India seemed torn by it—pleased to have her brother's company a little longer, but perhaps less than pleased to have his. He'd definitely disconcerted her today. And in truth, she'd disconcerted him as well: how did they move forward? Or did they? Perhaps they ought to deal with the past first, assuming the past could be dealt with?

It was clear that for her the outcome of those questions had been a heightened sense of wariness, but for him the outcome was different. It had stirred curiosity. The more India revealed—intentionally or otherwise—the more he wanted to know.

Sitting across from her at the table provided an opportunity to feed some of that curiosity. Unlike himself, she'd had the opportunity to change before supper. She'd traded her dark blue walking costume and half-boots for a light blue gown with an open neck filled in with a delicate white lace fichu and a narrow belt at her waist. Her white-blonde hair had been reassembled into a casual pile of curls atop her head and threaded with a silk ribbon.

The image she presented was one of ethereal beauty. Pastels and iced colours had always shown her to perfection, taking advantage of her hair and porcelain skin. She managed to look both ready for a London table *and* completely at home for the impromptu country supper served *en famille*.

'You own the carriage works in town, I hear,' Godric Blackmon said affably, refilling his wine glass with an excellent red. 'I do apologise for not being down to make myself known to you. My wife and I are only in residence part of the year and winter saps my motivation for being out and about meeting people.' Carrick thought that was a polite way of saying Godric Blackmon preferred to spend winter curled up with his wife.

'It's understandable, Blackmon. A carriage works isn't like an emporium where one might wander in hoping to find a variety of goods. One comes to a carriage yard only if they're in the market for a vehicle. Still, you are welcome to come and look around. Hal, here, can give you a tour.'

'Have you owned it long?' This next question was from Benefield. The question was harmless enough on its own. It was only in the context of his history with India that the question became dangerous. Was Benefield aware of it? When Carrick had accepted the invitation to supper, he'd not counted on being the one interviewed.

'Not long. I bought it a few years ago when the original owner wanted to retire from the trade.'

Benefield studied him with steady eyes. 'How is the trade these days? I imagine one reason the former owner was eager to get out was the railroad. People don't need coaches like they used to. This is only the beginning of what I believe will be the age of the railroad across the country.'

From another man, the question might be designed to be malicious, implying he'd made a poor investment, but Carrick could detect only interest on the other man's part. It was hard not to like Benefield. The man was well spoken and considerate, although Carrick would have preferred to find him lacking.

'I do make carriages for general use, but you are right. The coaching age is definitely diminishing and, if steam-powered omnibuses catch on in cities, it will diminish even further. But most of the vehicles I make are specialty vehicles for the express purpose of racing. There is still a strong market for the hobby carriage, as I like to call it. In fact, driving clubs are becoming even more popular now that a gentleman might hone his driving skill as if it were an art, or sport like fencing as opposed to a necessity or practical skill. I have hopes of building a showroom where demonstration designs can be displayed before people order.'

'Well said. That's an intriguing insight.' Benefield raised his glass. 'I see that you're an astute businessman as well as a craftsman. That is often a difficult combination to come by. Many craftsmen can create a beautiful product, but don't have the business acumen needed to position it in the market to best effect. I'm impressed.'

He glanced at Hal, 'I hope you're learning everything this man has to offer.' Benefield smiled benignly, but Carrick felt India's gaze lock on him. He could read the thoughts behind her wary blue eyes. *Perhaps not everything*, they said.

She was learning him all over again. India sipped from her wine glass, her eyes steady on Carrick, trying to figure out who he was now and what that meant to her in this new iteration of their lives. In many ways, her past knowledge of him was still valid. He looked the same—still in possession of the brawny build, the auburn hair and storm-grey eyes that exuded permanent restlessness. His conversation was the same, too, still lacking in subtlety and favouring the brazen directness that had set debutantes' cheeks aflame, only today, that brazenness had been directed at her.

He'd applied those techniques to great effect this afternoon on the picnic blanket, plying her with questions a mere acquaintance would not dare to ask until she'd given him far more information than she'd intended. How could she keep him at a distance when he *insisted* on drawing near? Not in terms of physical proximity, but in terms of something far more dangerous: emotional proximity.

Today, they'd shared intimate information with one another, things it was clear were not easily shared with just anyone. He'd told her about growing up in a large family, of his father's affection and what it had meant to lose that affection. She had reciprocated, offering him a glimpse into what her life had become, a glimpse she offered to only Elizabeth and Laurie. And yet, even with such intimate discussion between there was much more to unearth, much more that stood between them that needed to be addressed *if* they meant to be friends on their own without Landon to act as their bridge.

Now it was just the two of them: the former heiress and the former gentleman racer. Well, not quite just the two of them. There was also the accident between them. Who were they now, accident and all? Did it matter? Would this friendship extend beyond Carrick's obligation to Hal? And if he pressed Hal racing, would that nascent friendship survive?

India had no answer for that and it unsettled her as she drank her wine and watched Carrick across the table. Along with the Carrick she knew, there was also the Carrick she *didn't* know and *that* man was a revelation here at the dinner table just as he had been on the picnic blanket. This afternoon he'd spoken of his family, of his past, allowing her to see the side of him that intuitively understood the needs of a young man.

Tonight, he talked about marketing carriages for this new age in a serious and insightful manner that suggested he was a critical thinker, looking ahead into the future. It was a very different image than the man she'd known in London and it was unlike the thrill-seeking rogue who lived in the moment.

If she thought he'd changed, did he think the same of her? What did he see when he looked at her? The girl she'd been or the woman she'd become? What did she want him to see?

How can he see anything when you work so hard to obscure the truth of your life from him? The voice in her head was quick to point out the contradiction she'd constructed for herself. *And why does it matter how he sees you?* That little voice added a postscript. *Do you want to cultivate a deeper relationship? For what purpose? To recall the past? To awaken your old self?*

Hardly. There was pain in the past and the girl she'd been was no match for the world she now lived in.

'India, shall we leave the men to their port?' Elizabeth rose from the table and India joined her, glad to make her escape. Perhaps by changing rooms she might also change the direction of her thoughts. Too many of them had been about Carrick.

'You neglected to tell me how handsome Mr Eisley was,' Elizabeth said as they settled down to enjoy their own post-prandial glasses of sherry.

'He knows it, too. He is quite the flirt.' India laughed. 'He had a terrible reputation in London.'

'Did he flirt with you?' Elizabeth asked pointedly.

'Of course not,' India was swift to answer. 'I was engaged to his best friend. He was my friend, too, but only because of Landon.'

'I meant now,' Elizabeth clarified. 'He seems very interested in you. He studied you at dinner, as you studied him. It was like watching two dogs circling one another in the farmyard, each trying to take the other's measure.'

India felt herself flush at Elizabeth's implication that Carrick's interest wasn't entirely platonic. She did not need Elizabeth trying to play matchmaker. 'He is helping Hal, that is all.'

'That is *not* all,' Elizabeth argued. 'Helping Hal is akin to helping you. Why would he help Hal if not for the benefit of showing himself favourably to you?'

India set aside the small sherry glass, her drink untouched, determined to disabuse Elizabeth of her ideas. 'Because it's penance, Lizzie. He feels guilty over the accident and this is a way for him to assuage that guilt. He told me that when I asked him the same question.' Her tone was sharp, perhaps because her own feelings were so raw at the moment. She wasn't ready to talk about Carrick Eisley's reappearance in her life with anyone because she could barely process what it meant to herself.

'It means nothing, Lizzie. In a few weeks Hal and I will be gone. Hal will be off to university and I'll be too far from here to be of any consequence.' Women didn't hold Carrick's attention for long. There was always another pretty face to distract him from the one in front of him. Or had that changed, too?

It doesn't matter if it has. That's his business alone. Just as your desire to not marry is your business.

'Whatever interest he has in me is driven by his need for absolution.' Or perhaps by pity because he felt sorry for her. She hoped not. She did not want to be pitied by anyone. Was *that* how Carrick saw her? As a woman who'd been at the top of her game and now was…well, was not. She no longer dazzled in ballrooms. She no longer simpered and flirted and said outrageous things simply to gain a man's attention.

'What if you're wrong about that?' Elizabeth asked.

'I'm not, so there's no need to speculate,' India said firmly.

The door opened to the drawing room and the men came through, still talking about carriage designs amiably among themselves as if they'd been friends for years instead of new acquaintances made over the span of a dinner. How many times had she witnessed a similar scene, of Landon and Carrick walking with the other men after a supper, the two of them in the midst of the group, laughing, joking? Would she ever be able to look at Carrick and not think of Landon? Of what life had been like when it had been happy?

Life might have been happy, but it wasn't real. It was an illusion. You were living a pretence. Regardless of losing Landon, your father was putting on a show he couldn't afford, the family finances would still have been in difficulties. You simply didn't know it at the time.

It was an oft-used reminder when she sought to paint the past rosier than it truly was.

'Hal and I must be off. We have an early day tomorrow.' Carrick shook hands with Laurie and Godric.

'We can't entice you to stay for cards?' Elizabeth asked.

'Cards would be fun,' Hal put in hopefully, but Carrick was quick to stand his ground.

'Morning will already come too early,' he said firmly to Hal before he smiled his regrets at Elizabeth. 'Another time.' He had all of India's attention now. This was new. Carrick Eisley turning down a game of cards in lieu of retiring early. Add to that the firm stance he'd taken with Hal, along with Hal's acceptance of that response and the short conversation approached noteworthy.

Carrick caught her gaze and offered her a nod. 'Goodnight to you as well, Miss Claiborne. I hope to see you again soon. Perhaps you'll come down to the carriage works. You are welcome any time to check on our progress.'

She would have laughed if it hadn't meant trying to explain herself. Just when she'd thought he'd changed, he'd gone and issued an unmarried woman an invitation to visit him. He'd even provided an excuse and she was tempted to take it. Perhaps leopards really didn't change their spots. If so, that said quite a bit about them both.

Chapter Eleven

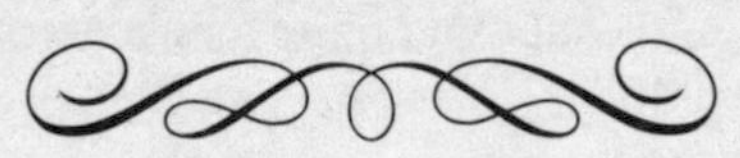

Would she come? She'd been considering it—he'd seen it in her eyes as he'd issued the invitation. He needed her to come to the carriage works, to see his life now, to see that he was changed and so that he could see her life, get to know her again. Carrick let Hal handle the ribbons in the dark. He offered the boy a couple of tips and then gave himself over to his own thoughts.

It wasn't just her life he wanted a glimpse of, he wanted to see *her* again if for no other reason than to continue building on the conversation they'd started on the picnic blanket. He wanted answers to his questions: what was life like for her now? What did she do with herself if she was not in society? Who had she become?

He could not imagine an India Claiborne whose social calendar wasn't filled with teas and parties. India had been the *ton*'s darling, who'd always been surrounded by people, a sparkling girl who'd thrived on company and who had relied on Landon for everything from fetching her refreshment at a ball to planning which entertainments they'd attend.

When Carrick had known her in London, India hadn't had to do anything alone, hadn't had to make a single decision. She was surrounded by men who did all of that for her. She only had to laugh, to look beautiful and to make witty conversation during the waltz. That was not who she was now.

She was still beautiful. In some ways, she was even more lovely now. Gone was the starry-eyed innocent who flirted without fear because she had none. She had no knowledge of what an unscrupulous man might do with her naive innuendos and invitations. It had been his job and Landon's to make sure she never knew.

Yet he could not imagine the woman who'd sat across from him tonight enjoying such a life any longer. Within six months, she'd lost everyone she loved, except for Hal, and she'd lost both the men who were to have looked after her. Her life was empirically different now. The death of her father had made it so. There was no one to arrange another match for her. Hal was too young for such advocacy on her behalf.

Carrick didn't need the details that had eluded him on the picnic blanket to guess the basics of that change. When a man died, the women in the family always fared the worst. They lost their protector, their shield from the world, their source of financial support. It had been that way for his mother when his own father had died. She'd had to get used to her oldest son assuming the title, to his wife assuming the reins of the household she had once run.

India's father had been well off by all accounts. Amid that knowledge, it was easy to forget a man's wealth would mean very little to the women in a family. Her father's death would have impacted her far less if she'd been married to Landon. But she'd been left by both the men in her life, becoming that most pitied creature in society: a woman without a man.

Whatever her father had left behind would go to Hal. Carrick slid a sideways glance at boy beside him, a question forming in his mind. Without the benefit of marriage to Landon, what did India have that was entirely her own, that was not dependent upon Hal? He reframed the question again: without Hal, what did she have? Who inherited the Claiborne estate if not Hal? That certainly put a different spin on her sisterly protectiveness.

It wasn't just Landon's death that had her concerned over Hal's racing. Hal was risking his life, but he was also risking her security. It was far worse to be a woman alone than it was to be a man. A man might make his own fortune, but a woman...? Especially a woman like India who hadn't been trained to be anything but beautiful. She ought to have remarried by now. It could not have been for a lack of offers. But instead, India had chosen a different course, one that he was not privy to.

Carrick supposed he could ask Hal for the specifics of her situation, but it felt dishonest, as if he were going behind her back. If he wanted to know, he ought to ask her directly. But would she tell him? Today, she'd not been entirely forthcoming with him, showing great reserve, and he'd already acknowledged gaining her confidence would take time, time he might not have.

'Did you talk to India about the meet?' Hal asked casually once Foxfields was behind them. They'd had high hopes for the picnic at the castle ruins. It had seemed a chance for India to see Hal's success and a chance for Carrick to win her confidence so that she would agree to let Hal race at the upcoming meet in Wallingford.

But something had happened on that picnic blanket. The conversation had moved from Hal to her and there'd been the tiniest glimpse of who she'd become. He'd followed her down the path, eager to see where it led even at the expense of the conversation moving away from the direction he'd intended.

'No, next time, though, I promise. The time wasn't right. She's still wary of me and this arrangement. She fears it will take you away from what she has planned. I want her on our side before I tell her Logan wants you to race at a meet, or else she'll see it as proof that she was right.'

She would withdraw before he'd fully peeled back her layers, fully come to know her in this new iteration of herself, or perhaps simply discover her truly for the first time and before he could atone for the role he played in forcing that transformation. He was not ready to let her go. It was selfish of him.

'Do we have that kind of time?' Hal slid him a disbelieving look.

'We'll *make* that kind of time. We've issued our invitation. She'll come. If she doesn't, we'll find reasons to come out here.' He smiled over at Hal. 'Don't worry, we'll win her over.'

'How can you be so sure? You don't know my sister.'

Ah, but he did. At least he used to and, if he was lucky, he might get to know her again. He found the prospect carried an edge of excitement to it for reasons he couldn't explain except for the chance to be with her, knowing that he could do something for her at long last. It made him feel as if he was coming back to life after walking in a fog for so long.

She did come, three days after the supper. It was, in Carrick's opinion, a carefully calculated span of time designed to set his sense of anticipation to jangling each time the bell over his shop door tinkled, while allowing her to avoid looking over-eager or as if she was hovering over Hal.

The first time she came, she brought Elizabeth Blackmon with her and a lunch basket, as she did the second time. The third time, she came only with the basket. It was a practice Carrick heartily encouraged. He liked Mrs Blackmon well enough, but it was difficult to have any meaningful conversation with India with her friend to hand and he desperately needed meaningful conversation with her if he were to win her approval for Hal to race.

Are you sure that's the only reason? Are you sure you don't crave her conversation for yourself as well?

His conscience was forcing him to be brutally honest about his growing connection to her, a connection that was fast becoming that most dangerous of all things: an attachment.

He found himself looking forward to lunchtime with far more enthusiasm than the usual and it wasn't only because she brought fare superior to what the White Hart provided him. Carrick found himself watching the clock as it neared noon and lingering closer to the front of the shop.

* * *

Today, she was late. It was five minutes past twelve. At ten past twelve, the bell jingled and he looked up, feigning pleasant shock as if he hadn't been anticipating her arrival since nine that morning.

'Ah, you've come. I wasn't sure if you would. This is a lovely surprise.' Carrick untied his leather apron and set it aside. He strode forward to greet her, taking the basket from her and hefting it appreciably. 'It's heavy. What have you packed today? Stones?'

'Chicken pot pie and I cannot claim any credit for it. Elizabeth's cook must get all the accolades.' She laughed up at him from beneath the brim of a bonnet trimmed in bright blue, the colour of the sky, the colour of her eyes. She was doing more of that in his company, laughing, smiling, relaxing her guard. It warmed him to see it, to know that she was coming to trust him and yet he wondered how long that might last. It would be tested soon in a variety of ways. But not yet.

'It will just be us for lunch, Hal's off on an errand for the shop.' He flashed her a smile, his hand dropping automatically to the small of her back, falling into old habits, as he ushered her across the yard as if it were a ballroom of old. 'I want to show you something, come with me.'

The work yard was empty now of his apprentices who'd gone to seek their own lunches. He nodded at a carriage in a state of near assembly, a low-slung vehicle with its front wheels sticking out well ahead of the body.

'The construction allows for the body to be slung lower to the ground. It's for the Earl of Dartmouth,'

Carrick explained. 'His gout keeps him from being as mobile as he'd like some days. I've designed the vehicle especially for him. This way he can still get in and out of the carriage with ease. He can also drive himself if he'd like.' A design to salve an ageing whip's pride while keeping him safe. It might be a design he'd have to make use of himself some day if his knee gave out entirely.

'That's quite clever.' She looked up at him from beneath the brim of her hat, something akin to perplexed appreciation in her gaze. He'd like to see that gaze in all its unadulterated splendour without the damn hat getting in the way.

'That's not what I wanted to show you, though.' He continued on to the back of the shop where it gave out into an alley. A sleek, black-lacquered Whitechapel cart stood at the ready, two coal-black horses harnessed in tandem, one in front of the other. He watched her gaze rove over the horses and land on the eye-catching seat. He held his breath, watching her for a reaction.

'Oh, what a darling vehicle!' she exclaimed softly as if the words were uttered against her will and perhaps they were. Perhaps it was a kind of heresy to her to appreciate a carriage. She turned to him, a little furrow creasing her brow. 'But pink leather? Is that practical?'

Carrick laughed. 'I don't think practicality is a priority for the lady it's ordered for. Lord Dartmouth commissioned it for his wife's birthday. I am delivering both carriages together. She's more interested in how she looks driving it than whether or not pink leather needs to be cleaned after every outing to keep the dust off it.

Shall we try it? It needs a test drive and the weather is perfect.'

He didn't wait for an answer. If one gave India Claiborne a chance to protest, she would. He'd learned the best way to gain her compliance was to simply move forward. Carrick set about the business of departing. He put the basket on the rear seat and turned the crank that moved the entire seat back from the front footboard.

'This allows the driver to adjust the balance. When the cart carries four people, the seat can be cranked all the way forward. However, since it's just the two of us, we need to readjust the balance of our weight over the wheels.' Satisfied that the seat was in proper alignment, he offered India his hand. 'Up you go. I want your impressions. This is meant to be a lady's vehicle.'

He came around and jumped up, taking his seat and gathered the reins. 'What do you think of the bench position?' He manoeuvred them on to the road leading out of the village and let the horses pick up their pace. The blue ribbon on India's hat fluttered in the breeze like a kite streamer.

'We're surprisingly high up, higher than I anticipated for a dog cart. That's what this is, really, a creative version of a dog cart put to good use.' India's hand went to her hat to steady it. 'But, oh, my—how far I can see down the road! It has excellent visibility.'

Carrick chuckled and flicked a glance her way. 'It needs to have it, with the horses in tandem instead of side by side.' There were other features he was proud of, too, on the vehicle, like the deep-blocked springs which allowed the driver more control, an important feature with a cart balanced on two wheels instead of four. He thought it best to keep that to himself. India was enjoying herself.

The ribbon on her hat fluttered in his face and he brushed it away as she apologised. 'Take your hat off, India, if you'd like. There's no one to see and the October sun is hardly warm enough to be an issue for your skin,' Carrick laughed, daring her to this one small rebellion. 'The drive isn't a long one.'

She slanted him a look that said she knew what he was doing, how he was tempting her, *and* much to his delight that she was up for it. Her hands worked the ribbons loose and lifted the hat from her head as she turned her face to catch the full force of the sun. 'Oh, that feels wondrous. We won't have many days left like this one. It will be winter, too soon.'

It was a good thing the road was deserted, otherwise he might have been in danger of crashing. It was hard to keep his eyes on the road with India Claiborne sitting beside him, head raised, eyes closed as the sun bathed her face in its autumnal glory. It was a profile that begged to be touched, its lines traced with the caress of a gentle fingertip. The straight precision of her nose, the sweep of her elegant jaw, the firm curve of her chin, the long length of her throat.

A man's hand would not want to stop there. It would want to continue on to the fair skin beneath the white lace of her fichu, to the delicate, narrow valley between her breasts, to feel her tremble from the lightest of touches. She *would* respond. She was an elemental creature, made for sunshine and laughter, even if she was currently in denial.

Carrick pulled his thoughts back from the unseemly.

Had he really allowed himself to think of seducing India Claiborne as if she was another of his former London women? Certainly not. She was more than another physical liaison or a game to be played. She was a friend who needed his help and, if truth be told, he needed her help, too. He needed her permission for Hal to race, he needed her absolution for Landon's death. These were not things that could or should be seduced from a woman.

And yet there was no denying there was an attraction between them. Did she feel it, too? This new potent thing between them, this indefinable something that hadn't existed between them before, perhaps because it could not have existed in a friendship based on disparity. But now, the inequality had narrowed between them. She was no longer an innocent girl in need of a protector. This new relationship they were building together was a scintillating clash of equals and he found the potential of it intoxicating.

'Where are we going?' India smiled at him, unaware of the direction of his thoughts.

He gave her a teasing glance. 'Perhaps I shouldn't tell you. It's not much further. We're going to my place, my farm. I thought you'd like to see where Hal and I spend the weekends.' Carrick turned on to the lane that led to the property, feeling a burst of pride as the stable and small manor house came into view, both done in neat red brick, white fences partitioning off the paddocks, and the green meadow where the horses ran free in the summer.

They pulled up in front of the stable and a boy ran out to the take the team as he helped India down, keenly aware of how his hands fit at her waist, of the soft autumn scent of her—all vanilla and cinnamon—mingled with the fresh air. She smelled like home, at least the way he'd always imagined a home smelling. 'Let me show you around.' He set her down on the ground, his hand once more resting at the base of her spine.

He showed her the ten-stall barn with its clean swept aisles, the tack room that smelled of leather and saddle soap, the brood mares in the paddocks, talking the whole time about his small breeding operation, his plans for the house and anything else he could think of, while his mind raced. *What did she think?*

India was used to living on a grander scale. Would she think his property, his pride and joy, a trivial thing? At last, he showed her the track, the dirt oval only a short distance from the house. She was uncharacteristically quiet and he was aware that he was talking overmuch to fill the silence and perhaps to ignore the signs. She was withdrawing—the happy, sun-drenched, hat-free India was retreating. His heart sank. Had the tour been that unimpressive to her?

'So, this is where you race.' She was suddenly wary with judgement as he ended the tour. He heard the criticism in her voice.

'No, actually. This is *not* where I race. This is where I raise horses and this is where your brother practises on the weekends under my supervision.' He was sharp with her before it occurred to him that she didn't know. How could she? They had not talked of the accident and they never talked of racing other than that first day in the work yard.

He fixed her with a long, serious stare. 'I don't race,

India, not any more.' Not in three long years, even though it was still in his blood, even though his hands itched to hold the reins of a team and let them fly down the road, testing the limits of a vehicle, even though he missed the thrill of it every day.

A dart of anger pierced him at her assumptions. 'I am retired and I have been since the accident. Did you really think I had kept racing all this time? That Landon's accident had changed nothing for me?' It was a reminder that, for all they'd shared, they still knew each other so little, that the old days, the old façades still held sway.

He could tell from the shock on her pale face that was exactly what she'd thought. The world fell silent. The soft chirp of the birds in the trees suddenly resembled a deafening roar as they stared at one another. Disappointment was not nearly an adequate enough word for what he felt in that moment, standing there with her. He'd not understood until now what his purpose had fully been for bringing her here.

He'd wanted to impress her, not just for Hal's sake, but also for his own. Her opinion of him mattered. How had he not realised it when he'd spent the last three years craving her absolution? That search for absolution was behind every carriage he made, every safety feature he engineered. 'Dear God, India, do you think I am that shallow?'

Chapter Twelve

'No, I don't think that.' She uttered the words, aghast at what she'd done, trying to deny what he thought and the realisation that he was not entirely wrong. A wave of sickening horror swept her. She was entirely off balance, unsure of what she knew, of who she was, of who he was or what she was doing here with him. What had she'd been thinking to come out here alone with him? She didn't know what she thought these days when it came to Carrick.

Who *was* Carrick Eisley? The reckless rogue or the serious business owner? He'd entirely upended her world with his reappearance and then turned it over again, shattering expectations and assumptions, making her past knowledge of him irrelevant, forcing her to build her assumptions anew, forcing her to *choose* to forge new paths with him. In response, she'd lashed out with her unfeeling words.

While she struggled to gather her thoughts, something flashed in his eyes amid the stormy depths of the anger she'd provoked. *Hurt*. Understanding struck her like a blow hard to the solar plexus. For a moment even breath escaped her. She'd once believed Carrick Eisley was impervious to hurt. He'd spent his years among the *ton* deflecting their barbs, fully cognisant that he was good enough to dance with the *ton*'s gentle innocents, but not to marry them. He'd been a gentleman long on charm and short on blunt.

But this hurt was not that. It came to her as they stared at one another, each grappling with the sudden onslaught of awakened emotion that it was not her words that had hurt him. It was *her*. *She* had done this. The horror swept over her again, a sob threatened. She gave a shake of her head and fled.

She sought refuge in the stable, the building closest to them. She sank down on a hay bale and gave full vent to her sobs, giving in to the confusion that roiled in her. She was confused as to who she thought Carrick was. A friend, or the man responsible for her fiancé's death? One of those men deserved her mercy, perhaps the other did not. But perhaps her focus was misspent. Perhaps she ought to focus on understanding who *she* was? What sort of a woman insulted a man after he'd shown her his treasure, the things that were important to him? And she'd done it in five words. *This is where you race.* Those words had belittled a man's pride in the place he'd established, indicated that it wasn't enough. More than that, those words *accused* him of being a man who had continued on his wicked ways after the death of his friend. The sort of woman who did those things was a woman who'd come to believe the worst of people.

Was that the sort of woman she'd let herself become? A woman so jaded, so cynical, that she could not see the change in a person until it was spelled out to her?

I am retired. I haven't raced in three years, not since the accident. He'd had to put it to her bluntly before she'd understood.

That man—a man who'd given up the thing he'd loved the most when his friend died, who'd come to see her only to be turned away, who comprehended his own culpability in that accident, who had shouldered responsibility for it and had been changed by it, perhaps even reformed by it—*that* man was deserving of her mercy, but she'd given him her hatred, nursed that hatred over years of misunderstanding. Perhaps it had changed her as surely as Landon's death and her father's death had. And yet Carrick had brought her here. He had not given up on her.

Bootsteps announced Carrick's arrival. She looked up, tears staining her cheeks, her breathing ragged. Would he give up on her now? He would be justified in doing so, to turn her away as she'd turned him away the day he'd called at the town house. Carrick's eyes had calmed. His voice low, his words simple. 'You are not the only one who mourns him, India.'

He took a seat beside her on the hay bale, the heat of his big form warming her. 'I miss him every day,' he offered without preamble. Somewhere in the distance, thunder rolled. He reached for her hand and she gave it. They sat in silence, listening to the autumn storm come in, watching the early splatter of raindrops outside the stable door replacing blue skies.

'I'm sorry, Carrick.' She breathed the words softly. Would they be enough? Those words seemed overly simple, hardly able to encompass all she regretted.

He raised their hands, palm pressed to palm, and

slid his fingers between hers. 'You have nothing to be sorry for, India.'

'I don't believe that. I turned you away the day you came to the town house. I could have stood up for you, but I refused to see you when you were the one person I should have seen. I should have shared my grief with you and, in doing so, given you a place to share yours. We both loved him.' Her rejection of him had been a double repudiation, she saw that now in ways she'd not understood it before. Closing herself off had caused hurt to others, stolen from them a chance to grieve the tragedy.

'You are too hard on yourself. You blamed me for his death. How could you receive such a man?' He drew a deep breath. 'You blame me still.' This was part question, part statement. Whenever she imagined discussing the accident or the aftermath with Carrick, she'd not imagined it like this: quietly, solemnly on hay bales in a stable while a storm rolled in, a conversation tinged with sadness and regret.

She'd thought it would be more like the storm outside that drew ever closer: loud, angry, the hurling of harsh words like Zeus's thunderbolts. A war, not an armistice, a recognition that the war had been perceived on her part only. She might have been at war with him, but he'd not been at war with her. Yet he was the one asking her for absolution.

'I should never have blamed you. I should have listened to you when you came.' A thought came to her as she uttered the words. What would the last three years have been like if Carrick had been beside her? Standing as her friend through the difficult days after her parents' deaths? Would Cousin Victor even be a threat to her now? She scolded herself for the thought. She'd had Laurie Benefield's support. Why would Carrick's presence have been different?

She slanted him a look, taking in their joined hands lying between them. A friend had no legal authority, but perhaps she was not imagining him in the role of a friend, but something more… A role she would not have considered three years ago in the wake of her grief over Landon. No. Elizabeth's comments were getting to her. There'd been far too much talk of marriage on this trip. She was as uninterested in marriage now as she had been when she arrived.

'I can't forgive you, Carrick, for something I should not have blamed you for in the first place.' Blaming had been an act of desperation, an attempt to explain the inexplainable.

Carrick quirked an eyebrow. 'Are you sure? I was on the road with him, I made it impossible for him to pass. I forced him to consider the alternative if he wanted to win.' India was quiet. She'd not heard even that much about the accident.

'Did no one tell you?' Carrick asked in a low growl.

'No. I was to be shielded from the details of the tragedy.' That had made it that much worse. She'd been left with nothing to hold on to, not even an understanding of those final moments, or how they'd come about. 'Only that Landon had been forced into the verge and the phaeton had flipped.' It had been easy to jump to conclusions from that scrap of information. To be forced had implied to her grief-stricken mind that it had been done deliberately, that Carrick had instigated it.

'I blamed myself, too.' Carrick's voice was full of quiet pain and her own pain renewed. 'It took Logan a year of telling me that it was a fateful coincidence that the Richmond coach was coming around the corner at that exact time, that Landon chose to pass on his own accord, knowing the risks of passing on the inside. But still, I will probably always blame myself for setting up the circumstances. I put the choice to him. I don't know that I'll get over that.'

Landon had collided with the Richmond coach, not Carrick's own carriage as she'd assumed. Remorse swept her yet again. How wrong she'd been. 'I didn't know.' More inadequate phrases to add to 'I'm sorry'. Then, she added softly, 'I wasn't allowed to see him afterwards or to attend the funeral.' Women didn't attend funerals, especially not young ones. Even death was a domain reserved for men. She cast an expectant glance at Carrick and asked with no small amount of timidity, 'Did you? See him?' She had no right to ask, to make him relive those moments.

Carrick ran his thumb over the back of her hand in a soft gesture. 'Yes, but he was gone before I reached him.' He was hesitating, for her sake, not his, and she knew this was her chance, that Carrick would tell her what others had not, but she needed to ask. He would stand the pain of dredging up those memories for her and that realisation spoke volumes of the quality of his friendship, of what he'd endure for her and perhaps what he had endured for her. Maybe that was all she needed to know. If Landon had been dead when Carrick reached him, there'd been no last words, no last message to her. She needn't make Carrick tell her what she should already deduce.

'Thank you,' she said, her voice a whisper beneath the thunder. The rain outside was falling harder now. 'Can you forgive me, Carrick? For turning you away, for believing the worst of you, not only then but now?' She'd accused him and Logan of exploiting her brother for money.

He lifted her hand to his lips and kissed her knuckles, a gesture he'd made countless times before, a little smile teasing his mouth, but this felt less playful and, when his lips brushed over her skin, a tremor of awareness skittered up her spine. 'I will always forgive you, India.'

She gave a breathy laugh. 'I hope I won't need you to.'

'Well, one never knows.' He chuckled, his eyes holding hers in an unspoken declaration of victory. Together, today, here in this stable, they'd overcome the obstacle between them of Landon's death. They'd slayed the demon of grief and the dragon of blame. India felt a quiet elation rise inside of her. Her friend was returned to her. 'Carrick, I missed you.' She smiled as she said the words.

'I missed you, too.' He grinned back and rose, dusting at his breeches. 'I want to show you one thing more.' He pulled her up to join him, never letting go of her hand. She didn't mind. It felt right to be like this with him, to be together. He led her down the length of the stable block to a stall at the end looking out over the track. A black-maned bay poked his head over the half-door of the stall. He nuzzled at Carrick's hand until Carrick fished a treat out of his pocket.

India reached out to pet his soft face. 'What a sweet boy you are,' she crooned as she stroked him. 'Look, you have a little star, here on your forehead.' Her hand stilled, her voice catching. 'Landon's horse, King, had a star. The smallest amount of white featuring allowable on a true Cleveland Bay.' She looked at Carrick, a wild wave of hope rising up. 'This is King, isn't it? You saved him. How?'

No one had spoken to her about the horses. She'd assumed they'd not survived, those two beautiful boys whom she'd loved on sight, whom she'd imagined tooling around Hyde Park with Landon beside her. That was another lifetime ago. She looked around, glancing into the stall next to it, hoping beyond hope. 'And Sabre?' She glanced at Carrick long enough to see Carrick's smile falter.

'We could not save Sabre. His leg was broken and he could not rise up from the ditch where the carriage had overturned.' The words dampened her earlier elation. She could see they pained him. His throat worked, his words choked. 'Sometimes I think Sabre took the brunt of it on purpose, knowing he could save King instead of them both perishing.'

'Oh, God, Carrick,' she whispered, as if her words could take away his pain. Carrick loved horses, even better than people sometimes. They had that in common. Even when faced with her father's debt, she'd refused to sell the horses. It would have destroyed Carrick to see two innocent animals injured simply because they'd obeyed their master.

She saw Carrick's shoulders tighten. 'Landon should not have risked them.'

It was her turn to comfort him and she was glad for it, glad for a chance to give back. Carrick missed his friend, grieved him, but there was anger beneath it, anger over Landon's foolishness, anger for risking the team. She placed her other hand over his. 'I get angry at Landon, too, sometimes,' she uttered the secret that lay deep in her heart, the one she dared not share with anyone. Who would understand? Everyone thought she and Landon were perfect.

'I get angry at him for risking so much on so little. He risked his horses, his life, me. I would have thought I mattered more to him than winning a race.' It had been rather sobering to realise she'd not, which had been followed by another realisation. He'd decided to take the risk, on her behalf, and that married life would always be like that, with Landon, or any man. Men would always be deciding her life on her behalf. She could not allow that.

'You did matter to him, India. He adored you,' Carrick was quick to reassure her.

She shook her head. 'Then why did he do it? To me, to Sabre, to King? To you? Did *our* lives matter so little? Did he even think of us at all? Or were we all just things he collected? You would think if he loved us, he'd not have left us.' Her voice cracked, the chasm filled with self-doubt splitting open.

Carrick's arms were about her instantly, drawing her against the breadth of his chest, shielding her from her sorrow. 'Three of us are here, though. You and me and King. We are alive,' he murmured, pressing a kiss into her hair where her head lay against the steady beating of his heart.

Yes, alive and alone, she thought. But, no. Alone no longer. Carrick was here now.

Chapter Thirteen

He'd meant only to hold her, to place a chaste kiss in her hair, as a gesture of comfort. But his mouth had other ideas and his body had other wants. They moved independent of his mind and his good sense. A kiss dropped on her head led to a kiss along the delicate curve of her ear, another along the gentle sweep of her jaw and yet another down the long column of her neck.

Even then, he might have stopped there if it hadn't been for the soft mewl of delight that purled up from the depths of her white throat, or if her body had not pressed into his, her hips hard against him as if their bodies knew better than their minds what was required in the moment. His name was a whisper on her lips, the last word they uttered before his mouth claimed them.

She was honey and sugar to his tongue, all sweetness and necessity, a luxury he could suddenly not live without. She gasped beneath his mouth and his body moved to deepen the kiss, his hand digging deep into the depths of her hair, anchoring itself at the nape of her neck, to guide her and to steady him.

Her tongue licked at him and the kiss became reckless, ruthless, consuming everything in its path, driving out all thought of consequences beyond the moment. There was only this moment, only this kiss. It was as if he'd waited his entire life for this one taste, for *her*. And yet, how had he not known until now this was what he'd been waiting for? She was a live, burning flame, white hot in his arms, the heat of her kindling them both. It would be the work of an instant to have her against the stable wall, giving them both the release their heat sought.

Yes, yes, take her here, now.

His body strained in answer. Overhead, thunder boomed, the storm fully arrived. King whinnied nervously in his stall, nature's intrusion distraction enough for reason and realisation to assert themselves, for his mouth to drag itself from hers, both of them drawing a sharp breath. India staggered backwards, steadying herself against King's stable door, her eyes wide with shock, desire, disbelief.

'India,' he said, 'I…' He was what? Sorry? No. Never that. He groped for words and came up with none.

She stepped towards him, putting a finger to his lips, her white-blonde hair falling about her shoulders like a cloud. 'Say nothing, Carrick. We both wanted it, needed it.'

Need? Perhaps. Wanted it, yes. Had to have it, had to know. Definitely. He was still rock hard with that wanting and with a new longing. He raked her with his gaze, looking for a clue. What would she say if he said he wanted more than a kiss, that he wanted to be inside her, wanted it badly enough he was willing to forgo a bed? That he wanted to give her a pleasure that would wash away the pain of the past three years? Would she say it was a lie? That nothing could wash that pain away?

That last went a way to dampening the evidence of his ardour. He could make her scream. He had no doubts. Empirically, he was a good lover. But could he make her forget? Is that what he wanted? For her to forget their friend? Did he want to supplant him? Did he have a palatable choice? Was there an alternative, something between supplanting and tolerating the ghost of another man, the ghost of a friend, in her bed?

Even now, her blue eyes still burning like sapphire brands, she was weighing those same thoughts. She was looking for obliteration, was desperate for it and she wanted him to give it to her. He'd felt it in the press of her hips, the heat of her body. But was she ready for it? Would she regret it once it was done? Would that regret destroy this newly restored friendship between them, still fragile? As much as he wanted her, he wanted that friendship more. He would not risk it.

Outside the rain was as unrelenting as her gaze. 'Shall we make a dash for it? We might make the house without being drowned.' He took off his coat and wrapped it about her. 'Perhaps it's a good thing we didn't get around to eating lunch.' He chuckled, but it sounded hoarse, unnatural, his body still trying to shake off the throes of desire. 'We can eat the chicken pie for dinner instead.'

'Dinner?' she asked the question with a laugh that didn't fool him. The import of their situation was suddenly apparent to her and there was worry in her eyes.

He worked the buttons of the jacket to give his hands something to do that approximated touching her. He let his gaze skim hers. 'We can't drive back to town in this weather. The Whitechapel cart has no roof top and I won't risk the leather in the rain, to say nothing of the wheels in the mud.'

He grinned to put her at ease. 'It's the housekeeper's day off, but we'll be well fortified at the house, never fear. There will be fire, and wine, your basket and blankets.' He gripped her hand. 'On the count of three we'll make a run for it.' He looked out into the barnyard and grimaced. It was a sopping mess of mud and pools. Her boots and skirts wouldn't survive it. 'On second thought, I'll run and you come along for the ride.' In a fluid motion he swung her up into his arms, laughing at her startled protest.

'Put me down, I am capable of running in the rain on my own!'

'I disagree.' He flashed her a rakish grin and made a show of juggling her for better balance. He ignored her protests, darted out into the rain in hopes the deluge would be exactly what his body needed to cool.

They were drenched and laughing by the time they reached the house. It had been a riskier proposition than he'd expected. He lost his footing in the mud and nearly dropped her, which wasn't all bad since it led to her giving a playful shriek and wrapping her arms tight about his neck.

'I don't think you saved me from any raindrops.' She laughed, swatting droplets off her skirts as he set her down in the narrow hallway of the house. 'And you are certainly the worse for all your gallantry.'

He was. His shirt clung to him and water ran in rivulets from his hair. He shook his head like a dog, sending a spray of water about the hall, mostly to make her laugh and to hear her give a girlish squeal as she jumped out of the way. 'Carrick! Don't!' Good lord, she was delightful like this, a mix of the carefree girl she'd been and the woman she'd become.

The spark from the barn was still there, unquenched by the rain. Caught up in her laughter, he advanced, his arms bracketing her to the wall. He grinned down at her. 'Why not? If it makes you laugh?' He stole a kiss, short, sweet, playful, for fun, for the sheer pleasure of being able to do so. 'I like it when you laugh, India. You need to do more of it. You used to laugh all the time.'

Her smile faltered. He'd said too much, pushed too far. He tugged her hand before the moment could turn serious. He wanted her to laugh, to play, to smile at him. 'Come into the parlour, I'll stir up the fire and you can help me with my boots. Do you remember the last time we were caught in the rain?'

'Sommer's picnic.' She tripped behind him, trying to keep up with his long strides.

'The three of us had sneaked off to hunt for strawberries while everyone else was napping.' Carrick laughed as he squatted before the grate and set a fire. 'We took refuge in the gamekeeper's cottage.' He tossed her a grin over his shoulder, but the grin froze at the look in her eyes. 'It's all right to reminisce, India. The past is about more than him.'

She gave a little smile. 'Of course it is.' Her gaze slid away, but not before her eyes had betrayed her and the coals in the grate weren't the only things in the room to catch fire.

India looked down at her hands, her flaming cheeks hidden by the tumbling, tangled veil of her hair. She was given a reprieve in his misunderstanding. She'd not been thinking of Landon. That in itself was disconcerting. Was it disloyal? Instead, she'd been thinking of Carrick, of how the thin linen of his shirt clung to the muscled planes of his chest, of the firm curve of his buttocks on display in wet, tight breeches as he squatted before the fire, of that smile and those eyes as he glanced at her over a broad shoulder. She thought, too, of how she'd seen that body on display once before in the gamekeeper's cottage.

But that had been before he'd kissed her against a stable wall, before he'd lifted her in his arms and carried her across a mud-flooded barnyard, the strength of that body on display for her quite intimately, and before she'd been able to fully appreciate what that body represented, what passions lay locked within it. Passions for *her.* Her body still reverberated with the echoes of that knowledge.

A man who kissed like that could only wreak havoc with the female mind. Even more so, when the particular mind in question was hers and she'd thought her mind was set, that she'd put herself beyond men and their inevitable disappointments.

But that was before...before she'd lost her head in the barn and couldn't find it within herself to regret what followed. Or what might follow still if she continued to stare at Carrick as if she wanted to devour him. Devouring was out of the question in the life she lived now.

But is it? the easy recklessness of her youth whispered. *Only if you're caught.*

'We were soaked to the skin that day.' Carrick rose from the fire, his hands ineffectual with the knot of his sodden cravat.

'Here, let me,' she offered instinctually, moving from the overstuffed chair where she'd perched. Perhaps her thoughts would redirect themselves if they had something else to think about and if her body had something else to do besides burn. She stood before him, working the tight, wet fabric loose, convinced that he was tormenting her now on purpose.

'We stripped out of our clothes and wrapped up in old quilts in the gamekeeper's cottage, do you remember? You didn't want to, but we dared you.'

She glanced up at him, feeling compelled to defend herself. 'It was dangerous. If we'd been caught, it would have been devastating. A girl caught alone with two naked men?' The fabric loosened and she unwound the cloth from his neck and hung it before the fire.

'One of them was the girl's fiancé and better to be dry than to contract an ague.' Carrick pulled his soaked shirt over his head and hung it beside the cravat, revealing a chest that would have stunned a London ballroom into silence. Gentlemen didn't have chests like that, furred with auburn hair across strong, developed pectoral muscles, defined abdominals that descended to narrow hips that made no secret of where their chiselled perfection led.

His upper body was, in fact, much like an arrow, narrowing to a single defined, male point beneath his breeches. No wonder, men wore so many layers: shirt, waistcoat, jacket, overcoat. To hide their deficiencies in some cases, no doubt, in other rarer cases to perhaps shield a woman from the sheer virility of what lay beneath. London's women would swoon at the sight of all this masculinity on display.

She gathered her wits and looked away. 'Regardless, it would have been the scandal of the Season, of the next *two* Seasons. Do men understand nothing? It would have been devastating to me at least. To you it would have been a lark, lived down in a week or so, helped along by the next daring thing you were applauded for.' She threw him a scolding glance. 'Women have no such recourse, Carrick.'

'They have men who do, though. Surely that is enough.' Carrick tugged at his boots, hopping from one foot to another. She envied him his ease with his body, his right to strip out of wet clothes without worry.

'I don't. Not any more,' she said quietly.

'You have me, India.'

'No, I don't. I could not lay claim to your honour without calling attention to my scandal. What right would you have to defend me that wouldn't raise society's eyebrows? You are neither fiancé nor brother. Anything you did on my behalf would only make matters worse.'

'Is that why you choose to stand there shivering in damp skirts?' Carrick reached into a blanket trunk beneath the window and drew out a quilt. 'Take this, I'll turn my back and give you my word as a gentleman that I won't peek. In fact, I'll do better than that. I'll go upstairs and find something dry for us both. This is far more decent of a situation than the gamekeeper's cottage where we sat around in our undergarments beneath quilts waiting for our clothes to dry.'

India thought decency had never felt so decadent. In the end, they had ended up before the fire, a bottle of wine and the chicken pie between them, he dressed in fresh breeches and a clean shirt open at the neck, his feet bare, and she dressed in a shirt of his that covered her quite decorously from neck to knees as surely as a nightgown. But it was the undertones of the afternoon that stole the decency from the simple acts of taking shelter from the rain and eating a cold supper.

She'd kissed Carrick and her body had thrilled to it, as had his, and the knowledge of that simmered beneath every line of conversation as did the question—what was to be done about it? Always the answer was the same: nothing. Nothing could come of this. No one could know of this. This was dangerous. If Cousin Victor ever learned of it, he would make trouble for her. That damage was already done, would have already been done even if there'd been no kiss, no removing of clothes.

Carrick leaned forward and refilled her glass. 'What's troubling you, India? You've gone quiet.' The firelight played over him, illuminating the body beneath his shirt.

'How dangerous it is for me to be here.' She had to impress the peril on him, although it could change nothing. Even if the rain stopped, the darkness made the journey back to the village implausible. They were past the point of no return in terms of the weather and the clock. The night would be spent here. 'If someone found out…'

'No one will find out. Who would know who would seek to harm you? Hal? Elizabeth?' Carrick paused, considering. 'The honourable Lawrence Benefield? Is there an understanding between you?'

She was quick to shake her head, shocked he would think such a thing after what had transpired in the barn. 'No, Laurie would never doubt me. If I told him nothing happened he would believe me. Besides, Laurie and I are friends.'

Carrick quirked an eyebrow at that. 'Perhaps more than friends? I can't imagine a man wanting only to be friends with you, India.'

'Perhaps you should expand your imagination, then.'

'Perhaps you should expand yours.' Carrick was not put off by her reprimand. 'You might be friends with Benefield, but I'd wager Benefield has more than friendship on his mind. He's stayed on at his sister's, put his business on hold and he was not happy to share you the day Hal and I brought the picnic.'

'He was perfectly civil,' she countered, not wanting to give Carrick's words credence. Hadn't she also noticed subtle changes in Laurie's behaviour towards her since the house party? There'd been that near-quarrel in the garden the day of the tea and the conversation they'd never got around to having. Hadn't she also cautioned herself not to give him undue encouragement just in case? 'Besides, even if he felt prompted to propose, it would only be out of duty. He doesn't love me, not like that.'

Carrick chuckled and took a swallowed of wine. 'Then he's a fool.' His eyes danced over the rim of the wine glass, 'What other jealous hearts are you dangling on a string, India? Who would care if you spent the night here, tucked up chastely in a guest room?'

'Not everyone is head over heels in love with me.' She tried to deflect the conversation. 'What of you? Is there any lovely lady who might not appreciate that you had a woman here without a chaperon or purpose?'. She asked with a coy laugh designed to disguise the sudden flutter of nerves. Perhaps now was the best time to ask such a question. What if he did? What if there was a woman?

A certain answer would definitely douse the flame ignited in the barn. It would contextualise that kiss as a one-time event. She could never be a woman who shared a man nor the sort of woman who took a man from another. The Carrick she'd known had always had a woman, or two. He had always been off to a bed or fresh come from one. Or had that changed, as well?

His grey eyes wore that sombre expression so new to them. 'There's no one, India. There hasn't been for a long time. A few casual liaisons to ease the loneliness on occasion, if you must know.' He chuckled softly in the firelit darkness. 'And I think you must. You've a loyal heart, India. You always did have.'

She shifted uneasily, tucking the shirt more tightly about her. 'Don't look at me like that, Carrick.'

'Like what?' His voice was a low drawl, his gaze lingering in defiance of her words.

'Like you can see all of me, right down into my soul. A girl needs her secrets, Carrick.' She clutched at the neck of the over-large shirt out of instinct, but it wasn't her body she was worried about exposing.

'I am trying to figure out what you're hiding, India. What is it you don't want me to see? And why?' He finished his wine and fixed her with a grave stare. 'Not everyone is head over heels for you, you say. I must conclude, based on your words, if there is no friend, no lover, who else would disapprove of you being here, then, enough to set you to worrying?' He quirked an auburn brow. 'There must be an enemy.'

'Carrick, I must insist we drop this line of questioning.' Because it put her in all sorts of danger: danger of telling him, the danger of laying her burdens down and allowing a man to shoulder them and, worst of all, the danger of setting herself up for disappointment again.

She reached for the dishes, thinking to gather them and rise. Carrick's hand closed about her wrist, his grey eyes steely. '*I* must insist that you have some more wine and tell me all about him, this enemy that has stolen the laughter from your life and the smile from your pretty face.' More dangerous words were never spoken.

She'd given too much away and the realisation that he was right made his gaze flint hard. His eyes narrowed. 'Tell me who the bastard is, India.'

She'd survived the last three years by holding to herself. Her problems were *her* problems. And yet there'd been a cost for her self-sufficiency. Her self-sufficiency had hurt those she cared for most. Hal. Elizabeth. Had she learned nothing from this latest round of mistakes? Her attempt to not burden those around her had resulted in Hal feeling betrayed and Elizabeth feeling left out.

Now, here was Carrick, asking for entrance into her life, challenging her not to make that same mistake again. More than that, he was asking her to trust him. What would it mean for their renewed friendship if she said no to that invitation? How could friendship exist without trust? She held out her glass. 'Pour.'

Chapter Fourteen

India took a healthy swallow from her glass. If she regretted this in the morning, she could always blame it on the wine. 'My cousin, Victor, is waiting for me to fail so he can swoop in and take the estate.' How was it possible that all of her troubles could be put into a single sentence? Alas, it didn't make those troubles any smaller or more manageable.

Carrick waited a long moment before he responded, his grey eyes thoughtful. 'A paternal cousin?'

'A second cousin of my father's. We had very little to do with him growing up. Other than a few obligatory letters over the years, I hardly knew about him until the funeral. My father's family came out of the woodwork for that.' There was a touch of acid in her tone. 'They swarmed Belle Weather like ants to sugar. Apparently, even a dead man in possession of a fortune is in want of friendship.' She gave a dry laugh, recalling the madness of those days, of being descended on by aunts and cousins full of feigned condolences. She studied Carrick carefully as she let out the first of her many secrets. 'Only there wasn't a fortune. The laugh was on them. They couldn't leave fast enough after the will was read and there were no bequests.'

'But not Victor?' Carrick probed gently, bringing her tale back to the intrusive cousin.

India let out a sigh and fixed Carrick with a steady stare. 'Victor figured out rather quickly that he had one thing all the aunties didn't have and that was a penis. It made him six inches closer to Belle Weather than anyone in the room except for Hal.'

It was rather gratifying to see that she could shock even Carrick. He choked on his wine and she let a little smile play on her lips. 'You know it's true, Carrick. I was Sir Randolph Claiborne's daughter, his oldest and technically next of kin, and I had no legal claim to the estate.' The reality still galled her.

'So, your father left everything to Hal?' Carrick asked.

'What there was of it, yes. Belle Weather will be Hal's when he comes of age at twenty-five and then, after Hal, Victor is the next of male kin.'

'What there was of it? May I ask you to clarify that?' Carrick's brow furrowed. 'I understood your father to be a wealthy man.'

That was the next big secret. She shook her head. 'Wealthy on paper: the estate, the land, the tenant rents. Nothing one could lay ready hands on like cash in a bank.' There was still bitterness over that discovery. 'There were a string of recent investments that had not paid out, also.' Fate had not been kind; the ship from her father's trading company in India had gone down, taking a fortune in silks and spice to the bottom of the ocean, and the sugarcane plantation in the Caribbean had been destroyed by a hurricane.

Carrick gave a low whistle. 'So, Hal inherited as much debt as fortune.' A thought crossed the planes of his face. 'What of your marriage settlements? Surely your father had made some provision for you?'

'Landon's father had given them back, of course. Hal and I needed every penny of them to meet my father's obligations.' That was the third secret. She dropped her voice low even though there was no need. 'I spent those funds to clear the debt and to maintain appearances.'

Carrick nodded solemnly, processing the rationale behind her choice. 'That way no one would guess there was no fortune.'

'It would have been a scandal and it would have tainted Hal's chances. Such news would have followed him to university and into society.'

Carrick fixed her with a rueful smile. 'You sacrificed yourself for your brother. I hope he appreciates it or is he even aware of it?'

'What do I need a dowry for?' It wasn't only her heart that was set against marriage. It was circumstances. Who would take a penniless bride who brought nothing but herself to the marriage? Perhaps it was for the best she'd already decided against the idea before her father's circumstances had been revealed. It had been less disappointing to her to realise marriage was now impossible.

Carrick looked up sharply at that. 'Do you not think that, in time, you might wish to marry? Hal will not need you indefinitely.'

She gave a soft smile. 'That is years away, though. I

have seven years to figure that out.' But when Carrick reached for her hand and squeezed it, she felt tears well up, the burden heavy tonight, perhaps because someone truly guessed what it cost her to bear it. 'It's not about whether or not I marry again, it's about keeping Belle Weather from Victor, keeping it safe for Hal. That's all that can matter at present.' She gave another shake of her head. 'You see now why it's a danger to be here with you. I have everything to lose, not just for myself but for Hal, too.'

He saw much more than that. This was not the only danger. It was a miracle she'd not faltered before this. She was beset by peril on all sides. Carrick ran a thumb over the knuckles of her hand. India had become a strong woman. 'Does Cousin Victor aspire to only Belle Weather?'

Something flashed in India's eyes and he had his answer. Something protective and primal unwound in him as she said, 'Cousin Victor does not care much for me. I am too independent for his tastes, although he pretends otherwise.'

Cousin Victor and his six inches, Carrick thought uncharitably, would not like a woman who dared to stand in his way. It didn't take much imagination to understand what Cousin Victor wanted. He saw an estate unguarded, a young man who could not claim his inheritance and who was in need of a regent until he could. All that stood in his way was one young, unmarried woman who'd proven harder to thwart than intended. 'If he can't go around you, he'd try to go through you.' He watched her for a reaction. Ah, so Victor had tried that, too; proposing marriage in order to control the estate through her.

'He's been thwarted thus far, so now his game is to just wait. Instead of being my enemy, he is waiting for me to be my own worst enemy. He's waiting for me to fail. With the estate, with Hal, with society. I will fall and he will be justified to rush in.' There was resignation in her voice as if she thought failure was inevitable, as if all she could do was prolong the inevitable and hope it would be enough.

'You think being here with me is failing.'

'It certainly is a risk. Do you understand now?'

'You used to take risks all the time.'

'Because I had nothing to lose, not really. I had Landon and my father. But now there is no one, Carrick. There is no one to catch me.'

There's me. I will catch you. He didn't dare say it out loud. They were only words. He wasn't even sure what they meant. How would he catch her? He owned a carriage works, he lived outside of society. His mother and older brother had despaired of him. What could he offer her? He hadn't a fortune to give her. Just a horse farm and a business.

He might have been born a gentleman's son, but he was in trade now. He made a living from work—work that brought him great pleasure, gave his life shape and gave him a solid income so he need not answer to his brother. But it *was* work, a gentleman's anathema, and none of it suitable for the likes of India Claiborne. He knew all this and yet his conscience whipped at him. He brought her hand to his mouth, kissed it. 'I should not have left you alone, my brave girl. I have not been a good friend to you.'

'You gave me what I asked for. When I turned you away, you left me alone, just as I asked. Perhaps it was necessary even if it wasn't pleasant. Good things have come of my trials. I've learned how to run an estate. I've learned the value of a pound. I've learned to economise, to live simply and cleanly. I've learned to see the world as it is and not the frill-lined fiction I'd been living in. These are not bad things, Carrick.'

'But at what price these lessons, India? Landon broke your heart, your father broke your life.'

'And gave me the chance to remake myself in my own image, a woman who wasn't reliant on a man. I had no idea how helpless I was until then and I swore I'd be helpless no more,' she replied softly. 'But, yes, Carrick, it came at a price. I'd be lying if I said I didn't miss the girl I was. I tell myself I've simply outgrown her, that I don't have time to indulge her. But I miss her.'

'What do you miss about her?' Anticipation made his question a collection of hoarse words as the fire popped and hissed behind him, a reminder that the evening was speeding towards night.

It was as if a dam had broken, the last of her restraint gone. 'I miss the wind in my hair atop a carriage seat. I miss taking a jump at full speed on the hunt field, the bunch of a horse's muscles beneath my thighs, I miss whirling about a ballroom so fast the room spins with the light from the chandelier. I miss being in another's arms. I miss being loved…'

Her voice broke and her eyes were in glassy earnest as their gazes held. He barely heard her words. 'I miss the thrill of being alive, Carrick. I feel like I died with my parents. This new warrior I've become lives on a battlefield. She fights every day to protect her home, her brother and she can never give up the fight, not even for a moment. Even though she's tired, so tired, Carrick. That makes me an awful person. I should be braver, stronger.'

He gathered her to him. 'Not at all. You *are* strong enough, brave enough.' He pressed a kiss to her mouth. 'You can lay you your burden down tonight. Tonight, it's just the two of us. You don't have to fight anything, nor anyone.' Her body melted into his, hungry for him, to be touched, to be with someone, to be loved. He could do the former, but not the latter—for her sake, not his.

If he took this to the conclusion her body was asking for, she'd regret it, she'd see it as weakness on her part and it would add to her burdens. But that didn't stop him from kissing her, from burying his hands in her hair. He would give her what comfort he could. But she had other ideas and the warrior in her wouldn't take no for an answer.

'Don't you dare stop, Carrick,' she whispered against his mouth, her arms a too-welcome vice about his neck.

'If I don't stop, there will be no holding back,' he growled the caution against her neck. But what his mind counselled, his body was less inclined to agree with. That body was reaching a point of no return, intoxicated by the woman in his arms, wanting to give her all she asked for, consequences and the morning be damned.

'Don't hold back, then,' she breathed, arching into him, her hips hard against his groin. 'Carry me to bed and make me forget.' Her eyes glittered with the dare and Carrick swept her up, her long bare legs dangling over his arm as he made for the stairs, well aware of what she was really asking for: not just obliterating sex.

India would never ask for something so meaningless. She was asking for much more, asking for him to bring her back to life, and *that* he would not deny her. He'd been dead for a while, too. He knew what it meant to move through the days without passion, without purpose. She deserved far more than that for an existence.

He set her down on the landing outside his chamber, his own hunger slipping its leash, their mouths devouring one another as he pressed her to the wall, his hand fumbling with the doorknob, his body on fire as she nipped his neck, her teeth as sharp, as intentional as the hand she slipped between them, finding the hardness of him and testing it in her grip. He groaned against her. 'I thought I was supposed to be seducing you, Minx.'

She gave a throaty laugh. 'You'd best hurry up, then. I think your window of opportunity is waning.'

He picked her up again and kicked open the recalcitrant door, ignoring the reverberating twinge in his knee, with a growl of a chuckle, 'No one ever accused Carrick Eisley of wasting an opportunity.'

Chapter Fifteen

This was going to be powerful, explosive and fast. Every bone, every nerve in her body knew it and strained towards it, like roots seeking water, like leaves seeking sun. Carrick set her on the bed, his own movements rough in his haste. The desire for obliteration was mutual, it seemed. He made to step back from her, to leave her alone on the bed and she reached for him, grabbing him with equal roughness and pulling him to her with a fiercely whispered command, 'No', followed by a hard, full-mouthed kiss.

'Trousers,' he managed to say the single word as their bodies entwined and her hands joined with his in a clumsy joint struggle to work fastenings and push the garment down over solidly sculpted hips, past thickly muscled thighs whose long sinews demanded to be traced, appreciated, on their own merits. Perhaps later, India thought, her mind and body hungry for other, more earthy delights in the moment.

The problem of trousers alleviated, she pulled him back down to her, legs wrapping around those hips, her body inviting him in, inviting him to stoke and then douse the fire raging through her, kindled by his touch, his mouth, his smile, his eyes, his *knowing.*

That last was as potent as any caress. Tonight, she'd been seen, been understood without being judged, without being fixed. Elizabeth and Laurie wanted to fix things, to help her. Not Carrick. With him, she had only to *be*.

She arched as his hands ran up her torso, pushing back the folds of her borrowed shirt, pushing back layers, revealing her both without and within. He put his mouth on her breast, taking her nipple with his tongue, the little prick of his teeth against the tender skin, and she gasped, her body arching up, thrusting itself further into his mouth, begging. She felt him smile against her skin.

'That's right, scream if you want to, *I* want you to, let her out, she's still there, that wild, passionate girl. Find her,' he whispered against her skin, his mouth moving to the other breast. 'Let her out,' he coaxed, his own body rigid in anticipation, the hard length of him nudging at her entrance, testing, readying and claiming, not that much of those things were needed. She was as ready for him as he was for her and the intensity of the moment was driving them hard.

There was no artistry here, no sophistication or a lover's finesse, only a joining, thorough and swift as he entered her, filled her. She cried out, in relief, in fulfilment as he pushed them both towards a fast-looming edge. *This* was what she'd been seeking, been wanting, to not be alone, to be safe. In Carrick's arms she found both and so much more, things she'd not known she wanted, not known were possible.

He looked down at her, grey eyes dark, the muscles of his arms corded and taut with the tension of his weight as his hips moved against her, his manhood moving in her, pulsing and hard as he pushed them to the edge and took them over, a primal growl ripping from his throat to join her own cries as they fell together like boats going over a falls, rushing towards oblivion, to shatter first and then to float second, in a tranquil pool of their own making.

She lay in his arms for a long while afterwards, eyes closed, her head on his chest, her body and mind reluctant to leave that pool. Why rush? They had all night. She didn't want to think, didn't want to compare, but as the pleasure ebbed, the thoughts came, wading into the pool of tranquillity with her.

She had not known such intensity was possible. She'd not thought such pleasure would accompany the need for an explosive joining. She and Landon had enjoyed what she'd once thought of as 'explosive joinings', sneaking away to alcoves and dark libraries at balls once their engagement had been finalised.

But now, those interludes seemed better classified as furtive than explosive, exciting perhaps not for their inherent pleasure but for their risky nature, the thrill of potential discovery. At the time, she'd not made the distinction. Couldn't make the distinction. To do so required comparison, something a well-bred young lady wasn't supposed to have.

But now...she had the comparison. She'd lain with London's one-time most notorious rake. Now she knew why women swooned for him, why women begged for his attentions even when they knew he could not offer an advantageous marriage by society's standards. She knew, too, why mamas kept their pristine daughters from him. He was dangerous to a girl's virtue and a parent's expectations. He was dangerous to other things as well—like Landon's memory and her own loyalty to it. The first vestiges of guilt twinged in her.

'You're thinking about him, aren't you?' Carrick's fingers idly combed through the tangles of her hair. Even an idle gesture such as this roused the embers of her desire. Here was a man who knew how to touch a woman, to rouse her with the merest effort. She ought to remember that. This pleasure was new to her, but not to him. He might experience it with anyone he chose, whenever he chose.

'Yes.' She looked up from his chest to meet his gaze. She would not hide the truth from him. Would he judge her for it? Would he be disappointed? But there was neither in the gaze that returned hers. There was only a smile on his lips.

'And feeling guilty?' he guessed with a soft laugh that made her smile. Perhaps he read her thoughts so effortlessly because they were his thoughts as well. 'You needn't feel guilty about comparing, or about having taken a lover.'

'Not just any lover, though. You. His friend.' She shifted her position so that she could prop her head up on one hand. 'Do *you* feel guilty?' she asked quietly, not sure she wanted to hear the answer.

Did he have some deep-seated masculine sense of territoriality that asserted he'd trespassed on a dead man's land and that was wrong? A betrayal of a friendship? She hoped not. That hope was tellingly indicative of how much she wanted to meet him on their own grounds, not grounds riddled with memories and a past that could not be changed, only confronted. Ghosts were made in such ways.

Carrick didn't give her a direct answer. 'He would not want you to be alone, India. How many nights did he entrust you to my care at a ball or a *musicale* when he couldn't attend? Perhaps this is no different? If you are to take a lover, why not a friend? Someone you can trust and someone Landon trusted to see you cared for?' She wondered though if his words were to assure her or to assuage him?

She couldn't help but smile. 'You could persuade the sun it was made of ice, Carrick.' She traced a whorl of auburn hair on his chest. 'It was the pleasure I was thinking about.' She couldn't quite meet his eyes. 'It was different this time. More…inherent…' She felt her pale skin blush at the intimate confession. This was what had felt most disloyal, that she'd enjoyed this more with Carrick than she had with Landon, a man who'd promised her everything, while Carrick promised nothing.

She half expected Carrick to gloat. She knew men did crow about such things like being a better lover. But Carrick merely fixed her with one of his soft, kind smiles, the ones that went to her toes, that said, *I see you, all of you, and I understand.*

He drew her down to him once more. 'Do not doubt that Landon loved you and that you pleased him greatly.' He planted a kiss atop her head as he wrapped an arm about her, holding her close to his side. 'Landon was looking forward to marrying you.' She could feel his chest rise beneath her hand as if he were gathering himself. 'That day at the race, all he could talk about was you. Logan and I were teasing him that you'd let him out of your sight. He said, "This time next week, I'll be a hen-pecked husband", and he was smiling the whole time as if he could imagine no better fate. He was lucky in love to have you, India, and he knew it.'

She smiled against his shoulder. Could he feel it? She wasn't sure she wanted to meet his eyes. 'Thank you, Carrick,' she murmured softly. 'I was happy to be with him, too.' But he was gone and the happiness she'd known with him was gone, and tonight she'd come alive again in Carrick's arms. What did that mean? Did it have to mean anything? *Could* it mean anything? She knew the answer to that before the question was even asked. Did Carrick know it, too? She ought to clarify, to make it clear with him, but the wild girl in her was still awake, her hand reaching between his legs and stroking him into arousal once more, ready to return to pleasure's pool while she could.

He took her once more before dawn, this time a slow, savouring of bodies. He'd let his mouth drink from her breasts, sip the nectar of arousal from between her legs before he'd fitted himself to her once more. If revenge was best served cold, passion was best served hot. The night had been nothing short of passion's feast, presented in early courses of heated, fast, couplings that ended in an explosion worthy of fireworks.

Later courses, once their bodies were assured passion wouldn't escape them, had been slower, more languid, a chance to taste one another, learn another through caresses in the dark, through fingers that traced and trailed over one another's bodies, through mouths that kissed birthmarks and scars. The rush and heat had been replaced by something softer, more reverent, but no less intense for that softness.

Could he ever recall a time when he'd been so exhausted, yet so fulfilled? Carrick looked down at India sleeping in his arms, her white-blonde hair spread haphazardly across his chest, mixing with his own auburn, a study in opposition, dark and light.

And yet her light had been hidden these past three years. Out of a necessity to survive, to escape the clutches of a greedy man who would take her home from her, and who would take more than that if given the chance, a man who would take her freedom. What was to be done about that?

He ran a hand idly along the length of her arm. And what was to be done about *this*? This new-sprung passion between them? He could guess what India would say about it. He wasn't sure he'd agree. He stifled a yawn, wanting to hold back sleep, knowing that when he awoke, the night would be gone, taking the passion with it. If he could just stay awake, perhaps the passion would live, too… But a man who'd made love all night had spent his stamina elsewhere.

It was well past dawn when Carrick awoke. The space beside him in bed was cold and his arms were empty. How had she managed to disentangle herself without waking him? But she'd not gone far. He lay still, listening to her move about the room, taking consolation that she'd not be dressed yet. Her clothes were downstairs, still draped over the furniture in an attempt to dry. He cracked open an eye and found her sitting in the chair beside the fire, the sight of her causing both eyes to open. She'd rummaged in his closet and found a banyan of bright blue and his hairbrush. The banyan was belted at the waist but it was still loose enough to offer a tantalising glimpse of her breasts as she worked through the tangle of her tresses with his hair brush. Oh, God, those breasts—breasts where he'd lain his head, where he'd laved with his tongue until she'd cried out in wild delight He felt his body rouse at the memory.

'I hope you don't mind?' She held up the brush.

'No, not at all.' What man would? What man would be able to deny such a vision anything she asked for? Oh, to wake like this every morning, to this vision of blonde loveliness dressed in his robe, combing out Godiva-like tresses. But such a privilege required the sacrifice of marriage—not the sacrament, the sacrifice. It required breaking promises to himself, about opening himself up to loss once more because such happiness as the happiness he imagined with India could not last. To lose her would destroy him and if by chance she felt the same way, he could not bear to be the source of such destruction for her after she'd endured so much already. If marriage was the consummation of love, then it was also the very consummation of loss. *Till death do us part.* No, he did not want such loss again.

'Does the housekeeper come in the mornings?' India enquired casually, but there was a tension in her blue eyes and he understood immediately her concern.

'No, she won't be in until noon. We'll have to fend

for ourselves for breakfast.' He hoped she heard the reassurance he'd hidden in those words, that their secret was safe. No one came to the house during the week. Of course, there were stable hands who lived above the barn and saw to the horses full time, but he could manage them. He reached for his trousers and threw his legs over the side of the bed. 'I'll retrieve your clothes from downstairs,' he offered. It would give him a chance to get himself in order as well. He couldn't spend the day walking around with an erection.

Retrieving clothes and stirring up the fire had the desired effect, although he thought 'desired' was a rather ironic term when all he wanted to do was crawl back into bed with India. But he couldn't do that. It was the middle of the week. He had a carriage to deliver next Monday to the Earl of Dartmouth and other orders besides. There was Hal to consider as well and no more bad weather to hide behind. His carriage works would be expecting him this morning and people would be expecting India as well. Discreet friends would give her the benefit of the doubt for one night. But two days? That would raise eyebrows.

India joined him downstairs in the kitchen, her clothes no worse for the drenching yesterday, her hair contained in a simple knot at the base of her neck. When she reached for an apron and tied it about her waist, she looked like a respectable country gentleman's wife, as though she belonged here, *with him*. Yet he knew she was a woman who deserved so much more. Or was it that he did not deserve her? He had much to atone for when it came to India. To fall for her, to want her to fall for him, seemed too much to ask after all he'd taken from her. And yet the last thing he wanted to do was distance himself from her, even knowing it was what he ought to do before he hurt them both.

She moved about the kitchen, opening cupboards and removing items. 'We have bacon and bread and a few eggs left here in the bowl with the towel over it. I think we won't starve.' She set the kettle on the hob over the fire and set bread on a rack over the flames before turning to the stove, scrambling eggs and frying bacon.

'How did you learn to cook?' Carrick busied himself setting out plates and mugs. He should not ask such questions, should not seek such intimate details. It would not help him establish distance. It would only draw him closer.

'Necessity.' She threw the word over her shoulder with a smile. 'Our cook left after Mother and Father died. Apparently, Cook had no faith in our ability to hold on to the property. She had no desire to work for Victor and she left. For a month or so, before I could find a new cook, I did the cooking. We ate a lot of scrambled eggs and I became pretty good at baking bread and a few other things.' She laughed. 'You sound surprised.'

Carrick came up behind her, placing his hands at her waist and kissing her neck. 'Nothing about you surprises me, India. If you needed to go to the moon, I imagine you'd find a way to do that, too.' He laughed and then sobered. 'I'm sorry for it though, that you were alone, without the funds you thought you possessed and no one to fight your battles.'

'Don't be sorry. I fought my own battles, for the first time.' She turned in his arms, her own arms going about his neck. 'I discovered I like to cook and bake. I might not be great at it, but I *am* learning. There's a lot I wouldn't have learned about myself, Carrick, if not for the tragedies. It's not all bad, although some days it's harder to remember that than others.' She slipped from his embrace and turned back to the stove, dishing up the eggs and bacon on a platter before bringing it to the work table where he'd set out plates.

Carrick retrieved the kettle and the toast. 'Here's to us, then, and our resourceful breakfast.' She smiled, but said nothing in return. He gave her the space of three bites of toast to come out with it. 'What is it, India? Something is clearly on your mind and I don't think it's the eggs.' He tried to tease the smile from her again.

She set down her mug. 'Last night was enlightening, wonderful, exactly what I needed, but it cannot be repeated, Carrick.' She bit her lip, thinking for a moment. 'I thought you understood, Carrick. There can be no us.'

He'd been expecting this ever since he'd fallen asleep. Gone was the woman who'd writhed with abandon in his arms, who'd been wild for pleasure. In her place was the practical woman who'd carefully shared her secrets with him the night before, perhaps helped along by the wine. But expecting the words didn't make the news any easier to accept, nor did it make it any easier to discern what he wanted from this.

By rights, he would usually be thrilled for a woman to walk away after a night of passion with no expectations of him. But when that woman was India Claiborne, such an ending sat poorly, even though it was what he needed. Her leaving would give him the distance he ought to want. But he insisted on arguing against it.

'This is it then? You'll simply go home and pretend this never happened?' Pretend, not forget. She would not forget. He'd chosen his words deliberately.

She gave him a hard stare over the rim of her mug. 'What else can I do? If Victor were to ever learn of this, I would be ruined, Hal would be ruined. We would lose Belle Weather. Victor would use it as grounds to take it from me and "hold it" until Hal came of age. But by then, he'd have driven the estate into the ground.'

He hated hearing the very real fear in her voice. He'd like to deal with Victor Claiborne himself, but that was the last thing India wanted. She wouldn't want men, any men, not even friends, to undermine her hard-won independence. 'So, I am to let you go?' Despite everything that had changed, he felt he was back on the doorstep of the Claiborne town house again, being turned away. And like then, he'd go, because that's what she wanted. If it was all he could give her, then it was *what* he'd give her.

'There is no choice.' India's eyes softened, the only sign that she regretted this as much as he did. 'What would you have me do, Carrick? Have an affair? Risk scandal for myself and Hal? And all for what? For a few nights of pleasure?'

Carrick gave her a wry grin to cover the hurt, the frustration. 'Well, when you put it like that, India, a man has a very strong sense of his limitations.' Of course, she was right. What *was* the purpose of them being together beyond the antidote of a single night? What would make a scandal worth risking for her?

'Carrick, we must be practical. The risk we took last

night was risk enough. And I thank you for it, but if anyone should find out…'

'No one will find out, I promise, India,' he said fiercely, holding her gaze. He would duel the bastard who alluded to anything untoward if it came to that. He paused. 'When will you go?'

'Not yet. Not as long as we both can bear it.' She was laying down the rules. They must not give anything away. He must drive her back to town and go about his work as if nothing had happened, as if nothing had changed, so that no one would suspect that perhaps everything had changed, that something had happened. As long as they didn't repeat last night, she would stay, hovering on the periphery of his life, tempting them both.

'You understand it will be a special kind of torture to be with you, but not touch you.' What she wanted came with a price, too.

Her blue eyes flashed. 'Yes. But you will not be enduring it alone.' There was a ripple of desire, of tension that followed her soft words. They both wanted each other, something that at present was a futile, terminal desire. Perhaps it was indeed true that misery loved company. They would burn in this hell of their own making together.

Chapter Sixteen

Waiting was a slow kind of hell to burn in, Victor Claiborne decided as he finished an early afternoon tumbler of brandy at his club, Mackey's, off St James's, on Rider Street. He was a man who knew a little something about hell. The only difference between waiting and hell was that waiting would come to an end, eventually. The torment was in knowing when. He'd been waiting three years—three long years because he'd not expected to wait at all.

'Another, sir?' The waiter approached with a deferential air and Victor nodded.

Why not? London in autumn was deuced boring with no one about but diplomats and politicos and those who had nowhere else to go, as in those who didn't have estates of their own to retire to or invitations to go to someone else's. He was here for both those reasons and in hopes of rectifying that situation.

At least London wasn't hot. The Caribbean had been *hot* with a type of heat he'd never experienced before in his life and one he didn't particularly like. Still, he'd paid his dues, overseeing Cousin Randolph's sugar plantation on Bermuda for seven long years until the hurricane had destroyed it. Reid's Hurricane, it was called, a September storm that had done eight thousand pounds worth of financial damage to the island's plantations, including Belle Mont, one of the largest, and, until then, one of the most lucrative even after the overhead of paying for labour.

Slavery had been outlawed for nearly twenty years on the island, adding to plantation operating costs. Victor groused about it, but Cousin Randolph had championed the move. Freed labour or not, the storm had made such argument moot. Seven years of work and sweat had been wiped out in a matter of hours, as had Victor's rather lavish island lifestyle. He'd lived well at Belle Mont on money he'd grafted from his cousin. But now he had nothing to show for it. There had been no gratitude from Cousin Randolph, no remembrance in his cousin's will, no bequest of another estate or financial remuneration.

To be fair, his cousin probably hadn't planned on dying so soon any more than his cousin had planned on a hurricane wiping out one of his largest sources of income. Perhaps he should have. It wasn't as if there'd never been a storm in the Caribbean. But that hadn't been Cousin Randolph's way. He was a man who took risks, who lived fully in the moment and gave little foresight to the future. The man's whole family was like that, his two children pattern cards of their thrill-seeking parents. Which was why it was something of a surprise to have arrived at the funeral and discovered Miss India Claiborne had things well in hand. Too well in hand for his plans.

The waiter returned and Victor took the fresh glass of brandy, holding it to the light. He'd missed good brandy in the Caribbean. Rum was the local drink there and he'd never quite acquired an affinity for it. But he *had* acquired an affinity for high living and ready funds. For that, a man needed a regular source of income and in England, a man needed land, an estate. It was no secret the estate would go to young Hal.

But Victor had been hoping Cousin Randolph might have named him guardian for young Hal. After all, he'd proven himself in the Caribbean, even considering the amount of profit he'd quietly pocketed on the side and, besides Hal, he *was* the male next of kin. Who better to handle matters and show Hal the ropes of estate management than he?

Meanwhile, he'd have access to the Claiborne coffers, there'd be the town house in London from which to enjoy the Season and its vices, and in the autumn, he could retire to Belle Weather for hunting at his own estate, no longer dependent on the invitations of others, no longer welcome only at mediocre clubs like Mackey's, but at the better clubs, maybe even the Travellers.

He grimaced into the depths of the amber brandy. Fate had seen fit to rob him on both accounts. First in the form of the revelation that the Claiborne finances had been devastated by multiple losses. But even then, Victor had thought the financial setback might have worked in his favour, the loss of money and an estate teetering on financial ruin, unable to naturally cover its debts, would have overwhelmed India and her brother. He'd liked the idea of stepping in and playing the hero. But India had wanted that role for herself.

Instead of being overwhelmed by loss and debt, she'd managed to convince the solicitor to turn the reins of the estate over to her. And so the waiting had begun. Waiting for her to fail. But India had not failed. He'd waited for her innate Claiborne wildness to surface, for her to do something socially outlandish and cause a scandal now that there was no fiancé or father to protect her. But she'd retreated from society, sold the town house—much to his chagrin—and lived an obscure life in the country. From all reports, she only left the estate for church on Sundays.

That left him with only one option. If he couldn't fight her, he could join her. He was in town to meet with the solicitor and make a proper offer of marriage. If he couldn't run the estate, he could at least run it through her. With a marriage, he'd take on legal guardianship of Hal and the estate until Hal came of age. By then, he should have his own pockets lined and his own finances set up. And who knew, Hal might not even want Belle Weather, especially if he could persuade Hal otherwise.

There were other ways to prolong his marital regency as well. Even when Hal came of age, he could suggest Hal might benefit from overseeing estates elsewhere. He could send Hal to the Caribbean, for instance, or to study estate management somewhere else. And who knew? Hal might just like the Caribbean too much to want to come home. Atlantic crossings were dangerous. Anything could happen. It would be a tragedy, of course, for India to lose her last family member, but accidents *did* happen, boats sank, Caribbean fevers could be deadly, hurricanes, too.

'Mr Claiborne?' A slim-built, wiry man with greying hair and spectacles, dressed in the modest black suit of a working man, approached. 'I'm Arthur Moore, the Claiborne family solicitor.'

'Ah yes.' Victor rose and shook the man's hand, offering a smile meant to put the man at ease. His nerves were evident in the way his eyes kept darting about the club. No amount of long windows and leather club chairs could change the fact that this wasn't White's or Brooks, or the Athenaeum, or that one had to leave the well-trodden streets of St James's to reach it. Meeting at questionable clubs suggested the men who gathered there were questionable as well and that suspicion likely extended to the subjects they wished to meet about. But it was the best Victor could offer for now.

He signalled for the waiter to bring fresh drinks. 'Thank you for meeting me. What I want to discuss is best done in a more genial environment than an office.' Victor sat back down and got straight to the point. 'I am concerned for my cousin being out at the estate all alone and about the amount of work she's been putting in. I hear she's withdrawn from society entirely and that can't be healthy for a young woman her age.'

If she was going to play the virtuous martyr, he was going to use that against her. A woman in a man's world never won and it was time she learned that. 'She needs a man to ease that burden. I want you to draw up a marriage contract and present it to Miss Claiborne, offering myself as bridegroom.'

The man swallowed, perhaps already anticipating

India's response. But to his credit, he didn't argue. 'And where shall I send it, sir?'

'To Belle Weather, of course.' Victor furrowed his brow.

'It may be a while then before she sees it, but perhaps there is no haste.' The man adjusted his spectacles. 'You do know, sir, that she is spending the autumn at Foxfields with the Blackmons? I've been directed to forward all of her business correspondence there.'

Victor took a swallow of brandy to cover his surprise. He *hadn't* known, but that was an interesting and worrisome development. He wondered if Lawrence Benefield, Elizabeth's brother, was there. If Benefield was there, did his presence have anything to do with India's visit? If India had finally decided to marry again, he didn't want Benefield beating him to the altar.

'Let us send a copy to both Foxfields and Belle Weather, then,' he amended. 'Now that my mind is made up, I don't want to delay.' An India married to another man would put Belle Weather beyond his reach short of an accident that resulted in Hal's death, at which point Belle Weather would be his. It wasn't the first time he'd thought of it.

Perhaps you should be thinking about that option more seriously now. The devil on his shoulder was speaking louder than usual.

He'd refrained from thinking of it because it would look incredibly suspicious for a single person such as India to lose so much to tragedy in such short succession. It also wouldn't take much to look around and see who benefited the most from such circumstances. Marriage would be better than murder, given that one was a sin and the other was considered part of the natural social order. Marriage, too, had the added benefit of being a celebration. Not that he *wanted* to marry India. The woman would need some taming.

Marriage was, however, the best compromise to his problem of how to legally get his hands on the estate. The Bible verse *Better to marry than to burn* flitted through his mind. It referred to passion, of course, and not the hell reserved for those who committed deadly sins. But there were so many ways to burn.

He shook the solicitor's hand, thanked him again for his time and sat back down to have a think. Better to marry one's second cousin than to murder them. But needs must when the devil drives. What he needed right now was to know what was happening at Foxfields. He had men for that. He'd send word right away for someone to take up watch. He'd go himself, but he didn't want to confront India when she was surrounded by those loyal to her: Elizabeth, Benefield and Blackmon. He also didn't want to risk alienating Hal. The fewer witnesses there were the better.

He'd prefer to catch her at Belle Weather, alone and unsupported. Then, there would be myriad ways to convince her that marriage was the only option she had. Separated from those she relied on, she would have few weapons in her arsenal with which to fight him, physically, mentally or socially. If they were alone and she did not see reason until he spelled it out for her in whatever ways were necessary, who would gainsay him? It would be her word against his and a woman's word wasn't worth nearly as much as a man's. No one would ever know what had truly happened at Belle Weather, only that Miss India Claiborne had decided to marry her second cousin, a judicious match all around.

Chapter Seventeen

They were being judicious, careful of every moment they spent together, careful not to give anything away, careful not to deviate from the previously established patterns. India still came to the carriage works at lunch. They ate together with Hal. No one could find fault with that. She lingered afterwards, sitting on a stool watching their progress on various projects, ostensibly to be impressed with Hal's education under Carrick's tutelage. But in truth, it was Carrick she was impressed with.

While her eyes lingered on his body, too aware of the strength that lay beneath shirt and breeches, her mind appreciated the skill he brought to his craft. She spent hours absorbed with watching his hands work, forging hinges, mounting wheels, testing axles. Those hands had forged her anew, a broken blade jagged and sharp, but broken none the less, and turned her into something whole and new. But for what purpose? To simply carry on most likely. There was no other choice for her. To deviate from the norm was to risk everything she'd managed to build.

Watching him, though, working, talking with his apprentices, with Hal, offering instruction here, a correction there as carriages took shape, India feared 'impressed' might be too tame of a word to describe her feelings. But any other word would be too dangerous. She could be impressed with him, she could perhaps even esteem him for the quality of his work and his devotion to it. But she could not fall for him.

Well, she *could* fall for Carrick, but no one could know, not even him because nothing could come of it. She'd had her one night of indiscretion, one night of solace, of laying down her burdens, of flying free. It could not happen again. Then there was the other reality; she *had* to go home at some point, had to go back to her life. Belle Weather needed her.

'As long as we both can stand it' really meant she could perhaps delay until the end of November, but not beyond. She needed to be at Belle Weather for Christmas. Even now, a certain restlessness stirred within her, wanting to get back, and yet that restlessness knew what leaving meant: leaving meant leaving Carrick, leaving whatever it was that she'd found here—passion, solace, her sense of self.

Carrick glanced her way and flashed her a smile, looking far too potent with his rolled-up shirtsleeves and a leather apron. He gestured for her to follow him outside into the alley. As soon as the door shut behind them, he pressed her up against the wall, stealing a kiss and she let him because she wanted it, too; wanted to see if the passion would rise between them again, or if it lingered only in her imagination.

'I want you, India,' he murmured against her lips. 'I just wanted you to know.' She felt the hardness of him through her skirts. He kissed her again and this time all playfulness was absent, the kiss full-mouthed and rough, and it sent a delicious shudder through her. He moved against her and her resistance began to fail. Who was there to see? To know?

'I feel your eyes on me in the shop and I go hard.' His voice was a rasp at her ear, 'I watch you set out the lunch and I imagine your hands on me, that it's me you're laying out. You drive me to distraction, India.' He nipped at her ear, trailed kisses along her jaw, stirring her desire to a point of no return, a point of no denying. If she did not have him, it would be unbearable.

'Be quick,' she gasped her consent before she could think better of it and because her body couldn't stand much more before it felt as if it would explode. She had only the flimsiest of rationales. Surely, just this once, surely, for a few moments it would be safe to indulge.

And it was. His strong arms lifted her, the breadth of his body covered her, would have shielded her from anyone who might have passed by, but the alley itself was not oft travelled. His broad shoulder took the brunt of her cries as he thrust into her hard and fast. It was delicious and short, a rough, erotic pleasure and she laughed out loud in the aftermath, her head thrown back against the brick to see the glint of enjoyment in his grey eyes.

'Good Lord, that was too much fun, India.' He kissed her one last time and set her down.

Too much fun indeed. It could easily become addictive, the slippery slope into decadence she'd so desperately wanted to avoid. 'We can't...' She didn't get to finish. His fingers pressed against her mouth.

He shook his head. 'Don't say it. Never say never,

India. Instead, say yes, say you'll come to the farm this weekend with Hal and me. We're going to try out some carriages before they're delivered.'

She gave a laugh. 'You make it sounds so harmless, so safe. You are the very devil in sheepskin, Carrick, when you know very well it won't be harmless.'

'Hal will be there.' He was kissing her again, laughing against her neck.

'Hal is no kind of protection against *this*.' No protection against passion, against desire, of the way Carrick made her feel, of wanting to throw reason to the wind. 'You know if I come, we'll spend the weekend looking for ways to be alone.'

He nuzzled her neck. 'Will we succeed?'

'Probably,' she whispered back. Which meant only one thing. It would be time to go home.

'So, will you come?' Carrick asked, grey eyes smoking like banked embers.

'Yes,' she whispered, a new rule already forming in her mind. They would go out with a bang while she broke every standard she'd set for herself.

Carrick squeezed her hand. 'It will be worth it, India.'

'Tell me something I don't already know.' She reached up and kissed him once more.

'I'm taking India and Hal to the farm this weekend, to try out a new carriage before I deliver it and to try out the new racing design for Wallingford,' Carrick told Logan that night. They were upstairs in his rooms over the shop, Logan's syndicate paperwork spread out on a table as he drew up the roster for the next race.

Logan looked up. 'Anything else you're going to try out while you're there?'

Carrick caught the dryness in his tone and answered with a sharp look. 'What is that supposed to mean?'

Logan set down his papers. 'It means you've been spending a lot of time with a certain woman, but to what purpose? I thought I knew. I thought you were supposed to convince her that Hal should race. But now I wonder if you had another, more personal motive in mind. Perhaps Hal was just an excuse.'

Carrick felt his temper flare at the implication. 'I *did* convince her that Hal could study racing and carriage-making with me. That was the deal. To teach him how to race safely.'

'But I need more than that. I need Hal to race at Wallingford and you refuse to let that happen behind her back. I am trying to honour that, but it's deuced difficult when you won't do your part and get her consent. You are leaving me no choice.' Logan waved a handful of fliers. 'I need Hal for Wallingford. We've already advertised him. "Come try your hand against the hottest new whip" and all that.'

'That's not my fault.' Logan had overplayed his hand, but Carrick did not want to overplay his and pushing India on this would definitely do that.

'I bet on you, Carrick. I bet you'd come through with him.' Logan scowled. 'I have money, investors and my personal reputation on the line. People want to be a part of the syndicate, but I need Hal for the prestige.' He slammed the fliers down. 'Dammit, Carrick. Just dammit. I have a lot riding on this. The syndicate is just getting established. I can't handle a setback like this.'

He'd seldom seen Logan so upset. Usually, Logan was the epitome of cool reserve.

'I have a lot riding on this, too,' Carrick said in low tones that bordered on a growl. 'I don't want to lose her, Logan.' And he might. She wouldn't like the idea of Hal racing, but even more than that, if she thought for a moment that he'd seduced her for her compliance, she would not forgive him or herself. She would think him no better than her insidious cousin, Victor. And she would withdraw. The fragile flame that had just now begun to glow again within her would go out. He hated the thought of that more than anything else.

'Lose *her*?' Logan gave a hard chuckle of disbelief. 'A month ago she wasn't even a part of your world and now you act like she is the entirety of it, as if you would trade nearly twenty years of our friendship for her—a woman, I might add, who turned you away on her doorstep and has made no effort to contact you in three years, a woman who was at best an acquaintance through a mutual friend.'

Carrick stiffened at the rebuke. He could not let that pass. Those were fighting words. Logan never did fight fair. And his speech wasn't over. 'Remember who picked you up and dusted you off after Landon's death, remember who arranged for the carriage works and the farm, who made sure you didn't drink yourself into oblivion. It sure as hell wasn't her.'

Logan cursed again. 'You've changed. She's changed you,' he accused. 'Can't you see it? What happened to the man I knew who'd sworn off attachments? Who believed loving was the height of foolishness, the very definition of loss? Of deliberately opening oneself up to remarkable, inevitable hurt? You promised.' Dear God. Logan was jealous. This was about more than the syndicate. Logan was hurt and afraid. Afraid of losing him. It was understandable given what they'd both endured, the loss of their fathers at a young age and the gaping holes of grief that had never been filled.

'I'm not in love with her. I want to help her. That's all.' He tried for assurance but he wasn't certain who it was meant for. For Logan? To assure him that their friendship would always stand? For himself? That he was not setting himself up for a disappointment of the worst kind? *I am not falling in love with her.* It was the one thing he could not condone. Love hurt. Love meant loss. He knew it empirically.

Yet he knew the words for a lie the moment he spoke them. Against all his protections, love was worming its way through the walls of his defences, sneaking around his promises. When had atonement and penance become something more? When had he stopped seeing her as the girl he had to make it all up to and started seeing her as the woman he cared for and admired? A woman he wanted in his bed and his arms for more than a short-term liaison? What did 'more' mean in these circumstances?

That was the real question of the hour. Did more mean an extended affaire? Did more mean matrimony? Matrimony was no protection against loss. Married people died, married people left behind their families all the time, left those they cared for open to hurt and grief. Her parents had done it, his father had done it. It would eventually happen to them—either she would die and leave him alone to grieve, or he would condemn her to that same fate. How did love *allow* such hurt to take place?

'Good God, Carrick, you *do* love her. It's written all over your face, you poor sod.' Logan shook his head in disbelief, the heat of his anger fading to something akin to sadness. 'What happens next then?'

Carrick rose and poured them each a drink. 'I'm not sure.' How did he make Logan understand what he felt for India? Logan who'd never been in love? 'I only know I don't want to be in the position of having to choose between you and her.' He handed the tumbler to Logan. 'Pax, old friend? I'd prefer not to lose either of you.'

Logan took the drink. 'Pax, Carrick.' Perhaps Logan was already picturing how he'd have to be there to pick up the pieces when this fell apart. Logan was good at that. He'd picked up the pieces before and goodness knew Logan had too much practice with his younger brother, who was forever getting into scrapes Logan had to extricate him from.

Logan took a long swallow. 'I don't envy you. Just keep a straight head and remember you need to sell carriages to stay in business. You need this syndicate as much as I do. The carriage trade is for rich men with a hobby these days, now that we have railroads. Don't let her run away with your heart *and* your head.'

Logan gave a sigh of resignation and Carrick understood it was as close to an endorsement as he'd get. Logan was no good at articulating feelings beyond anger, one of the many scars he carried.

But Logan's question prompted a lingering question. What did come next? What was he headed to with

India? To bliss, to joy, to a satisfaction that begged to be repeated the moment it concluded?

Images of India with her neck arched, her head thrown back in the alley today, her legs wrapped about his hips as he thrust into her, ran riot in his mind in full colour. Those moments in the alley had been glorious beyond imagination. To what end indeed? India felt there was no future for them and the future was not something he'd spent a lot of time contemplating until now.

'So, you're taking her and Hal to the farm this weekend?' Logan picked up the older conversation as if their quarrel had never happened—another one of his scars, Carrick supposed. Logan often ignored that which displeased him by pretending it had never happened at all.

Carrick gave a sigh and took a careful sip of his brandy. It was his turn to be resigned. There was only one reason Logan had returned to this topic. 'I'll talk to her at the farm.' Somehow, when the time was right, he'd find the words for the sake of both his relationships.

'He knows you for a friend,' Carrick stopped inside the stable door to watch India pet King. The afternoon was crisp and bright and the sun slanted through the stable, capturing her in a nimbus of golden light that outlined her slim silhouette in a way that turned him hard.

He'd spent most of the weekend hard, in fact, and now it was late Saturday afternoon and he was no closer to broaching the subject of Hal racing than he had been Friday night when he'd sneaked into her bedchamber, or this morning when he'd awakened in her arms and decided that he wouldn't discuss it before or after love-making. But he was running out of time and choices.

She turned, embarrassed at having been caught. 'He's a sweet boy.'

Carrick leaned against the door frame. He could watch her pet that horse all day, but that wasn't the point. The point was that she *wasn't* watching Hal. 'Don't you want to see Hal on the track? He's doing well with the new phaeton.' How could he bring up Hal's racing if she wouldn't even watch her brother drive? He'd been counting on Hal's prowess with the ribbons to sway her.

She said nothing and turned back to stroking King's long nose. 'He's a good driver, India, and he's become a much safer driver these last weeks. He's learned a lot and he's using it.'

She held out a piece of apple for King on the flat of her hand. 'Phaetons tip over.'

'Not this one. I built it especially with racing in mind. It's heavier, better balanced than the usual high perch. The tongue features a special release so that if it should actually manage to tip, the horses can pull free and be out of harm's way.' It was one of the first safety features he'd perfected when he'd taken over the carriage works. 'Such a feature would have saved Landon from his own carelessness,' he added quietly.

There was nothing she could say to that and they both knew it. He pushed off the door. 'Come on, let's put a saddle on King and take him out. It's a beautiful day for a ride.' He motioned for one of the stable boys to get his horse ready and for another to get King's tack. India started to protest.

'Don't worry, he's an excellent hunter these days.

I trained him myself when it became apparent that he didn't want to work in the traces with any other horse than Sabre.' He grabbed a rope halter from beside the stall door and slipped it over King's head and led the horse out into the aisle.

'I don't jump any more.'

He'd suspected as much. Risk, thrill, had no place in her world any longer. He nodded non-committally and took the tack from the stable boy. He threw a saddle pad over King's back and situated it over his withers. 'That saddens me, India. You were a dream to watch on horseback, so in control.' He let his gaze hold hers across King's back as he fitted the saddle. 'We *can* just ride.' He buckled on the girth and cinched it, checking it twice.

'But Hal...' she said.

'Will hardly miss us,' he finished for her. 'Now come, give me your foot and I'll give you a leg up.' He tossed her up, then mounted his own horse and they set off beneath the late-autumn sun.

At the hunt meadow, King was frisky despite India's expert handling. 'He wants to run,' Carrick called to her, working to rein in his own mount. Who wouldn't want to run on day like today? 'How about it? My grooms walk the field every day, perfectly safe.'

He flashed her a grin and gave his mount a kick. 'First one to the other side claims a forfeit!' and he was off, hoping King and India's own innate desire to run wouldn't let her refuse. He heard hooves pound behind him and smiled into the wind. India never could stand to lose a challenge on horseback. He pushed his horse to an all-out gallop. This time he was going to win and he knew exactly what he was going to claim in forfeit.

Chapter Eighteen

Damn Carrick Eisley for provoking her! India kicked King with her boots and felt him gather beneath her for the chase. He was a smooth mover and her body fell easily into the rhythm of him. She gave him his head and let the wind catch her hat, let it get carried away, let the wind pull her hair loose as she crouched low over King's neck, the thrill of the race starting to claim her despite her earlier protests.

They were close to Carrick now; they would catch him. A log loomed and Carrick's big grey took it effortlessly. There was no time to think or to react and her body did so instinctively, lifting its weight from the saddle, feet thrust heels down deep into the stirrups as King followed the grey over the log. She forgot she didn't jump any more, forgot she didn't race neck or nothing. Only the race mattered. They were nearly even as the end of the field loomed, but Carrick's grey found a final spurt of speed and crossed first by a nose.

'Ha!' Carrick crowed, turning his mount in a circle. His hair was windblown, a wild auburn tangle, his face ruddy. She thought he'd never looked handsomer. He was a man in his element. He jumped down and looped the reins over his arm before coming to her side and helping her down. 'Don't jump any more? You're certainly not rusty.' He held her against him for a long moment. 'Tell me the truth, India—it felt good, didn't it?'

Exhilaration was riding her hard. Her cheeks were likely as flushed as his and she was laughing from the joy of it. 'Oh, I've missed that! King is splendid.'

'Then he's yours. You were made for each other.' Carrick laughed. It was too generous of a gift. There was no question of accepting, but she would argue with him about it later. For now, she just wanted to enjoy the moment, the thrill of the race, the thrill of walking side by side with Carrick, their horses in hand, in the gorgeous afternoon. 'I don't think there's a rider in the world who rivals you, India.'

'Even though you won?' India teased him. He made her feel alive even though she'd not realised until lately how dead she'd been these past years, how much she'd given up. They paused at a wide oak and let the horses graze. She leaned against the trunk and looked up at Carrick, letting her eyes flirt with him, tempt him before she said, 'Now, as to the business of your forfeit, what was it that you'd like to claim?' She licked her lips in invitation.

'As tempting as your offer is,' he answered with a tease of his own, 'I want to talk to you about Hal.'

'Hal?' She tried unsuccessfully to ignore the disappointment that welled up in her over the lost kiss.

'He's done well these last weeks at the carriage works and as a driver. I know you've seen it, too.'

She could not deny that. Hal was happier than he'd

been in years, really. 'I appreciate everything you've done for him, Carrick.' She tensed and searched his face, looking for clues. Carrick wanted something badly enough to challenge her to a race, to spend his forfeit on it when there were other more pleasant things it could have been spent on.

'I'd like him to stay,' Carrick rushed on, 'Say nothing, India. This is my forfeit to claim, remember? I know you want him at Oxford next term. I know it's what you and Hal agreed upon, but can you really imagine Hal at Oxford? Sitting through long lectures about Roman history and complicated sessions about poetry and literature he'll never use?' His tone indicated how preposterous he thought the notion was.

India narrowed her gaze and crossed her arms. 'If Hal is to run the estate one day, he needs an education. Gentlemen do business with gentlemen. He needs to mingle with those who will be his peers. *You* went to university.'

'For a while. I went because that's how it was done in my family.' He let her take that in, seeing the surprise register in her eyes. 'I was sent down after my first year. My marks were appalling and I never attended class, if you must know, and I think you must because it adds to my case.'

'And what case is that?' India was beginning to suspect there was more to this than just staying on at the carriage works. Worry began to crowd in on the lovely afternoon. 'He needs an education.'

'I agree with that, India.' Carrick gave her a warm smile that said he was on her side and she wanted to believe that, only she couldn't. He would not have asked to speak of this if he hadn't felt there was something to discuss, some ground to press out between them, which by definition meant there *was* something they did not agree on.

'True. But there are all sorts of educations and all different types of learners. Hal is a very tactile learner. Like me, he learns best by doing, by being active. If you force him to Oxford, it will be a dismal failure. Take my experience, for example; it's not for everyone, gentleman's son or not. I skipped class and went street racing. My mother and my older brother were adamant I attend Oxford but they couldn't make me stop racing. Like that old expression, you can lead a horse to water… My father would have understood that, but my brother did not. He couldn't control me and it infuriated him. It became a wedge between us, one my brother and I have never got past to this day. All he could do was send me there. He couldn't *make* me stay. He couldn't make me like it. He couldn't stop me from doing what I loved.'

The topic was not a new one. They had discussed much the same that first day she'd discovered Hal in his shop, discovered *him*. But the way in which he made that argument was different today, of what it had meant to grow up as he had after his father's death, to make the decisions he had made. To be himself had cost him his family. There'd been no room for him as he was and he could not stay and be otherwise. He was offering her a warning.

'Is that where you think Hal and I are headed? To an impasse where Hal feels he has to choose between me and his own hopes?' That was a very dire consequence indeed, one she had overlooked in her attempt to get

Hal to take the actions she wanted. She'd not thought beyond them.

Carrick nodded solemnly. 'Yes, I do because I've been there. I couldn't live the way I wanted so I left. I haven't seen my brother in maybe fourteen years. Unless one counts a brief sighting here and there in London those years I went up to town with Landon. I saw my mother once a couple of years ago when I showed her the property. I wanted to show her I had made something of myself, that I hadn't come to naught. But she was not as impressed as I'd hoped.'

'I've never met your mother, but if I did, I'd have a few choice words for her.' India reached out a hand and touched him on the sleeve. She could feel how much his mother's disappointment had hurt him. Whether he realised it or not, a part of the boy he'd been had no doubt wanted his mother's love to fill the gap left by his father. Something warm and protective unfurled inside her, an irrational desire to want to shield this man from any injury.

'Your horse farm is wonderful. You have done well. I know few men who could have bought their own property and established their own business.' Most gentlemen she knew relied on inheritance. Even Laurie had not started from scratch.

He took her hand and raised it to his lips. 'My fierce India, so ready to protect those she cares about. It's one of the things I admire most about you. That and your courage, and your bravery.' He smiled and the warmth in her stomach turned to a desire of a different sort, something beyond sexual: the desire to simply be with this man.

'You want to protect Hal, but perhaps the best way to help him is to let him find his own path.' Carrick pitched his voice low now as if he was murmuring secret truths to a lover. 'We can't control others, not really, India, and we certainly can't make decisions for them, only for ourselves.' He slid his hand behind her head, cupping the nape of her neck, angling her head, drawing her close, his mouth capturing hers in a strong kiss, as full bodied as dinner's wine, slow as a summer's day. This was a kiss for savouring.

Her mouth opened and her body quickened where his hand skimmed the long column of her neck, touching the fast pulse note at its base. But even as her mouth dared to engage the kiss she sensed there was a test wrapped within it. Her tongue mingled with his in a slow duel while her mind sought for answers. 'The kiss is not part of the forfeit,' she murmured.

'No, but it is part of the lesson.' Carrick released her. 'We cannot control others. We can barely control ourselves.' He gave her a wry grin. 'What has happened to all of your rules, India?'

'You wanted me to break them. I broke them for you.' But even as she said the words, she knew them for lies and she hated him for the lesson that was suddenly as much about her as it was about Hal.

'Are you sure about that? The alley, last night, just now. That was all only for me? Not at all because you wanted something that existed beyond your rules?' His hand closed about her wrist when she would have pulled away, would have taken her anger and run.

'Is that the point of this forfeit, Carrick Eisley? To show me I'm not as much changed as I thought I was?'

Her anger was boiling now, mostly at herself for being so taken in, but there was plenty of anger still for Carrick, for tempting her when he ought to have known better, when he ought to have let her be. 'Are you proud of yourself, Carrick? At the first real temptation, you got me to risk the life I've built back after losing Landon and my parents. What sort of man tempts a woman to do that? Knowing full well what it could mean to her?'

Dear God, had these past weeks been nothing but a game to him? A side trick while he was doing his penance? And here she was, agonising over leaving him, agonising over these new feelings he'd awakened in her.

'That is *not* why I did it,' Carrick growled. 'I want you to let Hal stay and to let him race if he wants. Let him find his own way.'

'*If* he wants?' India's temper hit its flashpoint. 'What chance does he have of knowing his own mind with you around to tell him what to think? If you can persuade a woman to abandon all reason when she *knows* what's at stake, an eighteen-year-old boy won't stand a chance.' Emotions and thoughts rocketed through her, her mind trying to grab on to them as they sped by.

One could not control another's decisions, but one could certainly influence them as his kiss had so aptly demonstrated. She'd felt the test in it and she'd succumbed to it any way. She'd made rules, promising herself she would not give into a full-blown affair with him, that there would only be one night, and she'd broken those rules for rough sport up against a wall in an alley because his influence had been that powerful.

He'd not made her break her rules, but he'd certainly given her reasons to break them. What other rules had he wanted her to break? She broke free of his grip and stumbled backwards, a horrible thought coming to her. 'Did you seduce me, thinking to soften me up? Thinking that if you could win my affections I would relent on Hal racing?' Had all of this been only a gambit to get what he and Logan had wanted all along?

'No, India, it was not like that at all.' Carrick reached for her again, but she stepped beyond him. If he touched her she'd be lost, she knew that too well now. She'd been wrong to stay. She should have left after their one night. Even better, she should have left the day she'd discovered him in the shop. Her instincts had been right. Carrick Eisley had never been anything but trouble and heartbreak to any woman. *She was no different.*

That last thought sent her stumbling towards King. She fumbled for the stirrup, got her boot in it and managed to pull herself up. She moved fast, clumsy in her haste, aware of Carrick calling to her, aware of his big body standing in her path as she turned King back towards the meadow. But she spurred the horse on, her gaze locked on Carrick's as King barrelled down on him until Carrick at last was forced to move. Then she was free. King was all speed, carrying her over logs, across the meadow, back towards safety, back to the life she never should have left.

Carrick watched her go, *felt* her go actually, the wind of her passing billowing his shirt and his hair as King swept past him. The little fool had tried to run him down. In her temper she might have if he had not stepped aside. He'd not wanted to take that chance. India in a temper was a force of nature and not open to reason. Not unlike himself.

There was a pit in his stomach. He'd botched everything and all over a silly request to let Hal race. This was why he'd not wanted to ask her. He knew what he'd risked. He'd just hoped she had felt enough for him, that their relationship had grown strong enough to dispel such suspicion on her part. Part of the pit in his stomach was because she *hadn't* felt enough for him.

And why should she feel anything? The two of you have not pursued a future, have made each other no plans or promises.

They were both operating on the assumption that this interlude would end. Even if that was not what he wanted, only what he *should* want. He wasn't a marrying man, he'd promised himself as much. He should want her to go. It would keep them both safe from heartache. Now he might have driven her away for good and he found he could not be happy over it. What he did next would be critical. Should he go after her or let her ride out her temper?

The wildness in him was tempted to the former. His mount would chase her down, but not before they reached the farm, where there would be a scene. In front of Hal. Which would lead to a lot of explaining.

I slept with your sister and now she thinks I did it so that she'd give permission for you to race with us. When in truth, I am falling in love with her and I don't know what to do.

That was another lie. He knew what he *wanted* to do and it went against everything he'd promised himself. Logan was right. India had changed him, changed him enough for him to want to throw away his fears. Such want was more reckless than anything he'd ever done.

Is she worth it?

Yes. Yes, she was. What would she say to that? What would Hal say to that?

Hal was as protective of India as she was of him. If Carrick went after her and forced a scene, the two of them might join forces against him. That decided it. He would give her a chance to ride out her temper, time to return to the farm and cool down. Then, perhaps after dinner, he would offer an apology, assure her that he'd not ever intended to use her affections against her for the furthering of other ends. Easier said than done. He swung up on his mount and began a long slow ride home.

India was not there when he arrived just as the sun was setting. Neither was King. But Hal was in the barn, putting away the carriage team. He looked up from grooming Sterope when Carrick came in. 'Where's India?'

Carrick sighed. 'I hoped she was here. We took the horses out for a ride. I wanted her to try out King and I wanted to talk to her about your racing.' He picked up a curry brush and began to work Sterope's other side. Grooming horses always helped him relax. 'The conversation didn't go well.'

'Because you like her, don't you?' Hal smiled at him across Sterope's back. 'Did you think I wouldn't notice how you look at her when she comes to the yard? I think she likes you, too. She's been staying longer when she brings lunch and listening to you when you get carried away talking about the vehicles.'

'I don't get carried away,' Carrick interrupted.

'Yes, you do.' Hal grinned. 'But that's not the point. You're in a tough spot. You like her and you like racing, but she doesn't.' Carrick busied himself picking out a hoof to hide his surprise—or was that mortification? He was definitely out of practice if he was so transparent a youth like Hal could see right through him on both accounts.

'I've been thinking,' Hal said, handing him a tail comb. Sterope was getting more pampering than usual, but grooming gave them an excuse to talk and an activity to keep their hands busy without letting the conversation become awkward. 'I think Mr Maddox is likely putting some pressure on you about my racing, wanting you to be the go-between for him and India.' Hal gave a small, rueful smile. 'I've been wanting you to be the same for me as well. Mr Maddox and I have both relied on you to get my sister's compliance. I feel that's unfair.'

Carrick's hands paused their work on Sterope's tail. 'Why is that?'

'I am eighteen. I might not be old enough to claim my majority at the estate, but I am old enough to make my own decisions. I would like my sister's approval, but I don't require it and neither does Mr Maddox. The two of you deferred to her out of respect. But ultimately, the decision is mine.'

Hal met his gaze. 'I want to stay at the carriage works and I want to race as part of Mr Maddox's syndicate. I've been worrying about what to do in the winter when my compromise with India is over. But I realised I was worrying needlessly. I don't want to go to Oxford so I won't. I'll stay here.'

India was not going to like that and it was easy to see who she'd blame for the decision, especially after this afternoon. Carrick began to comb the tail again in slow, thoughtful strokes. 'Your sister will disapprove.'

'She will.' Hal nodded. 'But she loves me. She'll come to understand my decision in time.' How confident Hal seemed in that. How simple the decision had become for him. Hal, unlike himself at that age, was not worried about losing his family over a disagreement because their relationship was built on something larger than a single issue. Perhaps that made all the difference.

Hal paused and Carrick sensed there was more he wanted to add. 'I hope she'll understand, too, that this is about more than racing. It's time I decided things for myself, that I can't live my life being tied to her apron strings any more than she should live her life tied to me.' It was a rather profound sentiment from one so young. 'Everything she's done these past years has been for me, to ensure my future. But she needs to think of herself.'

Carrick began to gather up the brushes. 'Have you thought of what happens to her if anything happens to you before you have a child of your own to inherit?'

Hal nodded. 'Especially that. I wish she'd consider marrying so that if something did happen, she wouldn't be alone. But she wants no part of marriage, not since Landon died.' Hal gave him a pointed look. 'Perhaps you could change her mind about that?'

'Me? Marriage?' Carrick made a warding gesture and forced laugh. 'I'm not the marrying sort, lad.' At least he hadn't been a few weeks ago, a few hours ago.

Now, he wasn't so sure. 'Besides, I'm in trade. She's used to finer things and bigger houses than I can offer. After today, she doesn't want any part of me.' That was all he was going to say on the matter. He wasn't going to explain the rest to Hal. He freed Sterope from the crossties and led him to his stall where supper waited.

Hal began to sweep the aisle. 'Once she realises the decision is all mine, she might change her mind about you.' He paused and leaned on his broom. 'Unless there's something more I don't know about? Ah, I see there is.' He swept a few strokes before adding, 'Well, then, I guess there's only one thing to do.'

'Damn right there is. In the morning we go after her.' Carrick shut the latch on the stall door, wishing he could cage his emotions as easily. Logan would be thrilled that his star racer was secured. But at the price of India feeling betrayed, a price that left him feeling bereft as well. He'd just found her. He did not want to lose her again. But how did a man like him keep a woman like her?

Chapter Nineteen

How had it come to this? The question pounded through her head as King's hooves ate up the road between Carrick's farm and Foxfields in a ferocious gallop, his pace mirroring the speed of her thoughts. But whereas his route went in a straight line and had a destination, her thoughts merely formed circles, looping back to the question: how had this happened? She'd been so careful. She'd lived quietly, discreetly, denying herself any pleasure outside the pleasure of responsibility.

She'd put her wildness away and yet it hadn't been enough. She'd let her guard down one single time and the recklessness had come roaring back. It wasn't only what she'd done this time that bespoke the recklessness, it was what she *felt* that had made the recklessness so notable. The feelings Carrick unleashed in her had awakened her with an intensity she'd not known before.

What Landon had roused paled by comparison or perhaps she saw those days, those feelings, for what they truly were: the throes of youthful infatuation, the thrill of being alive and carefree. In time, those feelings might have matured into something more. But they weren't *this*, they weren't what she felt now—an all-consuming fire that could be summoned by a single touch, single look from a man who offered pleasure but no expectations beyond the moment.

Such a combination was the last thing she needed. If her indiscretion was discovered, it would be her ruin, it would make the sacrifices of the last three years moot. It was absolutely reckless of her to throw such efforts away on the momentary pleasures Carrick offered. As long as she stayed within his reach, she would succumb to that offering again and again. She *had* to leave, had to get as far from Carrick as she could before her luck ran out.

In the stable yard at Foxfields, a groom ran out as she dismounted. 'Rub him down good, he's had a hard gallop,' she instructed with a pat to King's neck. He'd served her well, aiding her flight with his speed. His own race was done now, but not hers. She had miles to go.

Belle Weather was nearly a two-day journey from Foxfields. She could put some of those miles behind her tonight if she packed quickly enough and avoided detection. She was halfway up the stairs when Elizabeth caught her.

'India? What are you doing home so soon?' Elizabeth's words stopped her on the stairs, her friend materialising in the doorway of the drawing room, worry etched on her face when India turned. 'My dear, what is wrong?' Elizabeth came up the stairs towards her.

'I have to go home, Elizabeth. I have to pack.' India tried to keep her voice even and firm, but Elizabeth was not fooled.

'Not tonight you don't, not in this condition.' Elizabeth could be firm, too. Elizabeth looped an arm through hers and India knew she was momentarily beaten. 'You look as if you've ridden across country at breakneck speed.' Elizabeth reached up and removed a leaf from her hair, brandishing it in evidence. 'Whatever has happened, it has upset you.' She gently steered them back down the stairs towards the drawing room. 'I'll ring for tea and you can tell me all about it before we decide what to do.'

What India might have told her and what they might have decided to do would remain unknown. They'd no sooner poured their tea when they were interrupted by the arrival of a letter, delivered by Laurie, who took one look at her and exchanged worried glances with his sister. 'It just came and it looked…official. I thought you should see it right away.'

Official was one word for it, India thought as she opened the packet. Dangerous was another. It felt officious and legal with its thick sheaf of papers and that bothered her. She'd not had any legal work done recently and was not expecting any documents. India scanned the papers, at first puzzled by what she read, so extraordinary and unlooked for was it, and then going numb in shock as her mind processed the import of the words.

'What is it?' Elizabeth leaned forward in concern, but it was Laurie who took the papers from her fingers, his kind brown eyes going agate-hard.

'Victor Claiborne has sent a marriage contract,' Laurie said in terse tones. 'You don't have to sign it, of course. He cannot coerce you.'

India lifted her gaze to meet Laurie's. 'Can't he?' She

held out the notepaper that had come with the contract, written in Victor's own hand. 'He says it is unnatural for a woman to remain unmarried and suggests he'll press the issue on such grounds if I refuse.' In the wake of the initial shock, she could imagine what that case would look like to other men and how it would end. Badly. For her, at least. Women who didn't conform to social standards were simply put away, put beyond society, their freedom locked up with them. And that was assuming Victor didn't know what she'd got up to with Carrick. If he caught a whiff of 'immoral behaviour' on her part, she wouldn't stand a chance of keeping the regency of Belle Weather.

It was the last thought that broke her. After all she'd done, Victor could still take it from her. Nothing would ever be enough. Tears started to form. She rose quickly, not wanting Elizabeth and Laurie's concern or pity.

'No, you stay.' Elizabeth stood, motioning for Laurie. 'We'll give you some privacy.' Elizabeth reached for her hand with a comforting squeeze. '*Then* we'll talk. Everything looks better with more eyes on it. But you take a moment, or two. I promise, we'll sort it out just as we have everything else so far.'

India barely heard her friend's well-intended words, barely heard Elizabeth and Laurie leave, shutting the drawing room doors behind them. She didn't hear the clock chime off the half-hour and then the hour. Somewhere beyond the drawing room doors, the family was gathering for dinner. She'd be welcome, but she had no appetite. The tea tray in front of her had grown cold and untouched.

She was numb, positively senseless, floored by Victor's audacious attempt to manoeuvre her into marriage as yet another strategy to wrest Belle Weather from her and Hal. What was she going to do? For the first time since her parents died she was simply not enough and there was nothing she could do about it.

'India?' Laurie's quiet tones interrupted her thoughts. 'Are you all right? We missed you at supper.' He slipped into the room and closed the door behind him. Her gaze went to the mantel clock. The hands showed it was after eight.

She rose and smoothed her skirts. She had sat here for two hours and had no answers. 'I need to pack.' More than ever she needed to go home, to Belle Weather, her refuge.

'Wait, not yet.' Laurie strode forward and gestured for her to resume her seat. He took the chair nearest her and leaned forward. 'You needn't face this latest obstacle alone, India.'

India managed a soft smile. 'I know you and Elizabeth mean well, but this is not like the other times. This is about me. You can do nothing unless you can change me into a man. A man would be impervious to Victor's charges. Indeed, Victor would have no grounds on which to disagree with a man's custodianship of Belle Weather until Hal came of age,' she added remorsefully.

Laurie's gaze became intent. He reached for her hand. 'I cannot change you into a man.' He chuckled. 'But I can give you a man who will stand between Belle Weather and Victor.'

Her brow furrowed. 'You cannot conjure a man out of thin air, Laurie.' She laughed quietly, ruefully. It was hopeless. After all her struggling, she couldn't escape Victor.

'I don't need to conjure one. I offer myself, India. Now, listen to me before you start to argue.' There was an edge seldom heard to Laurie's tone. His grip tightened on her hand and her own nerves clenched in dread at what she saw coming, too late.

'I will marry you, India, and through that marriage, I become the regent for Belle Weather until Hal is old enough. Victor can have no complaint that would stand up in court. You can continue to run the estate as you have been. Belle Weather will be safe. You will be safe. Hal's inheritance will be safe. It's the perfect answer for you.'

Safety. Everything and everyone she loved would be protected. The offer was tempting—safety in all its guises, the very thing she craved, the very thing she'd fought the last three years for. She ought to accept. She ought to put herself, Hal, her home, beyond Victor. It wasn't as if there'd be another decent offer. Carrick would not offer for her. He'd made his position on marriage quite clear and, after today, she wasn't sure she'd accept any way. He'd been manoeuvring her, hoping to gain permission for Hal to race. Carrick was and perhaps would always be a rake. There was no reason to hesitate and yet she did.

'And for you? Is it a good answer for you, for your life?' India shook her head, trying to dislodge the growing sense of hopelessness Laurie's idea invoked. She would not find passion with Laurie despite all he offered her. 'I cannot ask for such a sacrifice from my friend. You would give up too much. I have already told you that my heart will not be engaged.' Even as she said it, she knew it was a partial lie. Her heart *could* be engaged, it just wasn't engaged by Laurie, not in that way. 'You deserve more than I could give you.'

Laurie's eyes darkened. 'You give me plenty, India. Are you truly unaware of the feelings I harbour for you? That those feelings run deeper than friendship?'

'Laurie, don't. Please stop,' she cried, feeling the urgency of real anguish. This was awful. She didn't want to hurt her friend, yet it would hurt him far worse if she were to accept his offer. 'Say nothing more. You will regret that you've told me.'

Laurie's jaw tightened. 'What I will regret is watching you suffer, watching you struggle, watching you be vilified by a man who isn't fit to challenge your authority, but who can take all you've fought for. Let me do this for you, for us. Surely, in time, our friendship will grow into something more, I am certain of it.' He paused, realisation haunting his eyes. India withdrew her hand, but it was too late to hide the truth from him. Her own gaze had betrayed her. 'There is someone else?' Laurie rose and turned away from her. 'The carriage-maker?'

'Not as you might think.' She shook her head slowly, careful with her words. She didn't want Laurie coercing Carrick into a proposal Carrick didn't want to make. 'I'm sorry, Laurie. It wouldn't be fair to you. I care for you as a friend, nothing more. I couldn't let you believe it would ever be different.' She rose. 'I must pack. I will think of something and if I need you, I will write.' She'd never told so many lies in a row and they both knew it;

she would not write, not after this. She would not think of something, her options were exhausted.

Laurie turned to her, his face a schooled mask, his expression stoic despite the emotions he must be feeling. 'Stay the night, India. Do not set off like this. Have a good night's sleep and leave at first light if you must. I don't want you on the road because you've refused me.'

She nodded solemnly. After all he'd given her over the years, after all he'd offered her tonight, the willingness to give up his own future for the sake of hers, she could make this one concession. She nodded. 'I will take your advice on that account. Thank you, Laurie.' For understanding, for not pressing her, and for so much more even at the expense of what he thought was his own happiness.

But he *would* thank her for this, some day, when he found the woman he truly deserved. She would survive this. Somehow. She would find the answer at Belle Weather. It would be her refuge, a place where she'd be safe. She was going home. She should never have come here.

She was gone when Carrick arrived at Foxfields the next morning with Hal in tow. He could feel it in the air without being told the way one feels the onset of a storm. One just knows it in their bones. Right now his bones were regretting not having come sooner, although it was only nine in the morning, the very earliest he could justify calling on the Blackmons without invitation. Perhaps he should have come last night, risking the darkness and India's temper. What had seemed like consideration in giving her space and good sense last night now seemed like a great folly. Especially in retrospect.

He hadn't slept at all, replaying their conversation beneath the oak over and over in his mind, dissecting each line, and word, seeing the conversation from her point of view and cringing at what appeared to be a misstep on his part at every turn. All he'd done led her to the conclusion that he'd seduced her to get to Hal, that he'd used their friendship and more to wear away her resistance to her brother's racing, establishing for her proof that he'd not changed after all. He was still very much the reckless rake, a man who lived in the moment. A man who could *not* be for her. When all he wanted, he'd realised in the dark of the night, was *to* be for her.

'You look like hell, man.' Godric Blackmon came out of the breakfast room, napkin still in hand, and met him in the hall as Hal scuttled off to fill a plate. Hal was their guest. Carrick noted there was no such invitation for him to come in, to join them at the breakfast table. He was not their guest. Perhaps after yesterday, he was even now considered the enemy. They were India's friends, after all. What had she told them?

He ignored the remark about his looks, refraining from saying that Godric didn't look all that sartorial either, sporting the pale, dark-circled complexion of the sleepless. Intuition suggested something more had happened here—'I want to see India'—even though that same intuition told him she wasn't here to be seen.

His head craned around Godric's big form, hoping to see her come out of the breakfast room while his mind replayed reminders of another time he'd come begging for her attendance and been turned away. 'I'd rather not have to go through you, but I will.' They were both big men. Carrick didn't think Elizabeth Blackmon's hallway would survive the encounter.

Godric shook his head. 'No need for that. I'd let you see her if she was here. Talking would probably do the two of you some good.' Ah, so his sense had been right.

Some of the tension went out of Carrick at the realisation there was no chance now of seeing her. All the things he'd spent the night planning to say, the arguments he'd been planning to make, were useless for the time being. Godric gestured towards a small sitting room off the hall. 'I know it's early, but perhaps whiskey in coffee wouldn't go amiss.' He rang for hot drinks and a decanter as they sat.

'Elizabeth and I tried to persuade her to stay, but she would have none of it. King is in the stable. She left him.'

'She didn't need to. King is hers.' Right now, Carrick didn't give a damn about the horse. 'Did she leave last night?' Surely she wouldn't have tried to travel alone in the dark with only a coachman for protection. But he wouldn't put it past her. India might be less of a risk-taker these days, but the impetuosity that once drove her was still there.

She could be provoked into rashness as their kisses had so deliciously demonstrated. That was the best kind of rashness, the kind that led to shattering sex in an alleyway, or a torrent of hot kisses in the stable while a storm broke overhead. Travelling at night unescorted was not part of that, though.

The coffee and decanter came. Godric poured them each a mug, two-thirds whiskey, one-third coffee. 'I know brandy is a gentleman's drink, but I do prefer a good whiskey out of Ireland with my morning coffee, especially on days when I have to do ledgers,' Godric confessed with a conspiratorial smile. 'Don't tell my wife.'

The man was doing his best to put him at ease, to help, Carrick noted, and he appreciated it. He needed a friend right now, and he wasn't sure Logan could be objective at the moment. 'We did manage to convince her to stay the night,' Godric said as they settled with their coffees. 'She was furious when she arrived. It was clear she'd ridden hell for leather, but Elizabeth got her calmed down.'

Godric reached for something inside his coat pocket. 'And then there was this. By the time we got this sorted out, there was no question of travelling.'

'What is it?' The long, folded document appeared to be a letter, a very long letter from the looks of its thickness. Carrick reached for it, but Godric held back for a moment.

'I am only showing you this because I am counting on you to act in her best interests. I don't need to know what happened between the two of you or the current nature of your association, but you were friends once. She will need all of her friends about her at present.'

Carrick took the document with no small amount of trepidation after that little speech. He scanned it, his brow furrowing as his mind adjusted to the content. 'This isn't a letter, it's a marriage contract.' He glanced at Godric for confirmation.

What sort of man would send India a marriage contract? But it was a rhetorical question only. He knew the sort of man: a man who had no consideration for her, no understanding of her, a man who saw her only as a placeholder or perhaps an obstacle to be overcome. He scanned for a name on the contract to affirm what he already knew. 'Victor Claiborne. No surprise there.' He set the contract down.

'So, she told you about him? You'll know then that he's been a continual thorn in her side since her parents died.' Godric took a long swallow of his coffee. 'We've helped her avoid his efforts to take control of the estate, but all it's done is provoke him to new levels.'

Dangerous new levels. 'This isn't so much a contract as it is a threat.' Carrick ran a hand through his already tousled hair. He could imagine too well how this had looked to an already upset India. That the document had been sent to her here at Foxfields, a place that she viewed as a refuge, was an invasion of her privacy at the very least. That she'd not been expecting it was an ambush of audacious proportions. That it threatened her freedom and her home made it a kind of blackmail. It was, in short, a declaration of war.

The desire to protect her burned strong. He wanted nothing more than to saddle a horse and go after her, chase her down on the road, take her in his arms and erase her cares. He wanted to take on Victor. A fist to the face would cool the man's avarice. He wanted to threaten him in return, not just for this egregious document, but for the three years of torture that had been a prelude to this. What had India said? That there were so many ways for a woman to fail? That Victor was just waiting? Godric gave a slow shake of his head as if the man had read his mind. *She needs you to act in her best interests.*

That meant Carrick could do none of those things. To touch her, to hold her, would ruin her. It would bring to life the very things Victor needed to condemn her. Carrick gritted his teeth. Lucifer's balls, he felt impotent, something he wasn't used to being. He'd been self-sufficient since the day he'd left home. 'She needs a champion.'

'She doesn't want one.' There was a rustle at the door announcing the arrival of Laurie Benefield. Looking like hell seemed to be going around this morning. If Godric had seemed exhausted, then Benefield was both physically and emotionally drained.

'I offered to be that champion.' He leaned against the door jamb with a shake of his dishevelled head. The look of empathy Godric gave his brother in-law suggested Benefield had offered much more than to simply return to Belle Weather with her.

Benefield settled his brown gaze on Carrick. 'You do understand that only marriage can save her now? Marriage to someone other than Victor Claiborne?' Ah, so the poor man *had* offered matrimony. Offered and been refused. He knew a little about being refused by India Claiborne, how it tore a man in two. No wonder Lawrence Benefield looked absolutely wretched.

He heard the challenge wrapped in Benefield's question as well and perhaps the accusation of the walking wounded. Benefield blamed him for India's refusal.

'She flees into peril.' Benefield pushed off the door frame and shoved balled fists into his trouser pockets. 'She should not be alone at Belle Weather. There's no one to protect her there if Victor comes. My hope is that if the document came here, then he won't be looking for her there.'

'She is his equal,' Carrick assured him, even as a tremor of fear moved through him. If Victor's document had found her here, was he waiting for her there? Flushing her towards home like a rabbit to the hunt? 'She can hold her own against him. He won't talk her into anything. She's not afraid of words.' He knew that all too well. India's mind and tongue were in a perpetual state of sharpness. But Victor might not stop at words.

'That's not what I'm worried about.' Benefield arched a meaningful, elegant brow, giving words to Carrick's fear. 'Victor Claiborne is done talking. He's spent three years talking and it's got him nowhere. And you're wrong, you know. A woman is never a man's equal, not even when she thinks she is. Not even when that woman is India Claiborne.' The quietness of his tone only underscored the dark direction of his thoughts.

'Then why are you still here?' Carrick returned Benefield's stare.

'Because she does not want me. I can do nothing for her. She is beyond me now.' Benefield looked away, the knowledge behind that confession still raw.

'She does not want me either.' Carrick studied the other man, feeling Benefield's pain even as his own nudged at him, reminding him that to love was to lose and he'd chosen it anyway. He'd chosen to love India, to protect India even at the expense of his own pain.

'She might not want you, but she needs you. She turned me down for a reason.' Benefield's glance returned to him, harder, fiercer, as if the man was screwing the last of his courage to the sticking point. 'She won't have me, because of you.' He shook his head. 'No, you don't need to deny it to salve my feelings. In truth, she's never looked upon me that way. I have always been her friend, nothing more.'

The realisation saddened the man greatly. 'But not so you. She's been different since she's met you, more alive, more like the girl she used to be and for the better. She'd given herself up entirely.' Benefield gave a little laugh. 'She's a woman of extremes, but she needs to learn to live in the place between them, a place of moderation where she can be both passionate and practical. Can you give her that?'

Could he? It was a lesson he needed to learn himself. 'What are you saying, Benefield?'

'I think you are the only one who can save her.' The only who could go to her, who could offer her the protection she needed from Victor Claiborne whom she might accept. If he could make amends for yesterday, if he could restore her trust in him. Carrick could see what the words cost Benefield. The poor man was giving the woman he loved into the care of another.

Carrick nodded, his mind already working through the details of what a swift departure would entail. 'Send me Hal and I'll need writing materials.' There were instructions for the carriage works and the racing carriages to be finished in time for Logan's big event in Wallingford and Logan to be placated. He hoped Logan would understand. He'd secured Hal for Logan, so that should go some way in soothing Logan's rather ruffled feathers.

'I can be ready to leave by noon.' It would put him

half a day behind India. But perhaps it would be best to catch her at home instead of on the road and it would give her time to think. And he, too. He was going after India because he loved her more than he feared his pain, because life with India, whatever that life was, was better than his life without her. Now, he had to make her see it.

Chapter Twenty

There was too much time to think when one was alone in a coach on a two-day journey. And she was very much alone. She didn't even have Hal for company. Only her thoughts and they seemed set on torturing her. Had she made a mistake? *Only one mistake? How about three mistakes?* Her thoughts were not being kind. They'd kept her up most of the night at the inn, too, refusing to let her seek refuge in sleep. At least tonight, she'd sleep in her own bed under her own roof for the first time in a long while. She might never leave Belle Weather again. Going out into the world had been disastrous. Look what had happened.

You refused Laurie Benefield, the best man to walk the earth.

Had that been a mistake? Every logical bone in her body screamed that it was. What grounds did she have for that refusal? He was wealthy, well situated, a man of property and business. He had no title, but neither had her father until he'd been over forty. She had no use for titles any way. What she did have use for was the financial and social security Laurie offered.

Marriage to Laurie would have effectively derailed the threat of Victor.

And she'd said no. Because she could not give him her heart in return, she could not give him the love he deserved. Because the passion and heat of being with Carrick, of feeling the possibilities of being alive again, still lingered in her blood despite the hurt that had rocketed through her that last afternoon. Because even feeling hurt was a sign of coming back to life.

Carrick. Had he been another mistake? Would she have been better off to have stayed dormant, to have kept her feelings banked? Instead, she'd opened herself up to him, taking an enormous risk.

And the reward was glorious, was it not? Her heart refused to be left out of the debate. *The way he made you feel, all that pleasure, all that release, not just physically, but mentally?*

When she remembered those moments with Carrick, it wasn't just the lovemaking that stood out, but the conversations, too. The things he'd shared with her in the stables. *'Landon adored you, he was proud he was going to be your husband.'* The things he'd shared about himself, about his own life growing up.

He gave you the closure you'd never had over Landon. He gave you a part of himself. He brought you back to life. You rode again, jumped hedges again, felt the wind in your hair again, lived as perhaps you were meant to live.

At a price. He *had* given her those things, but he'd wanted something in return. He'd wanted Hal to race. He wanted her to rethink Hal's future at Oxford. He wasn't looking to marry her. She ought to be grateful for that. Two men wanted to marry her: one to protect her, one to steal from her. But she wanted neither. She'd not even wanted to marry, had insisted that she'd never seek marriage again.

And here was a man who wasn't pushing for her to give that up and it sat awkwardly with her. Is that what she wanted? To marry Carrick? Or did she just want the proposal from him? Perhaps as a token that he did care for her? What would she say if he asked?

She didn't allow herself to contemplate an answer. It was a moot point anyway. They'd quarrelled, he'd used her to make an argument for Hal. They'd had a brief affair and heaven forbid anyone learn of the latter. It was all Victor would need to push his case. She needed to spend less time thinking about Carrick and more time thinking about what she'd do when she got home, back safe to Belle Weather. Her fortress.

India had taken a lover. There was no place safe for her now. Victor Claiborne smiled to himself with a cruel pleasure as he strolled the halls of Belle Weather. He stopped occasionally to pick up a statue or knick-knack, or to study a piece of art on the wall. India had sold some of it to pay off her father's debt. He could see some empty spaces on walls where pictures had hung. But why not sell it? Randolph Claiborne had been a near-obsessive collector. He had more art than good sense in Victor's opinion. One did not need art. One needed money.

If he'd had half the funds Randolph had spent on art, he'd have a small fortune. But Randolph liked to be surrounded by beautiful things. Victor wasn't so grand in his affectations, which was why he'd already set the staff to organising the books in the library into piles to sell in London the next time he went. Nothing was better than money. Not art and not rare first editions.

He ran a hand over a delicate china shepherdess and her flock of sheep, artfully arranged on the hallway console. This set had belonged to India's mother. Clearly India had kept the items that had sentimental value to her. It made touching them that much more of an intimate invasion.

Take that, India. You have put me off for three years, but now I am in your home, touching the things you love, the things that hold your memories and you can do nothing about it. Belle Weather will be mine at last as you will be.

The long wait was nearly over. All India had to do was come home. And she would because the marriage contract would send her fleeing back to where she thought she was safe. It was an irrational thought on her part, though. The threat to her was not one that could be kept out by bricks and walls.

Victor continued down the hall, pausing to consider the master's chambers. They would need to be redone. Perhaps he would take out the wall and expand into one of the current guest rooms. He'd definitely have the lock taken off the door between this room and the adjoining lady's chambers. He'd want unfettered access to India at all times.

He chuckled to think how it would keep her on her toes to wonder when he'd come through that door; he could come when he wanted—to watch her bathe, to watch her undress, to hold her accountable for her marital duty day or night. There would be other things he'd hold her accountable for, too, like every second of the last three years she'd kept him waiting.

He shut the door to the room and went down the steps of the curving oak staircase, smugly halting to salute the portrait of Cousin Randolph. 'It's all mine now, you selfish bastard, and your daughter, too.' Wherever his cousin was in the afterlife, he hoped it had just got a few degrees hotter.

Victor called to the butler, 'Painter, I'll be in the library, enjoying a brandy.' Painter didn't like him much, which made giving the man orders that much more pleasing. 'If Miss Claiborne arrives, tell her to attend me once she's settled.' She wouldn't settle, though. She'd come to him straight away once she knew he was here. Like the very best of dogs, India would run towards trouble instead of away from it and India was nothing if not a bitch.

A bitch in heat, apparently. Victor poured himself a large serving of brandy and wound his way past stacks of books waiting to be packed up to take his preferred chair by the fire. Sending men to Benson had proved to be far more informative than he'd anticipated. It wasn't the honourable Mr Benefield that he had to worry about. He'd been barking up the wrong tree, if he wanted to extend the dog metaphor.

Benefield might be on her scent, but she did not reciprocate his feelings. She was hot for the carriage-maker who'd turned out to be an old friend and that wasn't even the juiciest bit yet. The juiciest bit was that he used to be a notorious racer, the very one who'd been on the Richmond Road the day her fiancé was killed.

Some might even say he was the reason Landon Fellowes had been killed. To reunite with such a man cast all nature of aspersions on India's good judgement.

After three years of making good decisions, she'd made a very bad one. Such a reunion had all the makings of a lurid scandal. Gossip could be started easily with the merest innuendo. 'Sir...' Painter was at the door, a sneer on his face '...Miss Claiborne's coach has arrived.'

Did Painter think India could do anything that would prevent him from taking over Belle Weather? That India would throw him out? Perhaps he did. After all, Painter didn't know his mistress had been sleeping with the carriage-maker. But Victor knew and he also knew exactly how this little play was going to end. Nothing was going to go wrong tonight.

Something was wrong. India looked up at Belle Weather, the quiet elation of homecoming fading as she stepped down from the coach. There was a light in the library when no one was supposed to be home and she wasn't expected. Anxiety took up residence in her stomach. She'd hoped for a hot bath, a hot meal and her bed in that order. Those hopes seemed to be doomed. She hurried up the front steps to the carved double doors, which opened on cue as if someone had been watching for her, another sign that something wasn't quite right.

'Welcome home, Miss Claiborne.' Painter made her a small bow, but his eyes were nervous. Something *was* wrong. 'You have company. Victor Claiborne awaits in the library when you're ready to receive him.' Then

Painter added, 'He's been here since yesterday, miss.' The day after the contract arrived at Foxfields. He'd been very sure of her, then, and she'd played right into his hand even though her friends had begged her to stay at Foxfields and sort it out with them.

What if I'm never ready? What if I leave him there all night cooling his heels? What if I go upstairs and have that bath and unpack my trunk?

But she knew the answer. Victor would still be waiting for her tomorrow, only he'd be angrier. If he'd been here since yesterday, she needed him gone immediately. 'I'll see him now, Painter, thank you.'

The library was down the hall on the main level. She straightened her shoulders and hoped she had enough strength. She was tired, she'd not slept well.

Victor knows that, perhaps he's even counting on it. That's why he is here. You're vulnerable.

She entered the library without knocking, taking petty delight in the small element of surprise as Victor jumped up from the chair, splashing a bit of brandy from his glass at the sudden intrusion.

'Ah, Cousin, you're back at last. I didn't hear you knock.' He was all malicious equanimity, implying that she'd impetuously decamped for months of unbridled frivolity.

'I don't need to knock to enter rooms in my own home.' She pulled at the fingertips of her travelling gloves, her words and gestures curt. 'And you knew very well where I was. Your mail had no trouble in finding me.' The gloves were off in all ways.

'The contract reached you, then?' He moved from his chair by the fire to come towards her. She sidestepped to put the long study table between them, taking in the piles of books for the first time. 'What is all this?'

'I'm doing a bit of decluttering, my dear. There are too many books in here for my taste. I hope you don't mind? I'll take them to London when I go up next. I know a bookseller who will give us top dollar for them. This way there will be shelf space for my things.'

Of all the effrontery! To come into her home and start touching things, taking books down—what else had he done since he'd been here? India slapped her gloves on the table. 'There is no "ours", Victor, and there won't be. I am not signing your odious contract. Now, please leave. This is not your home. You are trespassing.' She hoped the idea of committing a crime would encourage Victor to depart, but he stood firm, an indolent grin playing across his features. Victor was not an unattractive man, but a life of selfishness had driven any token of warmth from his features. If cruelty could look a certain way, it would look like Victor: hard and cold. His jaw tightened. She'd upset him.

'I think you misunderstand the situation, Cousin. So, allow me to explain it. We have no time for romance and flowery proposals. I can see that my contract has offended you, but you should have thought of that before you'd carried on with the carriage-maker in Benson.' He grinned. 'Did you think I wouldn't know? That I wouldn't find out?'

India felt the blood drain from her face. She pressed her palms flat on the table to steady herself. He couldn't possibly know. She and Carrick had been so careful. There was no time for word to even get back to him...

unless he'd had her followed. Or unless he was bluffing, only guessing at what she and Carrick had done.

But it was enough that he even knew about Carrick to create real fear for her. This was exactly what she'd not wanted to happen, to have her most private information in the hands of her worst enemy. 'You know nothing. The Blackmons will vouch for my conduct. I was always chaperoned.' Mostly true, but she could bluff, too.

Victor lifted a shoulder in a nonchalant shrug. 'It doesn't matter what I know or what is true or untrue. It only matters what I tell the trustees at Peterson and Moore, Solicitors. If I tell them you've played the harlot with a tradesman, they will believe me and you know what that means.'

She did know. Her reputation in shreds, a scandal for Hal and loss of control of Belle Weather until Hal came of age. He gave a cold smile. 'Sign the contract, my dear. We'll be married and everyone will say what a judicious match you've made at last, the very best practical choice. Everyone will applaud you. It's certainly better than the alternative. Scandal, the asylum.'

He made an exaggerated frown while her blood ran cold. 'Surely you understand you can't win, that you were never going to win, India. Even if you could manage to convince the solicitors you hadn't done anything immoral with the carriage-maker, the martyr doesn't suit you any better.' He leaned towards her, closing the distance across the table. She could smell the brandy on his breath. How much had he had? The decanter on the table amid the book stacks was nearly empty.

'A woman who prefers to be alone, who rejects marriage offers, who doesn't want a home, a family, a husband, is unnatural. There are places for her where she can get treatment and the help she needs for the unnatural inclinations.' Malevolence glinted in his cold eyes. He held his hands out expansively. 'You are a woman who appreciates her freedom, her ability to chart her own course. I am giving you that chance, India. You can play the tradesman's mistress, the martyr or the married wife.' He began to move, coming around the table. 'You can choose, or I can choose for you. I'll put a child in your belly and there will be no more choice.'

She backed up. 'You would commit rape?' Of course he would. He'd already raped the library and he would continue to plunder Belle Weather until it was stripped of its splendour. The time for words had gone. She was desperate for a weapon. She would need to fight and then to run into the hallway where there would be servants, where someone might go for help. Behind her, her hand closed around the nearly empty decanter.

'One can't rape one's wife, my dear. It's simply not legally possible. Any barrister will tell you that.' He lunged for her and she swung, the decanter catching him full in the face, and then she screamed.

Carrick heard the screams as he mounted the steps of Belle Weather, his knee paining him from a day and a half of hard driving. He was dirty and tired, but all that faded when he heard her cry out. He banged on the door and then tried the handle, not wanting to wait for an answer.

The door gave and he rushed into the hall, pushing past the wild-eyed butler who couldn't decide what to do first: deal with the screams or deal with the intruder.

'Where is she?' Carrick scanned the wide entrance hall, the left hallway or the right? Or was she upstairs?

'The library, on the right.' The butler waved a hand.

There was another shout, the sounds of a struggle as Carrick neared the library. He threw open the door to chaos. Books littered the floor as if someone had swiped them off table tops, glass shards covered the floor, a chair was overturned as if a chase had gone on about the room. The chase was rapidly coming to a close, though, Carrick quickly surmised.

India stood by the fire in fighting position, brandishing a poker at a man who staggered towards her, a hand to his face, a jagged piece of glass in his other. 'I will cut you to shreds, bitch, look what you've done to my face! How will you like it?' He waved the jagged glass in a slashing, menacing arc.

'Leave her alone, step away from her!' Carrick yelled, rage filling him at the sight of India in danger. He raced across the room, ignoring the pain in his knee. His voice had the desired effect, a distraction. The man glanced his way just in time to see Carrick's form barrel towards him, catching him off balance.

Carrick bore him back to the wall, imprisoning the wrist that held the glass. He banged the man's hand against the wall until the glass shard fell from it. 'Who the hell do you think you are, attacking a woman in her own home?'

Carrick landed a punch to the man's gut. He wanted this bastard immobilised, although India had got a start on that. Whatever she'd hit him with had cut open his right cheek. He would need stitches for that.

'Her cousin.' The man spat blood.

Victor. He had been lying in wait for India. Rage surged again. The man hadn't just attacked her, he'd ambushed her, too. Given her no chance to defend herself.

'Carrick, please. Stop.' India's tone was quiet beside him, but he noticed she still clutched the poker. She was milk-pale and shaking.

'I will escort you out. You are not welcome here.' Carrick grabbed Victor by the collar and shoved the man in front of him, making sure he had no chance to get to India in a final attempt to harm her.

The butler had recovered his wits and held the door open. Carrick's own vehicle was still in the drive. 'I'll have a driver take you to the inn in the village. You can have a doctor see to your cut. Tell him you fell.'

He pushed Victor up on to the seat as a groom hurried out to drive. 'But if I hear you've spread a single slanderous word about Miss Claiborne and the cause of your injury, I will personally see to it that you are miserable for the rest of your life.'

Victor glared through his one good eye. 'This isn't over. You can't have her. I'll ruin her first. Belle Weather is mine. She is mine.'

'Not as long as I'm here.' Carrick growled, enunciating each word. He wanted Victor Claiborne to be certain of the knowledge that India had protection now that was stronger, fiercer than the guidance she'd received earlier from Laurie Benefield and Godric Blackmon.

Victor made a sneer that contorted his torn face. 'Well, that won't be for long, carriage-maker. I know who you are and what you've done. Don't think I won't ruin you, too. It's no wonder you disappeared from London and have lain low these past few years. I would, too, if I'd killed my best friend in broad daylight.'

'That is a baseless lie.' Carrick stepped back from the carriage, the choice to do so taking all his willpower. He'd like to haul Victor down and pummel him into oblivion, but that was exactly what Victor wanted. Right now, any violence done to Victor had been in defence of India. Victor wouldn't want that mentioned to authorities. But Carrick pummelling him on other grounds… well, that was different.

Carrick wouldn't give him the satisfaction of being able to overtly provoke him no matter how hot his blood was running at the moment. That didn't mean he *wasn't* provoked, though. Victor was attempting to threaten him and that could not stand. But first, there was India to take care of. 'Take him away.'

Carrick off sent the carriage with a dismissive gesture and went inside to see to India, his knee aching with every step, but the pain was worth it. He'd got there in time. *Just in time*. He didn't care to think what would have happened if he'd not.

Chapter Twenty-One

It only took one look at India's face when he came back into the house for his world to fall into place. She was standing in the entrance hall, still pale, still numb with the shock of the fight, her fingers still clenched around the poker, dragging it absently with her. Primal emotions not yet fully banked flared within him. Never again would anyone harm her. She was his to protect, beyond that nothing else mattered.

Tonight had driven that singular item home in vivid, dangerous clarity. Never mind that she would not want a man's overt, perhaps old-fashioned protection, never mind that she prided herself on her own self-sufficiency and she would see tonight as a blow against that. She needed him.

He would find a way to protect her, a way to rid her of her cousin's interference so that she need not live her life in fear. There had been too much fear for her for too long: the fear of being alone, of *not* being alone, the fear of financial uncertainty, the fear of failing, the fear of losing Hal.

Every decision she'd made in the past three years

had been guided by that fear. He saw that more plainly now than ever before. It was etched in every line of her beautiful face. He saw, too, how very close to breaking she was. *That* he could not have. He did not want India broken.

He loved her strength. He would not let that bastard of a cousin take it from her. Whatever it took. 'He's gone now, India.' He reached to take the poker from her hand, gently disentangling it from her grip.

Her eyes moved at his touch, looking down at her hand, perhaps realising for the first time she still held the fire iron. 'For now. He'll be back.' Her fingers were cold. He needed to get her warm, it would help with the shock, but he'd be damned if he'd take her back into the library and the wreckage. Servants had begun to mill about, sensing the crisis had passed, wanting to be useful, but not knowing how.

Carrick began issuing orders. 'Bring me a blanket. Is there a parlour with a fire laid? Stir it up, I want the room warm, and I want tea brought.' He wrapped an arm around India and followed Painter to a small parlour at the back of the house. He had only to step inside the pink and white room to know it was India's, the place where she did her work, where she came to think, to have peace. It was done up in her signature colour and, even at night, the pink and white room seemed to burst with light. The desk in the corner looked feminine but efficient with its pounce jar and inkpot at the ready.

Carrick sat beside her on the sofa, unwilling to let go of her. A boy came to light the fire. For a while, servants bustled in and out, bringing tea and blankets. At last, they were alone. Carrick poured the tea and placed a cup in her hands. 'Are you hurt, India?'

He'd been carefully looking her over, surreptitiously. She would not want to be an object of study or concern. She likely had bruises beneath the sleeves of her gown, but no other injuries were apparent. Still, not all injuries were physical and there was no arguing that India was hurting.

She shook her head and sipped the tea. 'I am not hurt.' But her voice trembled as if she realised how thin a line had separated not hurt from being hurt. 'If you had not come…' she said.

He took both of her hands and held them firm. 'It didn't happen, so do not think about it.' He fought the urge to gather her to him, to hold her close, but he sensed she would shatter if he did that and she did not want to shatter, not yet. She wanted to hold on to her strength a while longer.

'Every time from here on out when I look at him, I'll know what he is capable of, what he meant to do in order to have his way. There can be no pretence of civility between us now.' She huddled deeper into the soft blanket as if it offered a refuge.

'Perhaps that's for the best—to see him plain, to see his full hand revealed,' Carrick argued softly. 'He is wicked to his core and he does not deserve your mercy or consideration.'

He did not like to see her huddled within a blanket, pale and scared. 'Every day when he looks in the mirror, the effect will be the same for him. He, too, now knows what you're fully capable of. That gash you gave him will leave a scar.'

She shook her head. 'But it doesn't matter. I won a battle tonight, but I did not win the war, nor can I. I am not hurt tonight, but I am defeated. That is far worse. I was never going to win.' She covered her mouth with a hand as if she could keep the sobs locked inside. Her shoulders started to shake. Carrick took the teacup from her and set it aside.

'Everything I've done has served as nothing more than a weapon to be used against me. I eschewed the high life, London, balls, parties, pretty clothes, all the things I enjoyed, in order to avoid scandal, in order to shoulder responsibility. But by living discreetly and privately, managing my own business affairs, paying my family's debts and preserving my brother's inheritance, I am labelled an unnatural woman who can be put away by men who are frightened by a woman's ability to take care of herself.'

She turned tear-bright eyes in his direction and he was undone by the depth of her despair. 'No matter which way I turn, I am caught and I cannot escape.' She fell against him then and he took her in his arms, holding her close at last. 'It's hopeless. He will be back, Carrick, because he's a man and he has resources which a woman does not.'

'But you have me,' he whispered into her hair. She had a man and by extension she had all of that man's resources. He was the brother of a baron, the friend of a viscount. He would call on those resources if needed. For now, the best resource was bed. They needed to sleep, to clear their minds for the tasks that lay ahead in the morning. Victor was the most pressing, but by no means the only task they had to face. Carrick rose and then lifted her in his arms.

'What are you doing?' she murmured.

'I'm taking you upstairs and tucking you in. You'll feel better in the morning.' He hoped his knee would feel better, too. He'd forgotten about it until he'd stood up, the weight of India in his arms. His knee rebelled at that, but he'd already committed. He'd be damned if he set her down. She needed his strength right now, even if it was only a physical show.

He managed the stairs and found her room, deftly manoeuvring her through the doorway and laying her on the bed. 'I'll call for your maid.'

She reached for his hand. 'No, we'll manage fine on our own. Stay with me tonight, Carrick. Hold me? I don't want to be alone.'

Carrick swallowed hard. Did she know what she asked of him? Even vulnerable and tear-stained, she was lovely and irresistible. To lie beside her, to hold her, would be a privilege as much as it would be a torture. This was a night for comfort, not for lovemaking although his body was making a strong argument to the contrary.

'Of course I'll stay.' He offered her a smile and sat down on the edge of the bed to tug off his boots.

To his complete surprise, he slept rather well with his body tucked around India's for the duration. Perhaps it was because they had no pretences between them. On his part there was no need to pretend that she didn't rouse him, that his phallus could somehow sleep nestled against her without being in some state of semi-arousal, simply because he was a healthy male.

She was not bothered by it because, on her part, there was no need to feel that she must 'show her appreciation' for his efforts on her behalf tonight. She owed him nothing. It was a rather different arrangement than what he usually experienced with women. Most of his arrangements didn't involve any form of celibate but intimate contact, for starters, nor did they involve full nights wrapped in one another's arms. They were usually limited to a few hours of mutual exchanges of pleasures.

But different was good, very good. Too bad he didn't expect it to last. She'd left Benson under the belief that he'd manipulated her feelings for him to gain access to Hal, that their affair had been a game, nothing more.

Carrick tightened his arm about her and breathed in her scent, all vanilla, cinnamon and sleepy woman. Hopefully, last night had proven to her otherwise. A man who played games for personal gain was unlikely to have put himself in Victor's path. Not that Carrick was looking for gratitude and recognition. He was looking for much more than that from her.

If anyone was grateful, it was him. Logan was right, she *had* changed him, had made him question the assumptions and self-made promises he'd built his adult life on. She'd shown him what it meant to be entirely selfless. The love, the care, the concern she showed for her brother had shown *him* what his own promises to eschew attachments had cost him.

She had lost at love, too, losing her parents as he'd lost his father, losing her fiancé and the life that would have come with such a match. And while she was reluctant to trust others beyond a select few, she had not given up on love, had not set it aside and shut off her heart.

And that observation had spoken to him subtly over the weeks, tempting him to rethink the impossible—that he might be willing to break those promises he'd made himself, that he might be willing to contemplate love, attachment, if it were with her.

Face it, man, it might be too late to not contemplate it, that voice in his head whispered. *You love her and you can't stop it now, it has already sprung its cage.*

He *was* facing the truth and had faced it from the moment Benefield had confronted him and every mile since to Belle Weather. He had realised he was riding to her not only because she was in danger, but because he loved her, because he would have ridden after her regardless of Victor's threat.

He loved her.

How would anything or anyone ever compare to her? What would happen to him if he lost her now just when he had discovered he loved her? That was the new unthinkable and Victor threatened it. He had a plan, though, one that would keep her safe, *if* he could persuade her to agree to it. She would want to resist the idea, but he could not let her. Her own safety and his heart depended on it.

She'd slept in her chemise, and he caressed a bare arm as he placed a soft kiss on her cheek. 'Sleep well, my angel,' he whispered. He slid out of bed and dressed quietly, not wanting to wake her. She'd need all her strength today and he'd need all his wits to help her see reason. He'd start with a cup of strong coffee in the quiet of the breakfast room where he could gather his own thoughts before the storm broke.

Her mind was quiet when she awoke. India lay in bed for a long while, eyes shut, mind still, as long as she could hold on to the peace. Carrick was already up, she could feel his absence without opening her eyes. But his scent still lingered. The remnants of his touch still echoed on her body.

He was still *here*. With her. He'd held her all night. She wondered if he'd slept at all. She'd like to stop her mind right there and savour the idea of lying in his arms, safe and secure. But the reasons *why* she'd spent the night in his arms could not be ignored. *Because she was not safe and secure on her own.* She *hated* that realisation.

Other memories, darker memories, pushed at the security that warmed her. Victor had trespassed in her home, threatened her and, when threats had not got the result he wanted, he'd attacked her, determined to take by force what he'd been unable to manoeuvre. Carrick had come, though, and that had made all the difference last night.

The storm would not be held back now. India opened her eyes and sighed up to the ceiling. *Carrick had come.* It was something she would cherish as much as she despised it. He *had* come, but the very idea that his assistance had been necessary smarted, unwanted proof that a woman needed a man's protection, that she was not enough on her own.

It smarted personally, too, given how she'd left things

between them. He'd come even though she'd hurled insults at him and accused him of manipulation by seduction. *And still he'd come.* She could not recall ever having been so wrong about something in her entire life. She would have to apologise for that. And she would have to sort what that meant.

It would be far easier if Carrick had been manipulating her to get to Hal. Then she'd have every reason not to give him her trust and, dare she say, even her heart? Loving a Carrick who was honest and sincere in his regard was *intricate* to say the least. It demanded she find it within herself to trust a man once more with the direction of her life after two men had failed her. Did she *want* to do that? *Could* she do that?

India threw back the covers and forced herself out of bed. She could not resolve anything by lying about. She needed to dress and go down to face the day…and Carrick.

She found him in the breakfast room at the table nursing a cup of coffee with his shirt open at the neck and sleeves rolled up, auburn stubble bristling along his jaw, his masculinity on blatant display against the floral decor of the room.

He rose when she entered. 'India, how are you? Can I get you anything?' He was already loading a plate for her with more food than her stomach would be able to manage.

'Carrick, you needn't fuss over me.' She took the chair near his, suddenly nervous, and embarrassed, over what he'd witnessed last night. She'd been helpless. He'd *carried* her upstairs, for heaven's sake. 'If anyone needs fussing over it's you.' She took the plate he offered. 'I owe you an apology for the things I said in Benson. I leapt to conclusions and I said awful things.' She searched his face as he resumed his seat.

'I forgave you the moment you said them.' Carrick reached for her hand. 'You are under an incredible amount of stress. People are not at their best under those conditions. I did not understand the hold Victor had on your life until I saw that contract.' She felt his fingers press tight on hers. 'But you've been living with that hold for three years. It is no wonder you're on edge.'

He held her gaze and she felt a modicum of peace sweep over her. 'The question is, how do we want to break his hold for good? You cannot continue to live like this for the next seven years, nor do I think it's possible.'

She nodded. During her hours in the carriage, it had become clear to her that Victor could not be evaded any longer. The end game had arrived. But that didn't mean she had any idea how to fight him at this stage. 'After last night, I worry for Hal,' she confessed her darkest concern. 'I don't know why I didn't see it before. If Victor wanted to, he could simply eliminate Hal once Hal comes of age and he'd inherit. He could outflank me by outwaiting me.'

The fear that came with that knowledge gripped her. Carrick's other hand moved over hers. 'I can't stop him then, can't protect Hal.'

'Don't even think it, India. It is not as simply done as you might believe. There would be an enquiry, there'd be too much suspicion thrown his way given the history between the two of you and given the amount of disaster your family has already suffered. Too much bad luck draws the wrong sorts of attention.'

His thumb moved gently over the back of her hand in a soothing motion. 'Hal is safe for the next seven years though, yes?'

'Yes. I am the nominal property holder until he comes of age. Even if Hal died within those seven years, I'd still hold the property until the seven years expired. I had it set up that way, although not for the reasons I've just mentioned. It had just seemed like the thing to do, intuitively.' Now she was doubly glad she had. It was another layer of protection for Hal and it made her more of a direct obstacle for Victor.

Carrick's thumb slowed. 'So, Victor needs to remove you by marriage or by incarceration. Hence his latest threats. Remove you, and he could be named regent and have direct control of the estate while Hal attains his majority.'

Only Hal likely wouldn't attain that majority, India thought. If she was out of the way, Hal would be gradually eliminated. Not right away, there'd be no rush, but after any notice of her removal had settled.

'What would you like to do, India? How do you want this handled?' Carrick's words touched her. She looked up from her plate. When had a man asked her what she wanted to do? Her father had never asked. Landon had never asked. They'd merely assumed.

'I appreciate you asking. Truly, I do.' He was treating her not as someone to be protected, but as someone whom he saw as his partner. She offered him a small smile of gratitude. 'My position and Hal's position are so very fragile.' She sighed, wishing she had a better answer for him, 'And I fear I have no ideas left.'

Carrick nodded solemnly. 'As I see it, you have one option that will put you beyond Victor's ability to challenge your authority. I cannot vouch for what happens once Hal inherits, but my immediate concern is for your safety since it is through you that Belle Weather currently stays in the family and it is you whom Victor is attempting to have removed.'

He paused. 'You can marry. I know it's not what you want to hear, but it is what works and you have two good choices.' India furrowed her brow at that. 'You have Laurie Benefield's proposal, which it is not too late to accept, and you have mine.' His grey eyes were steady on hers, unblinking. 'Will you marry me, India, and allow me to keep you and your home safe?'

Marry Carrick? The thought was so shocking, she could barely process the words. 'It wouldn't be for the right reasons,' she stammered, trying to gather her thoughts.

'The safety of a friend seems like a good reason to me.' He lifted her knuckles to his lips, a smile curling on them, warm and teasing despite the circumstances ,but his next words were serious. 'There is also this, India. Without marriage, I am not able to help you.' She noticed he did not use the word 'protect' and she was grateful for that. 'In fact, without marriage, I am only a hindrance to you, another way for Victor to slander your name.'

Her stomach sank with the knowledge of that truth even as she raised her eyes to his. She wanted him, but she did not want him this way, as a sacrifice to the problems she'd failed to resolve on her own. His offer was no different on those grounds than Laurie's had been. 'My concerns are not your responsibility. I will not be a burden to you. If it were not for Victor's threat against me, you would not be asking.'

'And if it weren't for the accident, you wouldn't need me to ask. You'd have Landon as a husband and Victor would have no toehold.'

'How dare you!' India reared back, withdrawing her hand in a rapid movement. 'I will absolutely not be the object of your pity or your guilt.' That hurt more than the idea that he might have seduced her to gain permission for Hal to race. She rose too quickly, banging her knee on the table in her haste to want to get away, to put space between them. 'Whatever penance you sought to do here, that debt has been more than paid. You owe me nothing, you never did. I asked for none of this.'

His hand reached for her wrist, stalling her. 'India, that's not what this is.' There was a quiet desperation in his tone, but she pressed on.

'How could it not be, Carrick? You, who have sworn never to marry? Ever since I've known you, you've made no secret of it. Why should you suddenly change your mind if not out of guilt or pity?'

His eyes narrowed to charcoals, hot flames simmering in their depths that made her breath catch. 'Because I love you. Because marriage is the only way I can be with you without jeopardising you. I cannot give you better reasons than that.'

Chapter Twenty-Two

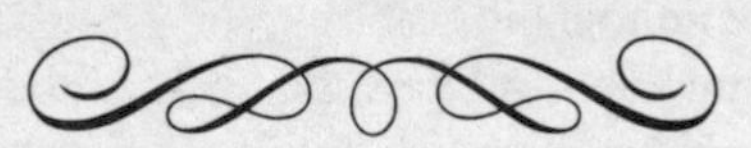

He'd stunned her first with his proposal, then with his pronouncement of love. In the stunning, he'd perhaps botched his proposal. No, there was no 'perhaps' about it. From the look on her face, he *had* botched it. He should have told her he loved her first and then proposed. But he hadn't and it was too late to change it now. So, he gave her what he could: space and time to process the revelations he'd sprung on her over morning coffee.

In the interim, he'd taken himself off to a quiet room in order to let her think. India prided herself on her control, her autonomy. That pride had been undermined severely last night by Victor. Carrick would not erode it further by badgering her into a decision with arguments she was already aware of, just as she might already be aware that there wasn't a decision to make as much as to accept.

Carrick paced the little room with its pastel colours and white woodwork. It had the look of a lady's sitting room, but it also felt like a room currently not in use. He paused before the painting over the cold fireplace, looking for something to take his mind off India, off her decision. It felt as if the whole rest of his life hinged on what that decision would be. This was what loving felt like, this was what he'd set himself up for. The pain with the pleasure.

'Do you love me or do you want to save me?' India's tones at the door had him turning around, painting forgotten. She offered him a half-smile as she moved from the door, but her features were drawn as if she'd just done battle. He did not want his proposal to be a burden to her when it was meant to be a solution and more. Perhaps she had done emotional battle with her feelings and realities, trying to align what she wanted with what she needed.

'Does a man have to choose?' Carrick replied, watching her make her way to the sofa. 'Can a man not wish to save the woman he loves? Or a woman for that matter,' Carrick added. 'Can she not also save the man she loves?'

India's brow furrowed at the last part. Carrick offered her a smile. 'Did you really think you were the only one being saved? I might be able to save you from Victor, but you have saved me from myself.' He moved to sit beside her, taking her hand. He wanted to touch her, comfort her.

'Have I saved you? I'd not thought of it like that.'

Of course she wouldn't think of it, she'd been too worried about not being a burden to others. 'Perhaps you should have,' he chided gently. Because if she did see that, she'd know he would have proposed without needing Victor's interference as a prompt. She would see that this proposal was motivated by want and not need. When she saw all that, she'd see the way to being able to say yes.

Thoughts were moving behind her blue eyes, her mind sifting his words. She raised her hand to his jaw, stroking the stubble there as she gave a little laugh. 'I think you specialise in turning my world upside-down and then shaking it until everything comes loose.' She wasn't far from the truth. He wanted to shake her until she had the good sense to accept his proposal. Her smile became resigned. 'Are you sure this is what you want? That you are in no way feeling compelled to marry me?'

Carrick captured her hand and kissed her palm. 'I've never been more certain.'

'Then I think I will accept. I think it's the only way forward.' Those were not exactly the jubilant words of a bride-to-be, but he'd take them. He wished her phrasing had been a bit more precise.

What did she mean by the only way forward? The way forward for them? Or the way forward in thwarting Victor? He'd prefer it be the former. He didn't want her to accept out of obligation any more than she'd wanted him to propose from it. But it was a beginning, he told himself as he claimed a kiss, a place to start from and all else could grow from there in time.

India was not as naive as to think a proposal would immediately fix everything, it was merely one step towards thwarting Victor. The next steps would be down the aisle. Then, and only then, would Victor be defeated. Yet India could not deny that in the days since Carrick's offer, she had felt her burden ease. They were alone at Belle Weather and could do as they liked.

That meant Carrick in her bed, waking beside her in the mornings, and making love to her at night. She liked the quiet intimacy of watching him undress in the evenings or standing naked before the basin going through his ablutions in the morning.

They spent their days walking the winter grounds of Belle Weather, visiting the stables, riding when the weather permitted and curled up beside a fire when it did not. She spent her mornings, much as she was spending this one, going over the ledgers while Carrick attempted to run the carriage works from afar, sending letters daily to Hal and to Logan.

She glanced at Carrick from her desk, to see his auburn head bent over paper, pen in hand, scribing another missive. It was a reminder that simply deciding to marry wasn't a magic wand that erased all their problems. In fact, quite the opposite was true. This marriage might resolve the issue of Victor's threat, but it opened up other issues for consideration.

She had an estate to manage and he had a business to oversee, not to mention his own horse farm. Belle Weather was an inconvenient two days away from Benson. He could not stay here indefinitely and expect his business to thrive. There was Hal to consider as well. Carrick and she disagreed on Hal's path in life between now and taking over Belle Weather. Would that come between them?

'India, you're staring. Did you need something?' Carrick chuckled, catching her out as Painter brought in the daily post.

'Ah, Logan's written.' Carrick sorted through the pile left on his table and slipped the letter opener between the sheets. 'I've been waiting for this. He should have news of my application for a special licence.' Carrick waggled his brows playfully. 'The sooner I have you wedded...' he teased, his eyes scanning the early lines of the letter.

She could tell something was wrong from the way his brow wrinkled and the smile slid slowly from his face. 'What is it?' A hundred possibilities ran through her mind: was it Hal? Was something wrong at the carriage works? If something had gone awry, he would not forgive himself.

He met her gaze, his expression resolute. She braced. 'Logan writes that Victor is making some difficulty about the race event at Wallingford this Saturday. He has entered a small team of experienced hired drivers. Apparently, he means to make a showing.'

India froze. 'What he means to make is trouble.' Panic gripped her. 'Thank goodness Hal isn't racing there. Those drivers out on the course could cause an accident. If Victor wanted to, it would be so easy...' Her words trailed off at the look on Carrick's face and she knew there was more bad news. 'Oh, Lord, he *is* racing.'

'It's something he decided on his own, India.' Carrick was quick to answer. 'He was going to tell you the night you and I quarrelled in Benson.' And then there'd been no opportunity for Hal. She'd fled without seeing Hal and now other issues had taken centre stage. She nodded, worry swamping her.

Carrick came around his table and crossed the room to her. She went into his arms, letting the warm strength of him ease her. 'If it's any consolation, I don't think he's going after Hal. I think he's coming after me.' Carrick sighed. 'This is not your fault, but mine. He's looking for revenge and targeting Logan's syndicate is the most assured way of drawing me out. He knows I won't let him strike at my friends or at Hal while I do nothing.'

But it was her fault, India thought, leaning against the broad strength of his chest. She'd involved Carrick in the mess of her life and now Victor was striking out at him, too. 'He wants you to come so that he can harm you,' she warned. 'Don't go. Surely Logan can look after himself? He's a viscount. Victor wouldn't dare anything.'

'Nothing directly, but do you think Victor ever deals with his problems directly? He prefers subterfuge and others doing his dirty work. He's been hiding behind solicitors and the law for three years now, trying to legitimise wresting Belle Weather away from you.'

She knew Carrick was right. 'Hal will need you, too. But I'm coming with you.'

'You needn't be brave, India,' Carrick protested but she was ready for him. She tipped her face up to meet his gaze.

'I'm not being brave. I'm scared and I don't want to be here without you, especially if Victor thinks you've gone and I'm alone.' It was all true. This threat to the race could be real or a decoy and there was no way to know. She knew, too, that going to Wallingford might very well be exactly what Victor wanted and they were just as likely to be walking into the lion's den. If so, at least they'd be doing it together.

She might have enjoyed Wallingford if she was the girl she'd been three years ago, always looking to be at the centre of the excitement. There was a vibrant air to the town as she and Carrick strolled two days later through the crowded streets lined with vendors who'd come to make money off the races. But she had too many cares to immerse herself in the lively atmosphere. Hal and Carrick were in danger and she could not lightly dismiss that she was the reason for it.

If anything happened to them it would be unbearable and to have it happen at a carriage racing venue was like losing Landon all over again, something she was sure Victor had not overlooked when he'd laid his plans. He'd chosen the Wallingford Cup race on purpose to torture her in both obvious and insidious ways.

'Are you eager to see Hal?' Carrick asked, stopping them at a booth to look at some leatherwork. They'd arrived last night, Carrick insisting on driving Sterope and Bronte and making the distance in record time. Logan was already present, handling entries and details for the race. Hal was slated to arrive some time this afternoon.

'Anxious more than eager—it's been a month since I've seen him.' A month since she'd fled Benson. Much had happened since then. She was engaged now, a fact that still seemed surreal to her. Hal had made his own decision about racing, an act she had originally viewed as defiance, but now saw perhaps as a necessity of his growing up. Even so, she couldn't shake the sense that she was losing her brother and it scared her to let him go.

Carrick thanked the leatherworker and they moved on, Carrick's steady hand at her back as he steered them towards the inn to check on Hal's arrival. Carrick had devoted himself to her tirelessly today, keeping her entertained at the booths and shops in an attempt, she recognised, to keep her mind off Victor. Given his way, she thought Carrick would have spent the day at the innyard with the other drivers looking over vehicles.

She slid him a studying sideways glance. 'Do you miss it? Racing?' Despite the unsettled nature of their circumstances, she'd not overlooked the energy that radiated from Carrick. He was excited to be here, although he was trying to keep that excitement tamped down for her sake.

'I did at first,' he confessed with a self-deprecating grin. 'I missed all the thrills; winning money is quite different than money earned. I missed the notoriety, the "fame". But I adjusted. I've found a way to live on the periphery of that world and participate through my racing designs and my safety features. I won't lie, though, it's in my blood.'

'It must be difficult to flirt with such distraction. Surely you're tempted?' India asked. How must it feel for him to be surrounded by other racers and be part of that crowd any longer?

He shook his head. 'My time is gone. My knee is a liability and I'm too much in my head, overthinking my strategies. A racer needs to react instinctively. To hesitate is to put yourself and others in jeopardy.' He leaned in close to her ear and whispered, 'Besides, I don't like to lose. Best to have left on a high note than to stay too long so that the legend is tarnished.'

He laughed, but India could hear the sad nostalgia beneath the laughter. He probably wouldn't appreciate hearing her own relief that he had given it up, that he, at least, wasn't racing tomorrow. It was one less thing for her to worry about.

Hal was in the taproom when they returned, his tow-head and lanky height easy to spot amid the crowd gathered around him, racers who had recognised him from the Benson contest. He spotted them and broke away from the group, 'Carrick! India!' He moved towards them, a smile on his face. Sweet Heavens, had it only been a month?

Hal seemed enormously changed from when she'd left. Today, he was dressed in riding breeches and tall boots and a green jacket, looking every inch the country gentleman. In other words, looking adult and grown up. He was in his element here, she realised, a driver among his peers, part of his own world, not her world. There was a catch in her throat as Hal swept her up in a hug.

'It's good to see you, Sister.' He offered his hand to Carrick to shake. 'I hear congratulations are in order. I'm happy for you both. Logan has a parlour in the back for us, shall we? There's much to talk about.' A look passed between the two men that India didn't miss.

'You go on with India,' Carrick said. 'I'll come a little later with drinks. You two have catching up to do first.' He gave her hand a small squeeze and let her go.

Hal was quiet until they reached the privacy of the parlour with its stuffed chairs and warm fire. 'Are you upset with me, India?' he asked, closing the door behind them.

He wasn't so far beyond her then, to still care about

her good opinion. The thought warmed her as India took a seat in one of the chairs. 'Not upset, Hal. Just worried.'

Hal took the chair opposite her, crossing a booted leg over one knee, a gesture he'd borrowed from Carrick. It made him look far older than eighteen. 'I went against your wishes, though,' he prompted. 'Are you upset I disobeyed?'

'Perhaps at first. But then I realised I cannot keep making decisions for you. You're too old for that. You *need* to make your own choices. I can only advise and even advising is a privilege, not a right.' Carrick had helped her to see that. 'I doubt this will be the last time we disagree on something. It's not easy for me to step back, Hal, but it is necessary.'

She debated her next words. He wouldn't want to hear them, but she had to try. 'Only, do you think you could just not race *this* weekend? Victor intends to make trouble and I fear he'll aim that trouble at you—an accident on the course perhaps, tampering with your vehicle.' She could imagine too well all the different ways Victor could cause harm.

Hal shook his head. 'Especially *for* those reasons I must race this weekend. Victor does not get the pleasure of dictating our lives. We will not give him the satisfaction of knowing his mere presence can direct our behaviours.'

Hal grew sombre. 'I know what he attempted with his marriage contract and what he tried at Belle Weather when that failed. The man has taken things too far and he must be put in his place. I see now that you've lived in his shadow much too long, India. I won't have that for you or for me.'

He leaned towards her, his voice low. 'Logan has the carriages and the horses under close surveillance. There is little chance of Victor getting near them. And on the course, I can handle Victor's drivers if they try anything,' he added confidently.

'I'd rather you didn't have to handle anything at all,' India replied.

Hal smiled. 'I must disagree, Sister. I think it's high time that I did handle a few things. Which is why there are other issues I'd like to discuss. Logan has offered me a place on his racing team. I can travel with the team and earn money of my own.' India braced herself. She knew what was coming. This was where he told her he wasn't going to university next term.

'I've accepted Logan's offer.' Her heart sank further. This was the third time Hal had called him Logan—not Mr Maddox or Viscount Hailsham. He and Logan were friends now, it seemed, as he and Carrick were friends. She couldn't fight them both.

'I've accepted. But,' he added quickly, 'I'm going to Oxford, too. This is the last race until spring. The school term will be over by the time the Season is in full swing and Logan needs me. I can race all summer and skip the rural meets in the autumn if I must. Although nothing stops me from joining the team on the weekends once the term is in session. With trains, I can be somewhere in a matter of hours instead of travelling for days. And it will only be a couple of years that Logan will have to share me with Oxford.'

'You have it all worked out,' India said with no small amount of surprise. It wasn't what she'd expected to hear. How could she argue with that plan when it gave her what she hoped for him? But she could take argument with that last part.

'Hal, you don't have to go to Oxford for me.' It was hard to say those words because she wanted university for him so badly, but she also wanted his happiness, wanted him to make decisions for himself, not for the happiness of others, even if that other was her. 'I should not have pushed you.'

Hal sat back easily in his chair. 'Of course you should have. Belle Weather is our home. It will fall to me to see it into the future. My mistake was in thinking that it had to be one or other, racing or university. I *can* have both.'

He gave her a long look. 'So can you, India. All things in moderation? You and I aren't used to living that way. Even in times of trouble, like after Mother and Father passed, we did not approach our situation with moderation, but head first. You ran at the debt Father left full throttle.'

She had. She gave her brother a sharp look. Hal's words threw that choice into a new light. She'd liquidated whatever could be turned into cash. She'd sold off the collections that weren't sentimental. At the time, she'd seen it as an act of necessity, but Hal's words added a new perspective. She'd always lived out loud, lived boldly and without compromise in her youthful naivety.

She'd not seen the choice of her grieving and her mourning as being an extension of that—of mourning in extreme. But it had been, hadn't it? She'd thrown herself body and soul into keeping Belle Weather together, she'd cast off all the trappings of her old life—the parties, the luxuries, the social whirl—and had exchanged it for a life lived alone, in a shell to keep the world out.

'It was necessary,' she said to Hal.

'Perhaps…' he shrugged '…but not any more.' He took her hand. 'Sister, you needn't fear Victor. You needn't be alone any longer. You have Carrick now and you have me. I'll be able to help at Belle Weather more and you'll need that help now that you have the carriage works in Benson to consider.' He gave her a wink as Carrick entered with a tray of drinks and Logan on his heels.

'Time to talk race strategy, Hal. If Victor means to try anything, we want to be ready for him.' Logan pulled another chair over to the fire and India nodded politely in his direction. One dilemma had been resolved, but the other remained. She and Hal had sorted out their differences—if only Victor could be sorted out as easily.

Carrick came to perch on the edge of her chair and take her hand. 'Don't worry, India, this time tomorrow it will all be over and we can get on with our lives.' She wished she could be as certain.

Chapter Twenty-Three

Perhaps Victor wouldn't try anything. India was finding the possibility more believable with each passing hour. She sat in the stands at the starting line, her hands clenched in her lap as Hal's curricle class lined up. It was the last race of the day and there'd been no sign of Victor, although his hastily assembled team of drivers had raced all day. To cause trouble, one had to be present, didn't they? She cast a look at the sky. It was good thing this was the last race. She didn't expect the weather to hold much longer.

Still, she was nervous. Perhaps Victor was waiting for Hal's race. He had drivers in this race as well and they were lined up on either side of Hal. Perhaps Victor would strike at Hal instead of Carrick. There was movement in the row and Carrick edged his way to his seat. 'So far, so good,' he assured her with a smile.

'Victor has drivers in this race,' she reminded him, unwilling to let her guard down until Hal was safe. She did not think for a moment that Victor had made an idle threat just to keep her on tenterhooks all day. She worried it was all a decoy and Victor was at Belle Weather right now. Perhaps that was what Victor wanted, her perpetually off balance wondering *if* he'd strike.

'At least we can keep an eye on everything. We'll see the whole race, just six laps around the track. They would have to be bold to try anything,' Carrick said as the starter sent the race into motion.

The first four laps went smoothly with Hal building a strong lead, Victor's racers close behind. Into the fifth lap, they narrowed the gap and India's nerves pricked. She gripped Carrick's hand, the two of them exchanging a look. Into the final lap, they'd come up on either side of Hal. 'Those wheels are too close,' Carrick muttered beneath his breath. 'If they mean to pass, they should pass.' A moment later he swore, 'They don't mean to pass. Hal needs to outrun them and hope he can hold the curricle steady.' He gritted his teeth. 'He's got to whip up the team, he's got to ask them for more speed.'

'And risk overbalancing?' India shot back. There were still two turns to take. 'Perhaps that's what they want, to force him to too much speed to take the corner.'

'It's a well-built curricle, it won't overbalance. He's driven it before. He knows what it can take.' But Carrick's words sounded more like a litany of self-reassurance. This was what letting go felt like, watching from the sidelines, unable to intervene, unable to stop what was happening. Only Hal could affect the outcome. They watched him navigate the first turn, then the second, pulling ahead in the stretch, the team at their maximum as they strained forward across the finish line.

Carrick and India were out of their seats, making their way to Hal, pushing through the crowd. They'd nearly reached him when loud tones called out, 'What were you thinking with that reckless driving! You could have wrecked my teams, you little upstart!' Victor Claiborne emerged from the crowd, charging straight for Hal. He swung, but Hal was ready for him. Hal ducked and came up swinging with a few choice words of his own.

'India, stay here,' Carrick growled, darting into the fight along with Logan to separate the two before it became a melee. In a crowd this size with emotion running high, it wouldn't take much for it to become a mob.

She would absolutely not stay put. India shoved her way to the front. For a moment it appeared Logan and Carrick had got everything under control. Hal was panting and resigned, but Victor was livid with anger. His eyes found her and she wished heartily she'd listened to Carrick and stayed in the anonymous depths of the crowd swarming the finish line. The scar on his face was red and shocking. Her stomach sank. She'd done that. She'd given him that mark. He would not let her go unscathed in retaliation.

'I should have known you wouldn't be far from your troublesome brother or your lover,' Victor snarled, drawing all attention her way. The crowd fell eerily silent, everyone craning to see and hear what would be said next and Victor was too happy to oblige. His gaze swung to Carrick. 'I see you've taught your protégé all of your tricks. He's become a dangerous driver just like you were. He almost caused an accident out there today, also just like you.'

'Your drivers boxed him in. They should have passed or fallen back. They knew the risks when they pulled alongside.' Carrick crossed his arms over his chest, his gaze steady.

'Just like Landon Fellowes knew the risk of passing on a blind curve? Is that what you tell yourself?' Victor raised his voice to ensure he was heard. 'You goaded him to it, drove him to his death and all so you could steal his fiancée behind his back. Or perhaps the two of you planned it together and you've been carrying on all this time, waiting for a decent interval before wedding.'

India blanched as the murmurs of the crowd rose. Three years was not so long ago that people were unfamiliar with the accident on the Richmond Road. Accusing glances were thrown her way.

It was Carrick who spoke up. 'Those are baseless, vile suggestions coming from the man who has been attempting to steal her estate, who has attempted to blackmail her into marriage and who trespassed in her home with the express intention of forcing a marriage one way or another. Why don't you tell everyone how you got that scar and why?'

Thunder rolled overhead and the first of the raindrops fell, fat and ominous, but no one moved. Everyone wanted to see how this turned out. This was precisely the kind of high drama India had attempted to avoid these past three years, but it had found her anyway.

'I should call you out for those wicked insinuations.' Victor was still trying to claim the high ground.

'I should call *you* out,' Carrick challenged. 'You cannot impugn the honour of a decent woman, a woman who will be my wife, without expecting repercussions. No man here would expect a gentleman to do any less.'

There was a smattering of applause from somewhere in the crowd.

No, she did not want a duel. They were illegal. Carrick would be sent away or, worse, he could be killed. But she wanted what happened next even less. Someone in the crowd shouted, 'Race!', and the crowd took up the chant. 'Race, race, race.'

India looked around wildly. Surely Carrick would not consider it. It was starting to rain in earnest.

'The weather makes it too dangerous.' Logan tried to intervene, but Victor saw an opportunity.

'I'll race you for her,' Victor declared.

India froze, knowing full well Carrick would not let that pass.

'I win, you renounce all claim to Belle Weather and you leave her and her brother alone.' Carrick's eyes were steely flints. She knew that look and how intractable he was when he made up his mind. His gaze flicked to Logan. 'Get my team. Sterope and Bronte in the stables. Hal, ready the phaeton if you please.'

'No!' India pushed towards Carrick, desperate to stop this, but no one was listening. The crowd was too busy placing wagers. She reached him, grabbing his arm. 'Carrick, listen to me, you are not going to do this. You do not think for a moment that he will play fair.' She dashed at the rain in her face, swiping away the raindrops.

Carrick gripped her hand and pulled her aside, impatient and earnest. 'Think, India, this is your chance to be free. Let me do this for you. Logan is drafting a gentleman's agreement right now. Victor will sign it.

He will honour it—there are too many witnesses if he does not.'

'And if you lose?' India persisted.

'I won't lose.'

'Your knee...'

'It will hold.' He pressed a finger to her lips. 'It is settled, India. I know it is not how you'd like it to be, but it is what must be done. Now, let me go and do it.'

Her anger broke then. 'Damn you, Carrick, I do not want to be a prize to be fought over. I never wanted any of this.' Fury was better than helplessness. Fury made her strong. 'This isn't about me, it's about you. You want to race. *You* want to be the great man.' She pounded on his chest with a fist, but he captured her hand.

'What I want is for you to be safe, India. The means justify the ends.' He kissed her cheek then and stepped away as Hal brought up the phaeton, Sterope and Bronte ready.

Carrick pulled himself into the high seat of the phaeton and chirped to the team. He did not dare a backwards glance at India. He hated leaving her this way, wet and miserable inside and out. But he needed to clear his mind. He needed to think about the two-mile course that had been used earlier for the cross-country race.

He squinted through the rain. He'd raced in worse than this—not much worse, though. The trick would be to avoid water-filled ruts in the road and to go fast enough that the wheels didn't have time to get bogged down in mud. The only part of the course that worried him was the hillside at the end. Water had saturated the ground and the rain had come on strong and sudden.

Conditions were prime for a mudslide. In terms of the rest of the course, he'd fare well.

Fortunately, Sterope and Bronte were mudders, as good in the rain as they were on a dry track. Carrick stretched out his leg, testing his knee. He caught Logan giving him a questioning look and nodded. It would hold. It had to.

Victor drew up alongside him in a sleek phaeton drawn by a prancing pair of pretty, high-strung thoroughbreds. Not the usual choice for carriage pulling.

Logan arranged the start and then they were off, each trying to surge into a lead. Rain dripped in Carrick's face, making it hard to see, but Sterope and Bronte were sure footed. Thank goodness. It gave Carrick time to focus on Victor, whose driving was making the race dangerous for them both. At the first curve, Victor surged into the lead, but gave it up when his carriage tipped precariously, his left wheels coming off the ground by inches. He had to slow in order to prevent it from flipping entirely.

Carrick cracked his whip and overtook him, making the most of the muddy straight that ended the first mile, Sterope and Bronte thundering towards the next curve, slowing and speeding alternately to negotiate the hairpin structure of the course as they approached the hill. The rain worsened. They were nearly halfway, the narrows approaching. Carrick was careful to make wide serpentines of the road to avoid being passed, but he wished for more speed.

He did not dare it, though. The road was starting to crumble as he climbed the hill. The edge of the verge on the right side, the side that sloped into the meadows below, was periodically crumbling under the weight of the water and the pressure of the carriage wheels. To his left, rivulets starting from the top of the hill had become small waterfalls, cutting muddy ruts in the dirt. If they went… It didn't bear thinking about. Short of building a dam, he couldn't stop them if they did. All he could do was drive.

Sterope and Bronte tossed their heads, as they sensed it, too. The storm was wearing on them. If he could just hold on another five hundred feet, he could close off Victor. But Victor knew that, which made these five hundred feet the most important. If a driver were to pass, it would be here or else he'd have to wait until the last bit of flat at the bottom where the road opened up again, where it could be too late if the lead was large enough.

Victor made his move and it was going to be trouble. He'd waited too long and now he didn't have enough room to pass before the road narrowed. A sane driver would back off, cede the road. But Victor did neither. His expression was set with grim determination as he pulled even with Carrick, his thoroughbreds lathered from their exertions through the mud. The mud made even a light phaeton heavy to pull and they hadn't the strength of horses like Sterope and Bronte who'd been bred to the task. Victor's horses were bred for speed and dry tracks.

The road could barely support two carriages. It was starting to deteriorate. 'Pull back! Pull back!' Carrick shouted, concern overriding his competitive spirit. Victor would never make the curve at this speed, with the road narrowing.

Victor's lips curled into a snarl as he yelled over the storm. 'The hell I will!' He whipped his horses and they strained, eyes wild with fright.

It was up to him. Images of the past flashed with the lightning: Landon, the curve at Richmond, Landon's stubborn determination. He should pull back, but how could he when it would mean India losing her chance at true freedom? She was counting on him at the bottom of the hill.

He tried for more speed despite the throbbing in his knee telling him he couldn't handle more. He hoped to force Victor to fall in behind him, but Victor pressed on. They were in the turn now, Victor's wheels on the very limits of the unstable road, Victor yelling with glee as he began to edge up on Sterope who had slowed slightly, while Bronte hugged the wall of hillside on the left. The turn sharpened and Carrick struggled for a lead, even a lead of inches would create more room, but there was no more room to be gained.

Then the sound of rushing water and mud frightened the high-strung thoroughbreds. Victor's carriage tipped, the horses out of control. The road gave out under the pressure of the wheels. Carrick yelled a useless warning as Victor, carriage and all disappeared down the hillside.

There was no time to think, to be horrified. He had his own crisis to contend with. The hillside had given out, triggering a mudslide that was taking out the road ahead of him at an alarming rate—a deadly rate—a rate he wasn't going to make. Would there be enough road left when he got there to get through? 'Come on, boys, it's now or never,' he said through gritted teeth. He leaned with all his strength to the left, his knee straining with the effort, to give the phaeton the weight it needed to stay balanced, while he gave the horses their heads and hoped his knee held. This couldn't be how it ended. Not when India needed him.

Chapter Twenty-Four

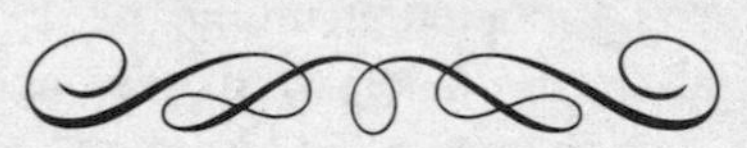

Dear God, the hill was coming apart! Around her, the volume of the crowd rose. India couldn't look away at the horror on the hillside—Victor trying to pass, the road giving out beneath his wheels, the horrible moment when the mud swallowed him whole, carriage, team and all in a wave of dirt and debris that triggered the whole hillside; mud moving like a house of cards, sweeping away everything in its path.

Hal passed her a spyglass and she put her eye to it, trying to gauge how long Carrick had before he ran out of road, before the mud swallowed him, too. If Carrick didn't get down the hill, it would be her fault. She shouldn't have quarrelled with him. She should have told him. *I love you.*

Hal moved suddenly beside her. 'He's picking up speed, India. He's going to race the mudslide. He'll make it, he will.'

She put down the spyglass and clutched Hal's hand. 'If he goes too fast, he'll tip.'

'He's balancing, he's throwing his weight to the left,' Hal argued excitedly. But all India could think of was his knee. If didn't hold, he'd fall down the hillside with Victor. And even that might not be enough. She gave a little scream. They weren't going to make it. Carrick was moving on his seat, reaching for something.

'The safety lever, he's going to separate,' Hal breathed. 'He's going to save the team.'

'No, no, no.' She knew what that meant. That Carrick knew he wasn't going to outrun the mud. There was a collective gasp from the crowd as the phaeton began to separate from the horses and Carrick's fate became clear. She snatched up the spyglass again. She wanted to look away, but she couldn't. If these were Carrick's final moments, she owed it to him be there in whatever way possible.

Then she saw him jump at the last opportunity, from the phaeton on to the back of one of the horses and grab the reins. A cry of disbelief went up from the crowd. She sagged in relief against Hal. Carrick had done the impossible. And now she had to find the courage to do the impossible, too. Victor was dead, she needn't hold Carrick to his promises. She was free and he could be free, too, free to decide if his proposal truly was motivated out of love or out of exigency to save her from Victor. He wouldn't want to hear it any more than she'd wanted to be the centre of that race.

India watched the victory celebration from the periphery, standing in the innyard beside the post chaise she'd hired. Around were the sounds of quiet victory, the festive day having taken on a subdued tone. Victor's body had been retrieved, his pretty horses buried where they'd fallen. The story of Carrick's miraculous drive was being recounted in hushed tones over ales in the inns around Wallingford.

The accident hadn't dampened all spirits entirely. There were other races and other victories to celebrate. Hal was in high demand and Logan had claimed him in order to make introductions. But that was fine. Hal knew where to find her and he had his life to live now. He could take care of himself. She would wait only long enough to see Carrick. She'd had only a moment to hold him when he'd crossed the finish line on Sterope.

'India, what is this? What's the coach doing hitched up?' Carrick wound through the crowd to her side, free from the attention at last. 'We will travel tomorrow.'

She shook her head. 'You needn't come with me. You've done enough.' Her words began to tremble. He'd done more than enough. 'You nearly died today. You should not have raced, you could have ruined the horses.' The scold came out choked, full of all the emotions from the day. It was not what she'd meant to say. 'When I saw the hillside start to go…'

'There were a few dicey moments, I admit. But we managed. The safety feature worked and we all came home safe.' Carrick took her hands. 'You're free now. I am sorry for the loss of your cousin, though. It was not what I intended.'

'I know.' She took a steadying breath. 'You are free now, too, Carrick.' This perplexed him.

'I was always free, India.'

'I mean you needn't feel obliged to marry me. You have time now to truly consider whether or not you are ready to offer such a commitment to me without the pressure of Victor's threat looming.' She put a hand to his lips as he'd done to her earlier. 'Carrick, I know what you think, but you need time to revisit it, to make sure. You owe me nothing.'

Carrick's gaze hardened. 'Perhaps it's you who wants the time to rethink now that you no longer need to accept.'

'Perhaps we both need time.' If that's what he needed to hear in order to let her go, she would allow it. 'This is what is best for both of us.' Because she couldn't do it, couldn't watch him risk himself for her, couldn't watch him sacrifice for her. He would come to resent her for it when they had to choose between Belle Weather and the carriage works or the horse farm.

If he had time to reconsider, he would see that it simply didn't work. She wouldn't give up Belle Weather for another seven years and he should not have to give up the business he'd worked so hard for.

He let go of her hand. 'If this is what you want, you shall have it.' He held the coach door open for her. 'You know where I'll be if you ever need me.' He shut the door behind her and signalled to the driver, sending her away. She tried to pretend her heart wasn't breaking over it. If she had everything she wanted, why didn't it feel better? Why didn't it feel *right*? Perhaps it would once she was home.

But it didn't feel better. Not the next day or the next. Or even a week later. November ended. December began. Early signs of the seasonal festivities were evident in the village near Belle Weather. But even the joy of impending Christmas and Hal's arrival didn't lift her spirits. She missed Carrick.

'You should go to him.' Hal said as they sat reading together one evening, the library restored from Victor's attempt to denude it.

'To whom?' She looked up from pages she'd not really seen, her thoughts wandering once more to the final day she'd seen Carrick, to those horrible moments when he'd decided to race.

'To Carrick, you silly head. I know you miss him. You haven't turned a page in half an hour.'

She sighed. 'He doesn't want me, Hal.'

'Are you sure? What did you tell him about marriage? Does he have any reason to believe that it was what you truly wanted? He knows you refused Laurie.'

She barely heard the rest of what Hal had to say. She was too busy replaying those conversations. What had she said about marriage? That she'd never seek to marry again, that she wanted to be free, that she didn't want his offer out of pity or duty? Was it possible that he thought she didn't want him now that she didn't need him? Hope flickered for a moment and then wavered. 'He's not the marrying sort, he's very proud to declare that,' she argued.

'But that was before you, India. He raced Victor—heck, he raced a hillside for you. Only a man in love would do such a thing, to give you everything you wanted.'

Everything she thought she'd wanted. 'I'm not sure...' What if she stuck her neck out and got it chopped off? What if Carrick refused her? But what if he didn't and she never knew?

'And you won't be sure until you know for certain,' Hal said firmly.

* * *

The bell over the shop door tinkled, announcing a customer. Carrick looked up from his work on a carriage meant as a Christmas gift for a wealthy man's wife. He wasn't expecting anyone today. The shop was quiet. His apprentices had left for their noon meal. He worked through lunch these days, lunch no longer holding the same allure for him as it had held this past autumn. God, he missed her. Was she well? Had she found the peace she was looking for? Was she happy at Belle Weather? Even now, were she and Hal planning for Christmas? He spent too much of his time day dreaming about her, imagining her at Belle Weather, imagining her at the farm, riding King, bringing him a picnic. But he'd had to let her go, had to give her what she wanted. She'd suffered enough.

'We're closed, for lunch,' he called out.

'That's why I've brought it,' a familiar voice called back. He froze, sure that his mind was playing tricks on him. He'd just been thinking of her and here she was. He stepped out cautiously into the front office, not daring to believe it was true.

'Carrick, it's me, India. I've brought lunch.' She worried her lip as she held up the basket, as unsure of her reception as he was of her reality.

Carrick recovered himself first. 'Lunch? All the way from Belle Weather?'

'All the way,' she said shyly. 'Are you glad to see me, Carrick?'

His throat worked. 'Yes.' He should say more than that. He should say he'd missed her, that he loved her. 'Come on back, we can use the work table for our picnic.' He watched her set out the lunch, not caring over-much what was in it, only that she was here. 'Have you come to visit Elizabeth?' He would die if she was only here for a visit to the Blackmons. It would be like rubbing salt in a wound.

Her hands stilled on the ham. 'No, I've not come to see Elizabeth. Just you.' Her gaze found his. 'I have something to ask you.'

'And a letter wouldn't do?' Carrick joked and then wished he hadn't.

She shook her head, her little gold earrings jiggling. 'It's not something for a letter. I need the truth, Carrick, and you've always been honest with me. When you decided to race Victor in Wallingsford, was it because you didn't want to marry me?'

A blow to the stomach could not have hit him harder. 'Is that what you thought? I raced him because you didn't want to marry me, because you deserved the right to make your own choices. I raced to set you free.' How could she begin to think he didn't want her? He'd shown her in every possible way with his actions, worshipped her with his body. But he knew why. He hadn't told her, hadn't said the words.

She nodded solemnly. 'I don't think anyone has ever given me a greater gift. But there's something I want more. I've had time to think, time to choose and that's why I am here, Carrick.' She came around the table and gathered her skirts and knelt before him.

'What are you doing, India? You'll dirty your skirt.' His mind was a riot, no small part of him remembering the last time she'd knelt before him which only added to his confusion.

She reached for his hand. 'I am proposing to you, if you will hush long enough. Carrick Eisley, of all people I can choose to be with, I choose to be with you. Will you marry me?'

Carrick felt a smile rip across his face. She was proposing to him. How…novel. How…incredible. How very right it seemed. 'Yes, I will marry you, India Claiborne.' He drew her to her feet and pulled her close, kissing her hard. 'You are a wild one indeed.'

'You're one to talk.' Her arms stole about his neck as joy caught at them both. He swung her about and set her upon the work table.

'Well, you know what they say, some are born wild and some have wildness thrust upon them.'

She laughed against his mouth. 'Then, thrust away.'

Epilogue

Eight years later

'Papa! Papa! Can I drive?' Ethan Landon Eisley came sliding down the farmhouse banister full of energy despite the early morning hour, bursting with anticipation at the prospect of spending the day at the carriage works.

Carrick scooped him up as he hit the end of the banister. 'Maybe part of the way, don't tell your mother.' He winked conspiratorially at his tow-headed son. Ethan might look like his mother, but the boy was definitely his. A wilder, more fearless imp Carrick had yet to encounter. The scamp had stolen his heart the moment he'd entered the world and Carrick had given it gladly.

Ethan threw his arms about Carrick's neck and whispered back, 'You're the best, Papa.'

'What is this? It looks rather suspicious.' India stood in the doorway of the dining room where the smells of breakfast indicated it was already laid out and waiting for them. She smiled and came forward. 'Just be careful,' she admonished.

'Of what?' Carrick teased, feigning innocence, his eyes meeting hers over Ethan's head.

'Of letting him drive.' India laughed. 'Don't think I don't know what you were planning. You're always letting him drive,' she scolded, but she wasn't angry.

He kissed her on the cheek and they set about filling breakfast plates. 'You'll come into Benson this afternoon for the ceremony, won't you?' Today was a big day. It was the grand opening of his carriage showroom. It had been some time in the making; they'd taken a loan from Logan for the construction and they'd had to wait for the properties adjacent the carriage works to become available, but slowly over the years, they'd acquired the space needed. It would be an elegant but modest showroom, allowing him to show four carriage styles at a time.

'Of course,' India assured him, helping Ethan with his plate.

'And you'll bring the baby?' Carrick poured coffees for them both. 'I want my family with me when we cut the ribbon.' Ethan had been followed five years later by a sister, Cecilia Rose, named for India's mother, and if his guess was right, Cecilia Rose would probably be followed by another sibling in about seven months.

There were those who would laugh to see him so tamed, so devoted to family. They'd hardly recognise the rake who'd bashed around town racing neck or nothing for something as insignificant as bragging rights and a pocketful of money.

Seven years ago, he would have laughed, too, over the prospect of giving his heart to not just one person, but to three and now quite possibly a fourth. Attachments didn't get any more personal than the ones he had to his wife and his family and he would not change one thing about it.

Ethan finished eating and scrambled down from the table to find his boots. India rose from her chair and came to sit on his lap. 'Are you nervous about today?'

'Yes, it's a bit of a risk and I'm taking it with someone else's money. But Logan assures me that people will come to Benson especially for my carriages whether the railroad puts a station here or not.' It was looking more likely that the Great Western Railway was not going to put a station at Benson. The coaching traffic between Oxford and London, which had sustained Benson for so long, was definitely down. Once, there'd been eight coaches a week that passed through on that route. These days, there were only three. Hardly ideal conditions on which to expand his business, but the racing syndicate had grown over the past seven years under Logan's management. Carriage racing was as popular as ever as gentlemen turned what once had been a necessary skill into a hobby. Customised carriages with Carrick's special features were all the rage among the elite who could afford a custom-designed carriage, a one-of-a-kind vehicle from one of the premier carriage makers in the country. If a gentleman raced, he preferred a Carrick Eisley racing carriage.

Logan and Hal had done their parts to popularise his designs and his safety features. Hal had been the premier racing face of the syndicate until last year when he'd turned twenty-five and had taken over the running of Belle Weather. It would be interesting to see how Hal would balance the two obligations this year. He was contracted to make a few strategic appearances at key races. 'Are you looking forward to seeing your brother?' Hal and Logan would both be on hand this afternoon.

'Yes, I miss him now that he's not underfoot.' India smiled and wrapped her arms about his neck. 'I do appreciate the privacy, though.' She gave him a soft kiss. 'It's often difficult to enjoy one's husband when one's brother is always stealing him away. I rather like having a place of our own and having it to ourselves.'

They'd split their time between Belle Weather and Benson over the past seven years; Autumn and winter at Belle Weather while Hal was at university and the spring racing season in Benson where Logan had headquartered the syndicate. The first two years Carrick had even run the syndicate while Logan was occupied with family matters. It had been awkward and on occasion it had required time apart to balance the two strands of their lives. But they'd known it would be temporary.

'We managed.' Carrick smiled against her mouth. 'Ethan and Cecilia are proof of that.' They'd done more than managed. They'd built a life together starting from the ground up, beginning with the establishment of trust and love between them, things that had been difficult for each of them to invest in. For India it had been putting her trust in someone other than herself and for him it had been opening his heart to love and all that came with it.

She was not the high-spirited girl he'd known in London, nor was she the hardened young woman he'd met in Benson. She was something beyond both, something better. She was his wife, the mother of his children, the forgiver of his sins, the keeper of his heart and the redeemer of his soul.

'What are you thinking?' she murmured, snuggling against him.

'That I wouldn't trade the past seven years for anything. They've been the best of my life so far.'

'Mine, too.' India smiled against his shoulder.

How foolish he'd been to think love was loss. In truth, the loss was in not loving. He'd almost missed out on the greatest risk life had to offer—loving another. Which would have been too bad. Only with the greatest risks come the greatest rewards. The woman on his lap, the child asleep upstairs and the one who was no doubt going to come barrelling through the hallway any moment now with his boots on, were all proof of that.

* * * * *

If you enjoyed this story, look out for Logan's story
His Inherited Duchess
coming soon

And make sure to read Bronwyn Scott's miniseries
The Peveretts of Haberstock Hall

Lord Tresham's Tempting Rival
Saving Her Mysterious Soldier
The Bluestocking's Whirlwind Liaison
'Dr Peverett's Christmas Miracle'
in Under the Mistletoe

COMING NEXT MONTH FROM

All available in print and ebook via Reader Service and online

LORD MARTIN'S SCANDALOUS BLUESTOCKING (Regency)
by Elizabeth Rolls
Since Kit broke her betrothal to Lord Martin, she's a changed woman. But when tragedy strikes, she turns to Martin for help, only to discover their desire still burns strongly...

A LAIRD IN LONDON (Regency)
Lairds of the Isles • by Catherine Tinley
Lady Isabella must wed and Angus isn't looking for a bride, but when he rescues her from danger, the attraction is undeniable! But his wild Hebridean home is no place for a lady...

A MATCH TO FOOL SOCIETY (Regency)
Matchmade Marriages • by Laura Martin
Society insists Jane become a debutante—so play the game she must! She agrees to a pretend courtship with notorious Tom Stewart but is unprepared when real feelings surface.

THE WRONG WAY TO CATCH A RAKE (Regency)
by Lara Temple
Phoebe knows entangling herself with Dominic, Lord Wrexham, is the wrong way to go about her mission, but the closer they get, the more she's distracted by their simmering attraction.

ONE NIGHT WITH HER VIKING WARRIOR (Viking)
by Sarah Rodi
When Northmen lay siege to Ryestone Keep, Lady Rebekah's shocked to see Rædan leading the charge! They'd once shared a passionate night, but can she trust him with her dangerous secret?

AN ALLIANCE WITH HIS ENEMY PRINCESS (Medieval)
by Lissa Morgan
Despite being enemies, Rolant is intrigued by the brave Welsh princess Gwennan. Forced into an alliance, he helps her petition the king. But the king demands a price neither expects!